WHAT WAITS IN THE SHADOWS

WIL FORBIS

Copyright © 2024 by Wil Forbis

All rights reserved.

No part of this publication may be reproduced, distributed, or transmitted in any form or by any means, including photocopying, recording, or other electronic or mechanical methods, without the prior written permission of the publisher, except as permitted by U.S. copyright law. For permission requests, contact https://www.thehorrorofwilforbis.com/

The story, all names, characters, and incidents portrayed in this production are fictitious. No identification with actual persons (living or deceased), places, buildings, and products is intended or should be inferred.

Cover Artist: Covers by Christian

www.coversbychristian.com

Editor: Macabre Editing Services

https://www.facebook.com/profile.php?id=100089191483156

First edition 2024

For my true believer, Ali Marae.

Contents

Prologue   1

Part One

    Chapter One   10

    Chapter Two   13

    Chapter Three   19

    Chapter Four   25

    Chapter Five   30

    Chapter Six   34

    Chapter Seven   38

    Chapter Eight   45

    Chapter Nine   48

    Chapter Ten   54

    Chapter Eleven   59

    Chapter Twelve   63

    Chapter Thirteen   69

Chapter Fourteen	73
Chapter Fifteen	78
Chapter Sixteen	83

Part Two

Chapter Seventeen	88
Chapter Eighteen	92
Chapter Nineteen	96
Chapter Twenty	99
Chapter Twenty-one	103
Chapter Twenty-two	108
Chapter Twenty-three	113
Chapter Twenty-four	116
Chapter Twenty-five	123
Chapter Twenty-six	125
Chapter Twenty-seven	128
Chapter Twenty-eight	133
Chapter Twenty-nine	137
Chapter Thirty	142
Chapter Thirty-one	148
Chapter Thirty-two	154
Chapter Thirty-three	157
Chapter Thirty-four	160
Chapter Thirty-five	169

Chapter Thirty-six	173
Chapter Thirty-seven	181
Chapter Thirty-eight	186
Chapter Thirty-nine	192
Chapter Forty	196
Chapter Forty-one	198
Chapter Forty-two	203

Part Three

Chapter Forty-three	206
Chapter Forty-four	211
Chapter Forty-five	216
Chapter Forty-six	222
Chapter Forty-seven	228
Chapter Forty-eight	233
Chapter Forty-nine	236
Chapter Fifty	238
Epilogue	243
Your Reviews Help	246
Acknowledgements	247
About the Author	248

Prologue

Leaning forward in his swivel chair, Derek Kallman set a silver-plated jewelry box on the corner of his desk. The container held items of no particular value—an eagle feather he'd found during a kayaking trip in Colorado, a nonfunctioning lighter imprinted with a 1950s pinup girl, and the Purple Heart his grandfather had earned in World War II—but he liked having them around. The mementos had been on every desk he'd worked at since college, and their placement marked the completion of the day's organizational efforts.

He settled back into his chair and gazed about the room. His new home office was small and dimly lit (he'd already filed a mental note to purchase a floor lamp from IKEA), but comfortable enough. And private. In his previous residence, a dilapidated two-bedroom in Toledo's Old West End, there had been no refuge when the pressures of work and family life boiled over. This new office, however, had a door that could be shut and locked, a clear indicator that Daddy was in desperate need of "Daddy Time."

Currently, that door hung open, and a figure appeared in its frame. Margarita Kallman wore a sleeveless camisole and shorts—clothing ideal for a day spent tearing open boxes and stuffing knick-knacks onto shelves or into dressers. Her tan arms folded across her chest, each palm cupping an elbow.

"Are you done?" she asked, her lilting accent the remnant of a Mexican childhood.

"It's looking good," Derek said. "I still need to pick up a few things, but I think this will be a great place for writing." He patted a sheaf of papers on the center of his desk—a printout of his latest article for Scientific American—ready for edits. When he'd studied chemistry in college, he'd dreamed of discovering breakthrough uses for plastic polymers, not reporting on those who did. But science journalism was what paid the bills.

A coy smile spread across Margarita's lips. "Any ideas on how to celebrate? It's our first Saturday evening in our new house."

Derek scooted his wheeled office chair closer to his wife and stood. "As a matter of fact, I do. I plan on getting you pregnant."

She raised an eyebrow. "That's a very ambitious proposition, Mr. Kallman. You sure you're up to it?"

"I haven't a doubt. My boys are raring to go, and your obstacle course of a uterus can't stop them." He placed his hands on Margarita's hips and nuzzled her neck. She laughed, languidly rolling her head back as her hand ran down his chest, past his mild paunch, stopping on the zipper of his jeans.

"Mmmm. I believe I'm seeing signs of life," she said. Derek chuckled and brought his mouth to hers, tasting white wine on her tongue. They'd put off the idea of expanding their family for several years, mainly because of lack of space. But the new house solved that problem, so it was time to enjoy the fruits of their labors.

They stood together in the doorway for almost a minute, their hands tracing the outlines of each other's bodies. Then they heard a scream. High-pitched and piercing, what one half expected to be followed by shattering glass.

"Oh, for fuck's sake," Derek said.

Margarita's lips flattened. "C'mon, Daddy Derry. It's a new house. She just needs some time to get used to it."

Derek released a heavy sigh. "We've been here three nights, and she's done this every time." He stepped into the hall, walked past two shut doors, stopping at a third.

"Somebody in there order room service?" Without waiting for an answer, he turned the knob and pushed the door open.

He fumbled along the wall in the dark bedroom and found the switch. An overhead bulb clicked on and light bathed the space. Posters of clowns, fairies, and unicorns decorated the walls. A small desk sat in one corner, covered with childish paintings, a palette of watercolor paints, and a jar of brushes. A wide window filled most of the wall directly across from the door. Underneath it, stuffed animals gathered together atop a three-foot tall bookshelf.

In the center of the room, Lisa Kallman sat upright in her bed, tangles of red hair curling down her neck. The seven-year-old wore an expression of wide-eyed terror.

Margarita stepped into the doorway. "Did you have another bad dream, honey?"

Lisa gaped at both her parents. "It wasn't a dream," she squeaked. "There's something in there." Her trembling finger pointed to the closed sliding doors of a walk-in closet.

Derek sat on the edge of Lisa's bed. "What, honey? What did you hear this time?"

"Scratching," she replied, her voice becoming tinier. "Something was moving around in there."

"Do you think it's a monster?"

"Derek!" Margarita exclaimed.

He looked at his wife in the doorway. "It's a perfectly reasonable question. If there's a monster in the closet, we should know about it." He turned back to Lisa. "The realtor never mentioned the house came with a monster. If that's the case, I think we should get a break on our mortgage."

The barest hint of a smile crossed Lisa's face.

Derek walked to the closet and placed an ear against one of the doors. "Hmmmm ... I don't hear any monsters."

He raised a silencing index finger to his lips. With his voice just above a whisper, he said, "The best way to get rid of a monster is to surprise him." He hooked one hand around the edge of the door and slid it open.

Inside the closet, Lisa's dresses and overcoats hung on wire hangers. Board games and photo albums perched on a high shelf. Several pairs of shoes, a ceramic bear, a child sized swimming mask and snorkel, and numerous books scattered across the floor.

No monsters were present.

Derek poked a finger into the morass of hanging clothes. "Looks like the monster left. Or maybe he was never here in the first place."

"Do you think you can get back to sleep now, honey?" Margarita's eyes were soft with sympathy for her daughter.

"Can you leave the light on?" Lisa bit her lower lip.

Derek frowned. "You're getting to be a big girl now, Lisa. You're almost eight. That's too old to sleep with the light on."

"But I never hear the monster when the lights are on."

"Just let her do it, Derek." Margarita crossed her arms.

"No." Derek rolled the closet door shut and walked to his daughter's bed. "There are no monsters anywhere in this house. There is no such thing as monsters. And I'm starting to have my doubts about Santa Claus as well."

A new smile crept over Lisa's lips, but it didn't quell the anxious look in her eyes.

He leaned down and kissed his daughter on the forehead. "You're going to be fine. You know Mommy and I are just down the hall." He brushed a hand against Lisa's cheek, then stood and joined Margarita in the doorway.

"Night, Pumpkin." Derek flicked the light off, stepped into the hallway and swung the bedroom door inwards, leaving it open a crack. He looked at his wife and then flicked his eyes to their bedroom door. "I believe we've got some unfinished business to attend to."

***

Moonbeams poured into Lisa's bedroom. The leaves of trees in the yard rustled in the wind, casting shadows that fluttered across the floor. The electric heater in the hallway emitted a low hum.

Lisa sat upright in her bed and stared at the doors of the closet. It didn't matter what her parents said—she'd heard something in there.

But was it a monster? She'd never actually seen a monster, either in real life or on the TV news shows that claimed to reveal the truth about the world. Maybe Daddy was right. Maybe there were no monsters. Maybe what she'd heard was not a monster, but a raccoon. Perhaps a raccoon that had lived in the house for years and had built a maze of tunnels to move from room to room. That would explain why there was nothing to see when Daddy opened the closet door.

She lay back on her pillow and looked at the ceiling. The past weeks had been filled with anxious, new experiences. First, her parents had announced they'd found a new home and the family would be moving. Then they'd embarked on a two-week process of packing everything in their old house into cardboard boxes that piled in the living room. But Lisa hadn't wanted to leave. Her parents had said the new house would have more space and be closer to city parks, but the house they were in was the only one she'd ever known. On the day before the move, she'd walked out to their tiny backyard and apologized to the shrubs and stones for leaving them behind.

When she'd arrived at the new house, its emptiness overwhelmed her. The rooms in her old home all had personalities and held memories going back years. The blank walls of the new house had only stared at her, offering no welcome.

There was also the matter of entering second grade at Piedmont Elementary the coming Monday. When she'd started school last year, she hadn't known anyone, but neither had any of the other kids and that had made it easy to make friends like Jenna and Akari. At this new school, all the other kids would already know each other, leaving her as the odd one out. She envisioned the classroom building in her head, conjuring up an imposing concrete structure with an infinite number of windows peering at her like the eyes on an insect's head. She wondered about the children at the school. What if they weren't like her? What if they weren't even human? What if they were raccoons, like the one that lived in the walls of her new house? In her mind's eye, she saw her new classmates—little raccoon children dressed up in the latest kids' fashions. She had only the vaguest sense that her imaginings were no longer her own, that they were taking the jumbled, narrative form of dreams, before she drifted off.

Awake! Lisa couldn't tell whether she'd gone to sleep, or had just been dozing, but this time she knew she'd heard something in the closet. It wasn't even a matter of hearing it, she could feel it, even smell it … a stink like burning tires or the public bathrooms at the broken-down park in her old neighborhood. She sat upright, her eyes fixed on the closet doors. She strained her senses for any hint of the unusual, anything that would convince her parents of the wickedness in this place.

There was nothing. No scratching, no muttering like she'd heard in previous nights. The doors were not clanking on their rails.

Maybe it was a dream. Maybe it was a raccoon again. Maybe there were no monsters.

A guttural monotone that smacked of phlegm and spit came from the closet. "Open the door, Lisa. I want to get out. Let me out."

She froze. Her heart hammered in her tiny chest.

Lisa clamped her mouth shut just as the scream that had rocketed up her throat was about to burst from her lips. What would happen if Mommy and Daddy rushed into her room and didn't find a monster? Daddy had sounded like he was running out of patience when he'd been here just minutes ago.

What should she do?

***

In the dark of their undecorated bedroom, Derek and Margarita coiled together under the bedsheets, their soft moans accenting the rhythm of their movements. Derek pressed his lips against Margarita's ears and neck, kissing his way down to her breasts. She encouraged him with a breathy sigh while she ran a hand through the curls of his hair.

"Aaah!"

Another scream from Lisa's room.

"Oh, for fuck's sake," Margarita said.

Derek rolled off his wife. "That's it. I'm just going to kill her. I'll kill her, and that will solve the whole problem. We were going to have another kid, anyway. Maybe the second time'll be a charm."

"Honey, come on. You don't remember what it's like to be a little kid in a new house. Give her a break."

"Sorry, dear." Derek hopped off the bed and pulled on a pair of boxers. "I'm going to kill her. I'll see you when I get out in twenty years. Fifteen with good behavior." He opened the door and walked into the hallway.

***

Lisa's arms were wrapped around her legs, her chin at her knees, when her father burst into the bedroom and switched on the light. She pointed a trembling finger at the closet door.

"The monster, Daddy! I heard it in the closet!"

"Goddammit, Lisa," he yelled. "How many times do I have to tell you there is no monster?"

Mommy appeared in the doorway wearing a fuzzy robe. She frowned. "Derek, don't raise your—"

Daddy yanked open the closet door.

"Look, there's nothing to—"

A muscular green arm shot out and grabbed him by the throat. The hand was covered in goo that looked like the snot Lisa sometimes saw dripping from dog's noses.

"What the fuck?" Daddy's eyes bulged in their sockets.

Lisa and her mother screamed.

The hand pulled Daddy headfirst into the mesh of clothing. A sharp crack cut through the air, followed by an animal roar. One of Daddy's legs began twitching. Blood poured down his back, soaking his shorts and spattering the floor.

His body lurched forward, pulled deeper into the closet.

Lisa sat frozen on her bed. Her mother stood like a statue in the doorway.

"Hey, Lisa," gurgled the voice. "Let's play catch."

Something—the shape of a partially deflated football—sailed out of the closet. It curved through the air and landed on the bed. While it was battered, bruised, and drenched in blood, it was recognizable.

It was a human head.

Her father's head.

Part One

Twenty Years Later

Chapter One

Lisa Kallman pulled her auburn locks into a ponytail and bound them with an elastic tie. Loose strands of hair had been irritating her for the past hour, either falling into her face or getting stuck in pieces of discarded packing tape. She'd remembered the fuzzy tie in the back pocket of her jeans only a moment earlier.

With that problem solved, she looked around her new office. Despite its small size—it barely had space for her mahogany desk, 1960s style leather couch, and white bookcase—the room exuded an antique kind of charm. Tongue and groove pine planks ran across the floor to peach painted walls. Dark-stained wainscoting and window moldings displayed a simple, timeless aesthetic. She was reminded of the lounges in old movies where Spencer Tracy and Katharine Hepburn would sip brandy and coo sweet nothings to each other.

Flattened cardboard boxes piled by the door, remnants from the last hour spent unpacking books and placing them on the white bookcase set against the wall. The furniture's bottom shelf now held numerous academic tomes on child trauma and psychology, as well as a dozen moleskin notebooks Lisa had filled during her graduate studies. The level above that was dedicated to political topics and European and American history. Several higher shelves held the romance paperbacks that satiated her appetite for fiction.

A final unopened box sat on top of her desk in the middle of the room. She sliced through the tape with a box cutter and pulled the flaps away to reveal a stack of framed photographs. Her face brightened when she removed two photos from the top. The first picture showed her college class throwing their graduation caps in the air. In the second, she stood in her black gown next to her boyfriend. David Hague's handsome face bore a wide smile as he gazed at her affectionately.

She strolled to the bookcase and set the photos on the top shelf.

When she returned to the desk and the next photo in the box, her jaw tightened. Her mother, gray-haired and bony, folded into a wheelchair, her thin lips pulled into a grimace over browned and clenched teeth. Standing beside Margarita Kallman was an Asian doctor and a Black nurse. The trio gathered in front of several oak trees, through which could be seen a building marked as the "McArthur Psychiatric Hospital."

Lisa placed the photo at the far corner of the shelf, away from the others.

With the next picture, her face softened. Two-dozen children and several adults gathered with Lisa on bleachers at a public park. Some of the children beamed toothy smiles; others dourly stared at their feet. Everyone in the photo wore a T-shirt with a logo that said The Montgomery Center.

At the bottom of the box lay the final photograph: her teenage self standing arm-in-arm with her therapist, Dr. Gretchen Stein. As Lisa stared at the matronly and plump woman, her eyes dampened. She wiped a stray tear aside before placing the picture with the others.

She returned to the desk, where she discovered one more item in the box.

"Oh no," she murmured, removing a three-inch ceramic figurine of a helmeted, muscular man holding a sword. She rotated the tiny statuette in her hand and ran her finger over two sharp bumps on its shoulder blades. Frowning, she felt around in the box's interior and pulled out two small wings. She fit the wings onto the stumps in the figurine's back, but they stayed in place only as long as she held them there. "Sorry, little guy. Some glue will take care of this." She placed the broken figurine on the bookcase's top shelf near the photos.

With the box now empty, Lisa turned her attention to the view outside her window. The sun was slipping under the horizon, leaving minimal natural light. Still, it was enough to illuminate a neighborhood of aging three-story homes with shingled dormer roofs and large wooden awnings. Giant, grandfatherly elm trees lined the sidewalks. A few couples walked along the streets, pushing strollers or being led by dogs on leashes.

It wasn't fancy, but it was a warm, hospitable location. The kind of place you could feel safe. The kind of place you could raise a family. The kind of place where—

"Hey, Lisa," came a loud cry. "Get down here!"

Chapter Two

Lisa blinked, jolted from her reverie by the voice. She let out a wistful sigh. Part of her wanted to stay in the room and enjoy the silence, to watch the last rays of the sun grace the walls. But she was needed down below. And what kind of host hid in her office while a party was going on?

She walked down a hallway to a staircase that formed a U shape as it dipped to the first floor. A ceiling-mounted chandelier lit her descent while bits of conversation—work gossip, relationship advice, and restaurant critiques—rose to greet her. At the bottom, she padded onto the carpeted floor of a living room filled with over two-dozen people, few of them older than forty.

David sidled up to her, a short-sleeved dress shirt and casual jeans adorning his athletic physique. Both hands held a flute of fizzing liquid. Tall as he was, he had to lean considerably to kiss Lisa's cheek.

"Where've you been, babe? I've been calling you. I was about to send out a search party."

"Sorry," Lisa replied. "I had some things to put away upstairs."

He handed her a flute, careful not to spill. "Here's the champagne. But don't drink it yet. I'm going to do a toast in a minute. And trust me, it's going to blow your mind."

She smiled. "I bet. You're always full of surprises."

"By the way," David added with a wink, "everybody loves the house. They can't stop talking about it."

The back of her neck tingled. If David was happy, so was she. And she was glad to see him excited about their new home. When they'd first talked about moving in together, she'd fretted. She loved her boyfriend of two years, but knew they exemplified the adage *opposites attract*. He was bold and gregarious, she quiet and reserved, and their aesthetic tastes seldom matched. But while she didn't mind when David chose what movie to see or where to have dinner, she had to have her way when it came to the house they would live in—possibly for the rest of their lives. She wanted a place that felt settled, with a past. Not one of the soulless, ultra-stylized modern homes she suspected he'd prefer.

As such, it had been a surprise when David had suggested they visit an open house in the Old West End. Once a hot spot, the neighborhood had fallen on hard times decades earlier when affluent residents had fled to the suburbs. It had revived only recently as cheap housing prices and city investments attracted young buyers.

When they'd first walked up to the American Foursquare painted sunshine yellow, David had commented it was the smallest on the block. Lisa waved his concern away; the building looked—at least from the outside—roomy enough for two people. This was confirmed when they entered and discovered the realtor had left a copy of the floor plan on the kitchen counter. The house had four bedrooms—one on the ground floor and three upstairs—enough to give each of them an office and still have a place for overnight guests. Or for anyone else who might show up in their future.

They took their time exploring, first drifting through the rooms on the ground floor, then climbing the stairs to the second level. As they examined the bedrooms, David read the real estate brochure aloud and noted the house had been constructed from a kit in the early 1900s, as was common in the era. Buyers would pick out a lot and then order a house to be delivered, in parts, by truck from the Sears mill in Chicago, Illinois.

As they stood in the biggest bedroom, Lisa knew she had found their home. And she was prepared to fight for it. She looked at David, a knot growing in her belly. He was a man of many talents, but appreciating simplicity was not one of them. What would he think?

He seemed to recognize the yearning in her eyes. A wry smile crept across his face. "Should we put in an offer?"

They did, and in the struggling economy, their bid was accepted without complaint. A month after their first visit, a moving truck pulled up to the house and burly workers began unloading their possessions.

"Darlings!" A musical voice broke into Lisa's reminiscence. Tim Fairway cut his way through the crowded living room, smoothing his well-trimmed silver hair with a perfectly manicured hand. His clothes—shimmering black slacks and a silk T-shirt—hugged his body, his gym-toned muscles pulling taut with every movement.

A younger man, thinner but just as well-coiffed, followed Tim. Tom Saltzman, Tim's boyfriend, held a black pug dog close to his chest. The canine's glassy eyes were filled with concern.

Tim continued in his singsong voice. "Look at you. Our new neighbors in their new home. And everything looks so wonderful."

"It certainly does," Tom gushed.

David smiled at the pair. "We owe it all to you guys. We wouldn't be here if you hadn't told us when this place went up for sale." Tim, a client of the law firm where David was a junior partner, had passed on news of the house the day it had gone to market.

"No problem," Tim said, patting David on the shoulder. He turned to Lisa. "Look what you've done with the place. It's beautiful."

Lisa knew Tim was being gracious. Neither she nor David had found the time to furnish or decorate the house; they'd set up only what was necessary for the party. The living room contained two plaid couches (one mostly green, one mostly gray), a leather recliner, and an entertainment center. Trays of potato chips, miniature pizzas, carrots and dip, and dozens of full champagne flutes covered a long coffee table that sat before the television.

While Tim continued piling underserved praise on the decor, Lisa glanced at the other guests mingling in the living room. Most of them were David's fellow lawyers or college buddies, only a small fraction Lisa's friends or co-workers. It was easy to tell the two groups apart. David's invitees had donned expensive jackets or chic blouses, putting obvious effort into their appearance. Lisa's guests, while not dressed down, lacked sophistication. For them, a housewarming party was a different kind of engagement than a night out at the clubs.

As her eyes darted from face to face, Lisa tried to recall the names of the people she saw. Many of David's friends she'd met only once or twice at office get-togethers or parties. She recognized his blonde secretary, Sharon, off in the corner, talking to a striking East Asian woman whose bare arms were covered with elaborate tattoos. Not far from them, David's college roommate, Jeffrey Something-or-other, had his arm around a date different from the last one Lisa had seen him with. She waved when she spotted her best friend from work, Meg, standing by the coffee table. The dark-skinned woman flashed a bright smile and returned the gesture.

Lisa was about to step away and talk to Meg when David raised his champagne glass and tapped it with a fork. "Everybody, everybody ... can I please have your attention?"

The room quieted and David stood to his full six foot four inches. "I'm sure a drunken lot such as yourselves have noticed the champagne," he said, nodding towards the coffee table. "Now's the time to grab a glass because we're about to have a toast."

He paused as the guests lined up for their flutes, only resuming talking when most people held a glass. "You all know Lisa and I moved into this house just a couple of days ago. We're extremely pleased you could come by and help us start creating some great memories here. So, while I want to toast our new house, I also want to raise a glass to you guys for helping to turn it into a home."

"To us," shouted a trio of David's college friends, who then erupted into laughter. Lisa rolled her eyes and took a small sip from her flute.

After everyone had taken a drink, the conversation in the room began to swell. But David again tapped his glass, then set it on the dining room table. He turned and looked at Lisa. Something about the inscrutability of his blue-eyed gaze made her stomach flutter.

"I think everyone here knows how Lisa and I met, but I'm going to bore you with the story one more time," David said, flashing a set of perfect teeth at the guests. "I was working on a case involving one of her kids, and I kept seeing her at the children's center every time I went out there. While the case was active, I was a perfect gentleman. But after it settled, I came back and asked if she was free for dinner. She wasn't, so about a week later I returned and asked again. She still wasn't free. After she refused my third invitation, I asked her what the problem was, and she said, and I quote, 'I don't go out with dopes.'"

Lisa was taking another sip from her flute and champagne almost shot out of her nose. She couldn't believe David had revealed a private comment to all the guests.

"*Dopes*, ladies and gentlemen," David said. "She didn't go out with dopes. And I was apparently one such dope." He paused for a beat. "I think that's when I fell in love with her. So I jotted down a little love poem and handed it to one of her kids and asked him to go to her office and read it to her."

"You didn't even write it," Lisa reminded him. "You found it online."

"Whatever. Anyway, after the little squirt told her it was from me, she couldn't resist, and finally, after four tries, she agreed to go out with the dope you see before you. As you might expect, she fell head over heels for me immediately."

Lisa giggled. In his own dopey way, everything David was saying was true.

But the laughter caught in her throat when he got down on one knee. He reached a trembling hand into his jeans pocket and pulled out a box covered in black velvet. He flipped it open and the overhead lights caught on a sparkling diamond connected to a gold band. Several people in the room gasped.

David looked up at Lisa. "I wasn't kidding when I said it took me only a moment to fall in love with you. Now that we've moved into this house, I know more than ever that I want to spend the rest of my life with you."

Lisa's knees quivered. She wondered if she was about to topple over. This couldn't be happening. Could it?

David plucked the ring from the box and held it in front of her. "I am asking you, Lisa Kallman ... will you marry me?"

Lisa wasn't sure if the room actually went quiet or if her brain decided to weed out all but the most crucial input. How had she not seen this coming? Sure, she and David had talked about their future, even going as far as discussing marriage. But those conversations had always felt like vague thought experiments. Not anything serious or real.

As David kneeled before her, each second ticked by with the thud of a falling boulder. Part of her resented him for proposing in public, for springing this on her in front of all these people. But he was also giving her a chance to be part of something ... a union. A family.

Wasn't that what she'd always wanted? Ever since ...?

She bent down and looked into David's eyes. "Yes. Yes, I will marry you."

The room erupted into cheers.

Chapter Three

With all eyes on the newly engaged couple, Katrina Chen checked her phone: It was 8:18 p.m. which meant the evening was going nowhere fast.

Normally she'd be getting ready to go out clubbing, or lying in a bubble bath with a glass of chardonnay. Instead, she was watching a bunch of strangers celebrate a home purchase. It was her old roommate's fault—Sharon Hewsen had called midweek, begging Katrina to accompany her to the party. It was being thrown by Sharon's lawyer boss, and the blonde secretary had claimed it was her first opportunity to mingle with a handsome paralegal she'd had her eye on. Naturally, she needed a wing woman. "Besides," Sharon had added, "there will be plenty of hot, rich lawyers to meet."

So far, Katrina had met no one. Not that she had any trouble attracting attention. She was confident in her beauty and knew her unique heritage—Chinese, German, and Russian—gave her a certain exotic appeal. On this night, she'd glammed it up, donning a low cut, blue silk dress that showcased the tattoos which ran down her arms and across the top of her chest. The pink streaks through her hair complemented the faux ruby earrings which she'd purchased from a curio shop for less than twenty dollars.

The stares and flirtatious glances being thrown her way were obvious and uninhibited, but so far, no one in the crowded living room interested her. Most of the guests looked like boujee hipsters who thought downing three

Jäger shots and snorting a line of blow meant they were living on the edge. The artists or musician types she preferred were nowhere to be seen.

The party had been tolerable, earlier, when she'd been chatting with Sharon. But now her former roommate had gone off to pursue her dream man, leaving Katrina to fend for herself.

She took another sip of middling champagne and looked at the newly engaged owners of the house. The woman—*was her name Lisa?*—was pretty in her own way, but she had no dazzle. She looked out of place and was obviously uncomfortable socializing, even in her own home. While people gabbed nearby, the redhead threw furtive glances around the room or stared into space, seemingly lost in her thoughts.

The husband-to-be, David, towered next to his fiancée, his athletic arm wrapped around her waist, as if to keep her from straying. It was obvious he held the power in the relationship—an arrangement Katrina would never allow herself to fall into. In her world, men were kept around only as long as they provided amusement. When that moment passed, they could be quickly dispensed with.

Still, she had to admit David was attractive. Nothing about his manner or dress separated him from the hordes of corporate drones circulating the room, but his cobalt eyes flickered steely ambition. When he spoke, he gestured in a way that seemed confident, even cocky.

Katrina had a weakness for cocky guys. They were usually good in bed.

Sharon reappeared, blocking Katrina's sightline of David. The blonde was playing her assets, rocking a low-cut red sequin dress that gave a full view of her voluminous cleavage. "C'mon," she said. "Let's go upstairs. The downstairs john has a line and I *really* have to pee."

"Well, I don't," Katrina replied, not moving.

"*Come on.*"

Katrina sighed and followed her up the stairs.

Sharon was abuzz with chatter about her desired paramour. "Ohmigod, he is so cute. The only problem is his sideburns. Did you think they make him look like a pirate?"

Katrina wouldn't have been able to pick the guy out of a police lineup. "Which one was he? They all look the same to me."

"Shut up. I don't know why you're so picky. There are plenty of hot guys here. Or girls, if that's your thing."

Katrina rolled her eyes. The comment did not deserve the dignity of a reply.

They arrived on the second floor and stepped into a dark hallway that stretched out before them. Sharon flipped on an overhead light and led Katrina to an open bathroom door.

"I'll be out in a sec."

"I'm not going anywhere."

Sharon shut the door and continued jabbering about her romantic pursuit. Katrina stood in the hallway, feeling more than a little ludicrous.

Several feet away, a doorway framed a small room where a luminescent half-moon shone through a window. As the moonlight passed through the glass, it took on a twinkling quality, beautiful and hypnotic.

She walked down the corridor and peered into a congested office space. In one corner sat a desk. A space-age couch ran along one wall. The shelves of a white bookcase were packed with books. The room's layout was functional but unbalanced, lacking an aesthete's sense of design.

There was nothing polite about snooping in people's houses. But Katrina knew she'd hear anyone coming up the stairs.

She stepped into the room and navigated her way past a pile of discarded cardboard boxes on the floor. A box cutter lay on the desk next to a sheet of bubble wrap. Someone had been in the process of unpacking.

Turning to the bookcase, Katrina saw several framed photographs on the top shelf. One showed Lisa and several adults chaperoning a group of children. Two other photos appeared to have been taken at a graduation ceremony. The next picture over was a teenage Lisa with a doughy, unattractive woman.

The breath caught in Katrina's throat when she saw the final photo. A gray-haired woman sat in a wheelchair in front of a nurse and a doctor. It was the expression on the woman's face that was so disturbing. Her mouth hung half open, madness glinting in her bloodshot eyes.

"What the hell are you doing in here?"

Katrina whipped around. She expected to see the female owner of the house standing in the doorway, her fiery red hair splayed across her face.

Instead, Sharon glared at her.

"Jesus," Katrina said, holding her chest. "You scared the crap out of me."

Sharon frowned. "Were you even listening to me while I was talking? You know you shouldn't be in here."

"I know. I'm sorry. But have you seen this? Do you know who this woman is?"

Sharon looked behind her to see if anyone else was around. Then she tiptoed into the room, mimicking the exaggerated gestures of a character in a Scooby-Doo cartoon. She stopped before the bookshelf. "What? Who?"

Katrina pointed to the picture. Sharon narrowed her eyes. "Ohmigod. That must be the mother."

"The mother?" Katrina repeated. "Like in *Psycho*?"

"No, no, no. David told me about this, but I'm not supposed to tell." Sharon paused, as if contemplating whether to gossip, though it was clearly all performance. In a hushed voice, she said, "When Lisa was really young—six or seven—she watched her father get murdered in her bedroom. Like, right in front of her."

"Oh my god. That's why she's so strange."

Sharon clucked, annoyed. "She's not strange. She's nice. You're strange."

Katrina ignored the jab. "What happened to her mother?"

"She was in the bedroom too. She saw the whole thing. And her mind just snapped. She like, totally shut down. She's been in some asylum outside of town ever since."

Katrina's shoulders sagged, as if burdened with an unexpected weight. "Whoa ... that's so sad." She simmered in the melancholy for several seconds, until a new thought caused the fine hairs on her arm to stiffen.

"What about the killer? Did they catch whoever did it?"

"Oh yeah," Sharon said. "The police found boot marks outside the house and tracked down some guy who was a neighbor of theirs. A pedophile. Like, super creepy!"

"What happened to Lisa? After the murder?"

"She went to child services, I think," Sharon replied. "She was fostered a couple times, but it never worked out. She was in some kind of orphanage when she turned eighteen. Then she just took out a shit-ton of student loans and dove right into school. She didn't stop until she got a master's in psychology a couple years ago. She's like a therapist of some kind. But for kids."

Katrina brushed her slender fingers against her throat. "What a sad story. I feel so bad for her."

"I know. Can you imagine? To have that happen to you when you're so young? The guy who killed her father is coming up for parole; that's the only reason David brought it up. The courts are having a hearing to see if he's ready for release. David wasn't sure Lisa should attend."

The photographs on the bookshelf drew Katrina's eyes again. She'd come into the room out of boredom, but now she saw the harm of her actions. There are reasons people expect privacy, reasons they consider the airing of their secrets to be the worst kind of violation.

She hooked a hand onto Sharon's arm. "Come on. Let's get out of here."

Chapter Four

As guests mingled around her, Lisa looked at the engagement ring on her finger for what had to be the hundredth time. Both the row of diamonds mounted on the sides and the enormous jewel in the middle twinkled in the light. David had spared no expense. And while the monetary value of the gems was not important, what they symbolized was.

She had never fully understood David's intent in their relationship. His friends dated posh, fashionable women, many of whom, though only in their twenties, were familiar with the blade of the local cosmetic surgeon. And she'd picked up enough of his history to know he'd sought similar partners in the past. So questions had burned in her mind. Why her? Why now?

But the ring showed his commitment was real, that he could be counted on as a lover and partner. She would not wake up one day to find him gone from her life.

She looked up from the ring and at David standing beside her, chatting excitedly with Tim and Tom. His left hand hooked around her waist and his right held a gin and tonic, from which he took frequent sips.

Over the next half hour, the party began to wind down. Groups of guests approached Lisa and David to offer congratulations, followed by the comment that "we have to be going." From what she could gather, a dance party was going on at a club downtown, an event she had no interest in attending.

She watched out of the corner of her eye as David's secretary, Sharon, and her friend with the tattoos came down the stairs. Lisa had assumed the pair had already left, but maybe they'd just been girl-talking in the upstairs bathroom.

Sharon caught Lisa's eye and she rushed over, the tattooed girl behind her.

"Congratulations, guys. On everything. Look at that ring. It's gorgeous."

Lisa blushed, uncomfortable being adorned with something that drew people's attention. "Thank you."

Sharon turned to her friend. "Guys, I want you to meet my gal pal, Katrina. We used to be roommates together."

The woman's silken black hair shined in the light as she moved closer to the circle and exchanged handshakes with everyone. She looked at Lisa with a strange, almost sympathetic expression. "Congratulations on your engagement. And your new home. It's so charming."

"Thank you," Lisa said. "I love your earrings."

"Thank you." Katrina smiled and touched one of the red stones. Then she looked at the panting pug held close to Tom's chest. "And who's this little fellow?"

"This is our son," Tim replied, tilting his head towards Tom to indicate his role as a co-parent. "His name is Mr. Beverly. I'm sure he's very glad to meet you."

Katrina leaned over and stroked the pug under his chin. "Aren't you the cutest little guy?" The dog let out a sound somewhere between a whimper and a groan, but the wags of his curly tail showed he loved the attention.

"I just thought of something," Sharon said. "Since you guys just bought a house, you should hire Katrina. She does feng shui. She can totally get your karma in order."

The tinge of pink flushed Katrina's cheeks. "That's not quite right. I don't do feng shui myself. I'm an assistant to a professional consultant."

"Whatever," Sharon continued, unperturbed. "You're like a feng shui apprentice. It's time for you to put on your sorcerer's hat and sprout your wings." She waved her hands in the air.

"It's not witchcraft, Mickey Mouse." Katrina looked at the rest of the group. "Feng shui is a way of organizing your living space to bring positive forces into your life."

Lisa pulled her lower lip between her teeth. Why did these words cause a jab of anxiety to flare within her? Was she so protective of this new house, this new *home*, that she didn't want to let a stranger come in and assume some control?

David turned to her. "Should we do it, babe? I've never been feng shui'd before."

She giggled. "Honey, it's not a verb. You can't be feng shui'd."

"Babe, I'm a lawyer. Making up words is what we do." He nodded at Katrina. "Leave a card or something before you take off. We'll give you a call once we're unpacked around here."

"Sure. Sharon can give you my number." Katrina glanced at her friend. "Should we get going? It's almost nine."

"I guess so," the blonde replied. "So, um, how safe is this neighborhood at night? We had to park about four blocks over."

"You'll be fine," Tim said. "Just don't get sucked into the monster mansion over on Fullbrook Street."

Sharon's eyes bulged. "Ohmigod. Are you talking about that super-scary looking house? We walked past it coming over here. What's the deal?"

Tim chuckled and waved a hand dismissively. "It's just some condemned, turn-of-the-century mansion. There was a fire in it about a year ago. Mostly smoke damage, but it's been empty ever since. They put up a notice saying it's going to be torn down in a couple of months. Nothing for you two to worry about."

Sharon grabbed her shoulders and theatrically shivered. "It can't happen soon enough. That place was creepy."

Katrina sighed and tugged her friend's arm. "C'mon, girl. I'll protect you from the zombies and ghosts." The two women gave their farewells and headed to the door.

Within a half hour, more guests, including several of Lisa's co-workers, came over to bid farewell. Lisa looked around, surprised to see Meg had left the party without saying goodbye. Had her friend felt neglected among the excitement? Hopefully any ill feelings could be soothed over when they saw each other at work.

Soon, it was just Tim and Tom standing beside Lisa and David at the dinner table, downing their drinks and engaging in random chit-chat. Then, at just after ten o'clock, they returned to their house next door.

"That was a good party, right?" David said, as he and Lisa stood alone in the kitchen.

"It was." She looked through the archway that led to the living room. The coffee table and sofa arms were strewn with paper plates of half-eaten food and empty champagne flutes. But the clutter, far from being an annoyance, made the space feel lived in, like it was already gathering treasured memories. "This feels like a home," she said.

David went to a collection of bottles on the kitchen counter and poured himself some gin. "I'm going to head upstairs, babe. You coming?"

"I want to clean up a bit. But don't conk out on me."

He smiled. "You know booze just fuels me." He flexed a bicep and laughed, then walked to the staircase.

Lisa gathered the containers of food left on the kitchen counter and put them in the fridge. Then she flitted through the living room, collecting champagne flutes and plates of half-eaten chips and vegetables.

When she returned to the kitchen and began wiping down the marble countertops, she became aware of an odd sensation tugging at her consciousness. It was neither of her frequent companions, anxiety or fear. In fact, she felt quite good. She searched for a word to define the feeling, frustrated that it seemed to float on the tip of her tongue, yearning for expression.

Then it came to her. *Normal*. She felt normal. Like a regular person cleaning up, living life. Not struggling to hide from the dread that had percolated in the back of her mind for years. Not trying to push back the knowledge that a terrible crime had once ripped her childhood apart.

Maybe, after all these years, she could be like everyone else.

Normal.

Boring.

Average.

It wasn't too much to ask for.

Was it?

Chapter Five

On Saturday, Lisa and David began settling into their new home. First, they loaded the entirety of David's skiing equipment into the attic. Then David set up a Wi-Fi network while Lisa hung replicas of 20th century French cabaret posters and photos of David's friends and family on the walls. In the afternoon, they laid a plush red carpet on their bedroom floor and stuffed clothes into their dressers. Afterwards, sweaty and spent, they showered and visited Tim and Tom for a backyard dinner. The group sat under the stars, sharing stories and drinking several bottles of wine.

The next morning, Lisa and David walked to a Greek bistro for breakfast. They each ate a large omelet and decided to burn off the meal by strolling to the nearby Agnes Reynolds Jackson Arboretum. When they got to the park, they lay together on the grass, looking up at the clouds.

"You seem to have run out of words, baby doll," David said while he stroked Lisa's cheek. "At least, more so than usual."

Her eyelids fluttered in the sunlight warming her face. "I'm just thinking, that's all."

"About the parole hearing?"

She rolled over onto her stomach and propped her chin on her hands. "Well, no. I wasn't. But I am now."

"You know you don't have to go, right? I've been to plenty of these things. It's just a bunch of people talking. It could be weeks before the board hands down their decision."

"I want to go," Lisa said. "I've never seen him before. I mean, in person."

"Well, except…" David stopped himself, but the meaning was clear. *Except when he killed your father.*

Her jaw tightened, teeth grating together. "How many times do we have to talk about this? I've told you I don't remember any of that."

David avoided her eyes and settled his gaze on a wooden gazebo in the center of the park. "Yeah, sure, I get it. I guess."

"I've told you, I don't like talking about … what happened."

Neither of them spoke for a minute, then David began passing on idle gossip from his office. Lisa found she couldn't keep her smile from making furtive but frequent appearances. When she and David talked about such trivialities, she felt they were just a regular couple, soon to be man and wife.

After a half hour at the Arboretum, they decided to return home. They passed through the entrance gate, walked for several minutes down Delaware Avenue, navigated a few intersections, and turned south onto a quiet street called Fullbrook. As they were gliding down the tree-lined sidewalk, David stopped and pointed.

"There it is."

A row of multi-story Victorian houses stood across the street, set back from the sidewalk by large lawns. Elegant and beautiful, the buildings looked almost identical to scores of other homes in the neighborhood.

"There *what* is?" Lisa asked.

"The house that burned. What did Tim call it? Monster Mansion."

The additional description enabled her to pick out the desolate-looking building that stood three-stories tall in the middle of the block. Brown paint peeled off heat-warped wood. Blackened shards of glass hung in skeletal window frames. The few sections of interior, visible through gaps in the walls or windows that hadn't been boarded up, appeared lifeless or shrouded in shadow.

Bright yellow "CAUTION" tape ran along the perimeter of the home's lot. The plastic cordon couldn't actually keep anyone from entering, but its message was clear. *Stay out.*

Still, the home maintained a claw hold on its former resplendence. The wide porch that stretched out from the front was relatively undamaged. The ornamental moldings and trim embellishing the building's exterior presented the broad strokes of elegance. Lisa half expected to see a well-dressed society maven peering from the handsome, gabled dormer windows that jutted out of the roof.

The most striking feature of the mansion was the cylindrical turret that stuck out from the right corner. It curled upward to a pointed tip, taking the shape of a sage wizard serenely inspecting his surroundings.

Lisa furrowed her brow. "It doesn't look scary to me."

"No," David agreed. "Just tired. And sad. It's a shame, really. It looks like it used to be a great place to live. Maybe we should have considered it. I would've liked a fixer upper."

She patted David on his belly. "Fixing you up is enough of a project for me."

He laughed. "Then you've got your work cut out for you." His fingers ducked under her arms and started tickling her ribs. She squealed with laughter and wrapped her hands around his waist, pressing her body to his. He leaned down and kissed her forehead. Then dropped his head lower, bringing his mouth to hers. For several timeless moments, their lips pressed together and fluttering butterfly wings cascaded against the back of Lisa's neck.

When they drew apart, she gave her fiancé a wide grin. "Wow. Now I remember why I keep you around."

He laughed and took her hand in his. "I'm also good at taking out the garbage."

A warm sun shone down, dulling the autumn chill. Chirping birds flitted through the air and the smell of freshly cut grass wafted from neighborhood lawns. As the couple walked together, their discussion turned to the coming workweek and the projects they were engaged in. Lisa was anticipating meeting several children who had been assigned to her care. David would begin researching a new case involving a client suing a local hospital for improper medical treatment.

By the time they turned away from Fullbrook street, any thoughts of the burned house in the middle of the block had faded from their minds.

Chapter Six

That evening, Lisa tossed an arugula salad while David prepared a dinner of Cajun salmon, butter-drenched asparagus and mashed potatoes. They devoured the meal at their kitchen table, then Lisa loaded dishes into the dishwasher while David moved to his first floor study to prepare notes for his upcoming case.

As the hum of the dishwasher filled the air, Lisa padded into the living room and clicked on the television, careful to keep the volume low so as not to disturb her fiancé. She seldom watched network TV, but Sunday was the night of her favorite program, *Caressed by Heaven*. In the show, four angels disguised as human beings traveled around the United States, helping people in need.

She'd been surprised to find herself so charmed by the series, especially since her own spiritual beliefs were vague at best. While she suspected there was more to reality than appeared to the naked eye, she had little notion as to what that might be. She also struggled to reconcile the prospect of a loving God, after the tragedy that had shattered her childhood. But, despite her philosophical musings not aligning with the Christian narrative of "Caressed by Heaven", the show's optimism and innocence drew her in.

As she settled back into a brown recliner, the episode began with a scene of a rumpled businessman standing atop a freeway bridge, preparing to jump to his death. Marcus, a leather-jacketed Black man who was one of the show's earthbound angels, pulled up on his motorcycle. He cajoled the man off the ledge and discovered the source of his suicidal ideation: large gambling debts owed to Las Vegas casinos. All four angels then convened and worked out a plan to help the businessman. After various convoluted plot twists, the man paid off his debts and reunited with his twenty-something daughter, a prostitute.

"Jeez," David groaned, having walked in for the final minutes of the show. "I don't know how you watch this stuff."

Lisa giggled. "I know it's dopey. I just like the idea of someone up there watching out for me."

"Well, you're going to need them," he said, approaching the recliner from the rear. "Because I am going to get you!" His hands reached down and wrapped around Lisa's neck.

She laughed and easily twisted out of his loose grasp. She stood up and ran over to the sofa. "You couldn't catch a mouse on a tiny motorcycle."

David rolled his eyes at the curious image and began chasing her around the room. She evaded his pursuit, then came to a stop near the television, watching as he started climbing over the sofas. As he awkwardly straddled the furniture, she sprinted up the stairs to the second floor. She could hear him rushing behind her, but she had a sizeable lead and was able to run into their bedroom and slam the door.

Lisa lay on the bed and awaited her "capture" by David and whatever activities, perhaps inspired by the bedroom setting, might follow. She looked over at the door and saw the handle jiggle, but it did not open. She hadn't locked it. Why couldn't he enter?

"Open the door, Lisa." David's jocular voice came from the hallway.

She felt her face drain of blood.

"Come on, Lisa. Open the door!"

Her heart thrummed against her chest. A layer of sweat coated her body, pulling an icy sting out of the bedroom air.

The handle continued to rattle, and David's muffled expletives filtered into the room. Finally, the door swung opened. David ran into the room and leaped on the bed like a wolf taking down an elk.

Lisa screamed. It was a shrill and cutting sound that probably had the people next door questioning the sanity of their new neighbors.

David landed beside her, a stunned expression on his face. "What the hell, babe? We were just playing around."

Lisa trembled, her heart beating rapidly against her ribs. Why was she having such a strange reaction? She rolled onto her side, away from David's wide-eyed gaze. She didn't want him to see her swelling tears. "I don't know …" she mumbled. "I got scared."

"Why didn't you just let me in? The carpet got stuck in the doorjamb. I had to use my nail file to get it out."

"It was something … something about you jostling the door. It freaked me out."

David placed a hand on her shoulder. "It's okay. People get scared sometimes. Especially in a new house." He shifted closer to her, the shape of his body pressing into her back, buttocks, and the curl of her legs. He moved a hand to her hip and let it rest for a moment. Then he drew it up over her belly, settling on her right breast.

"No," Lisa said, sitting upright on the bed and bringing her feet to the floor. "I don't want to."

David's hand patted the mattress. "C'mon, babe, don't leave," he said. "We can break in the new sheets."

"I said *no*. Are you not used to hearing that or something?" She stormed into the bathroom, where she slammed the door behind her.

***

Downstairs, the television, never silenced, continued its low hum of blather. An advertisement came on and a costumed ogre promised shockingly low prices on a living room sofa set. The voiceover on another advert begged viewers to try the best Chinese buffet in the Great Lakes area. A third bragged that the Channel 12 Action News Team was the best in Toledo.

As the TV chattered, David stepped down the stairs and walked to the green plaid couch. He picked up the remote and flipped through the channels, muttering private curses. Finding nothing worth watching, he clicked off the television and threw the remote onto the cushions.

He stomped into the kitchen, pulled a bottle of Irish whiskey from a cabinet, and poured himself a glass. He raised it to his lips and downed it in one gulp. Scowling, he set the glass down and let out a loud burp.

Then he poured himself another drink.

Chapter Seven

The next morning, Lisa awoke to a Pretenders song blasting out of her clock radio. Sitting up in bed, she saw the sheets on the other side lay flat. David had not come up last night, probably sleeping on a couch downstairs.

She picked her phone off the nightstand and read a text he'd sent an hour earlier.

`Went to work. See you tonight.`

In her head, she heard David speaking the words in a brittle voice. Her stomach knotted, pulling tight.

Great. Less than a week in the house and we're already sleeping in separate rooms.

After dressing, she trudged downstairs to the kitchen and microwaved a bowl of oatmeal. Most of the flavorless mush ended up in the trash, before she grabbed her purse and headed out the door.

Twenty minutes later, she nosed her SUV into a space in an uncovered parking lot in the commercial section of Toledo's North Towne district. She got out of her car, strolled several blocks east, and turned towards a single-story red-bricked building on a street corner. Above a pair of glass double doors, a giant sign said The Montgomery Center for Children with

Special Needs. As Lisa reached for a metal door handle, something scraped against the pavement behind her.

She spun. A few feet away, a woman no older than thirty stared with bloodshot eyes. Her frayed olive sweater and denim skirt looked ill suited for the chilly October air.

A small boy, perhaps six or seven years old, clung to the woman's leg. He, too, was poorly dressed for the weather, clad in a long-sleeved pajama top and beige pants.

The woman took a hesitant step forward. Tendrils of stringy brown hair stuck to her cheeks.

"Do you work here?" she asked.

"Yes. I'm Ms. Kallman, one of the Mental Health Counselors. Do you need some help?"

The woman's gaze drifted to the ground. "I ... I dunno ... It's my boy, Patrick.

The child looked at his mother through the scraggles of brown hair falling over his face.

"He don't talk," the woman said. "The social workers said I should come here. That you help children who have ... trauma?"

"We do." Lisa gave a smile. "Helping people is what we're all about."

The woman sniffled and tilted her face skyward, seeming to prefer staring at the bright sun rather than risk meeting Lisa's eyes. "It was his father. He's gone now ... dead. But we think he might have ..." Her voice trailed off.

Patrick gripped the loose folds of his mother's skirt. Unlike his parent, he stared at Lisa, his expression flat and inscrutable.

Lisa moved closer and kneeled down. "Hello, Patrick. I'm very pleased to meet you."

She could feel his eyes tracing the contours of her face. Then he turned his head, pushing his nose into his mother's hip.

Lisa rubbed her hands together and gave a shiver. "It's pretty cold out. Maybe you guys would like to come inside? Patrick, I bet we have a jacket you could wear. And we can all talk."

The boy looked up at his mother. "Ts'okay," she said. Then she turned to Lisa. "I'm Semone,"

"Follow me, guys." Lisa opened one of the glass doors and led mother and son into a small waiting area that held a couch, a coffee table stacked with magazines, and a wooden tray with a brewing coffee pot on it. A middle-aged woman seated at the receptionist desk stopped clacking on her computer keyboard and pushed her cat eye glasses up her nose.

"Have a seat," Lisa said to the pair. "Gabby will get you some forms to look at. And she can discuss some programs to help cover costs, if that's a concern."

A nervous smile blossomed on Semone's face, by far the happiest expression Lisa had seen since their interaction started.

A large cardboard box pressed against the wall in one corner of the room. Lisa rummaged through it and removed a blue, child-size puffy jacket. Swiveling to Patrick, she said, "I think this will fit you just fine."

The boy ambled over and pushed his thin arms out so that he formed a T shape. Lisa laughed and pulled the jacket over him. She patted his shoulder and said, "I bet we're going to be great friends."

His brow furrowed into a curious expression.

She looked back in the box. "Oh, boy, Patrick. I think we have the perfect finishing touch for your fashion ensemble." She reached in and pulled out a yellow fisherman's hat, sized for an adult. The brim sunk to just above his eyes when she set it on his head.

"Aye, aye, captain," Lisa said with a theatrical salute.

A hint of a smile crossed Patrick's face. Then he ran back to his mother on the couch.

Gabby stepped out from behind her desk, carrying a clipboard with the many forms that needed to be filled out. Within moments, Semone was "uh-huh-ing" her way through the receptionist's instructions. Confident things were well in hand, Lisa slipped away. It pained her to leave the suffering mother and child, but she had dozens of documents to review before her afternoon meetings with clients.

She stepped into her small office and sat on a ratty swivel chair, flipping open her laptop.

Her fingers were furiously tapping on the keyboard, a half hour later, when a knock sounded on the wall. Lisa turned and saw Meg standing in the doorway, a wide smile on her face.

"That was a banger of a housewarming shindig, Lisa. You and David really know how to party. Took me back to my college days."

"Oh, we tore the roof off the, um, sucker," Lisa said, making clear she recognized Meg's sarcasm. "I can't even remember half the night."

"Sorry I had to leave before we got a chance to chat, but there's no way I can look this fabulous without my beauty sleep. And I could tell you were caught up in all the glory of getting betrothed."

Lisa groaned. "You know I hate being the center of attention. I wanted to go upstairs and hide in my office the whole time."

"You wouldn't have gotten that giant rock, though." Meg said, eying the band of diamonds on Lisa's finger. "That's three months of sexy lawyer money right there."

Lisa flinched. Was that a pang of jealousy she heard in Meg's voice? They'd known each other for years now, but sometimes Lisa couldn't quite get a read on her friend.

She swallowed hard, contemplating whether to tell Meg about the fight with David. Could she even explain what had caused her frightened reaction when he'd attempted to enter the bedroom? And could she bear to voice fears that her dream of a family and a normal life was already slipping away?

Better to change the subject, she decided, looking back at the computer screen. "I always thought this job would be more helping people and less paperwork," she said while rubbing her temples.

"Girl, tell me about it. I've got a pile of reports as tall as the Tower on the Maumee. But maybe later this week we can do lunch at Salvatore's? I'm dying for that ziti."

Lisa frowned. "Probably not this week. I'm working extra hard to take Friday off."

"Oh shit. I forgot you've got that parole hearing coming up." She paused, her sympathetic gaze trickling over Lisa's face. "You still sure you want to go to that?"

"You sound like David. But, yeah, I want to see that bastard in person. And I want to make sure he stays where he is." She heard the knife-edge creep into her voice.

Meg puffed her cheeks out in an expression that seemed to mix concern and trepidation. Maybe she'd only prepared for small talk, and was not looking to converse on topics like murder and revenge.

"Ok," she said. "You know what you can handle. Maybe next week, then?"

Lisa forced a smile. "It's a date." She gave a small wave as Meg vanished from the doorway, and was soon lost in reports about the upcoming counseling sessions.

***

At 5:30 p.m. that evening, Lisa walked up the porch steps of her house and unlocked the door. David wasn't home, but it wasn't uncommon for him to work late. She threw her purse on the floor and lay on the couch to brood for a while.

Two hours later, she was chopping broccoli at the kitchen counter, when a key clicked in the front door. The nervous jolt that passed through her body set off a twitch that almost caused her to slice a paring knife into her thumb.

The door opened and David strode across the threshold. He held his briefcase in one hand, wearing a gray suit and a frown.

Lisa rushed into the living room. "David, I ..."

He raised a finger to his lips. "Don't talk, babe. I have something I need to say."

Nervous energy bubbled in her belly, her heart punching against her ribs.

"Last night was my fault," David announced. "Sometimes I forget what happened to you when you were a kid. I know that sounds stupid. I mean, *Jeez*, how could I forget something like that? But I just got caught up in the moment, you know? Chasing you around and everything. But I should be making you feel safe. Making you feel like you're not in danger. Because, you know, you're not."

Lisa released her breath. "Oh, baby ... I know I can be a lot to take. I don't know why I got so freaked out in the bedroom. But you shouldn't feel like you have to step on glass when you're around me."

David set his briefcase down. "Babe, I'll crawl through glass for you." He cocked his head thoughtfully. "Is that a thing? Crawl through glass? Crawl over glass? Like in *Die Hard*? Whatever it is, I'll do it." He chuckled and opened his arms.

"You're such a dork," Lisa said as she pressed her cheek to his chest and wrapped her arms around him. "No wonder you need to steal your poetry off the internet."

David let out a blurt of laughter and squeezed her. When they parted, he took her hand, guided her to a couch, and sat down next to her. He leaned down and his soft lips kissed her forehead. "I'm so glad that fight is over," he said. "I was a mess at work all day."

"Tell me about it," Lisa said. "I thought … " She left the sentence unfinished.

David frowned. "What? You thought I'd leave? No way, babe. I'm a lifer. You're stuck with me."

She smiled, her eyes lingering on his jaw and taut cheekbones. "You want some dinner? I was making a stir fry."

"That sounds extra-delish. But maybe we need to … you know? Work up an appetite?" He leaned in close, his body pushing her back. When his lips found her neck, Lisa felt her body relax as the tension she'd been holding melted away. She fluttered her eyes shut and fell into a pillow of hot breath and quick kisses.

Chapter Eight

During the blur of the next few days, Lisa and David became more comfortable with their new house. They learned the hinges of the cupboard that held the spices squeaked, the door to the linen closet needed to be pushed into the frame for the latch to catch, and the handle of the first floor toilet had to be jiggled to get it to flush. The nooks and crannies of each room started to become familiar.

Still, the weight of the upcoming Friday's parole hearing polluted the air with a sense of dread. Lisa held firm in her commitment to see her father's killer in person, and David cleared his schedule for the day. When Thursday evening came around, they went to a wine tasting/jazz concert at the Toledo Museum of Art. The fine merlot and melodious music provided enough distraction that Lisa did not find the expected knot of foreboding in her gut when they returned home. She and David went upstairs, took their respective turns in the bathroom, and then got into bed. After switching off the light, David placed a night mask over his eyes. He mumbled something about his undying love and was soon asleep, his chest rising and falling in steady undulations.

For Lisa, sleep proved elusive. The questions she'd been avoiding during the evening rose from the depths of her mind. What would it be like to see the man who'd murdered her father? Would he repent and beg forgiveness? Or would he stare at her with eyes devoid of remorse and any promise of closure?

Closure? Was that even possible? And was it what she really wanted? During all those years in orphanages and foster homes, a fire had burned in her gut, the visceral embodiment of her anger at a universe that had shattered her family and turned her life inside out.

No, Lisa decided. Closure was not what she sought.

She moaned and glanced at the clock on her nightstand. It was almost midnight. She turned and looked at her fiancé lying beside her, soft snores emanating from his nostrils. With each breath, his chest rose and fell and the folds of the sheet rearranged themselves like clouds changing shape. She focused on the undulating mass. What would it be like to be a tiny person, lost in the folds, buoyed by the easy motion? The thought settled in her mind and soon she found herself drifting … drifting …

Lisa looked down and saw sand so luminously white that it almost blinded her. She looked around, realizing she was standing on a sunlit beach, her body clad in a loose-fitting white dress. To her left, shimmering speckles of light danced across the flat surface of a blue ocean. To her right, a beach stretched out towards the horizon. Above her was a cloudless sky.

A trail of footprints had formed in her wake, going backwards in time. For how long had she been walking?

She looked forward and saw him. A figure strode across the sand twenty yards ahead of her. Even at this distance, she could see that despite his broad shoulders and male musculature, he was not human. He stood at least nine feet tall, with gleaming, marble white skin and a pair of giant, reptilian wings folded behind his V-shaped back. Though she could not see the creature's face, she knew he was gentle—a friend.

At once, the scene changed. The blue sea mutated into a polluted gray. The previously still waters of the ocean turned violent as frothing waves began crashing to the shore, drenching Lisa in a thick, viscous spray. Dark clouds spread across the sky, spitting lightning and belching thunder. Unless she fled the water, she would get sucked into the angry current. But what of her strange friend? He still walked ahead with an even gait, oblivious to the cacophony around him. She could not leave him to face nature's wrath alone.

Lisa cried out, but the waves and thunder drowned out her voice. As she ran towards the angelic figure, seawater lapped at her ankles, its fluid tendrils grabbing at her legs. A wave knocked her to the ground where quicksand eagerly absorbed her hands and feet. She struggled wildly, freed herself, and bolted upright. Again, she ran towards the creature.

The sea drew back, preparing for a final assault. Lisa was a dozen feet away from the white figure, then half that, as a giant wave roared towards her. As she reached for his arm and felt the polished texture of his skin, his throbbing veins began to darken, and cracks opened across his flesh. He turned and she caught the barest glimpse of a face, monstrous and abominable, before the wave fell upon her.

Chapter Nine

Lisa flew through the air, thrown by the wave. Her chest slammed against something hard and she dropped to the ground. Round edges dug into her shoulder, her forearm, her hip and knee. Her head flopped to one side and pain jolted her neck. Coppery wetness spread across her tongue.

She blinked, taking in her environment. Shapes pulsed in the dim light. A grid of lines. A railing. Stairs. She was lying on stairs.

The sea, the angel ... it had all been a dream. But why was she here, not nestled under the sheets of her bed?

A door squealed and she heard a patter of feet. She moaned and coughed. More of the coppery tang spread through her mouth like liquid pennies.

"Lisa?" It was David's voice.

She moaned again to call for him. He appeared at the top of the stairs in a T-shirt and pajama bottoms, slippers on his feet.

"Jesus, honey!" he exclaimed. "What happened?"

"I fell, I guess. I think I'm all right. Nothing seems broken."

"Don't move." David scrambled down the stairs and kneeled beside her. He ran his hands over her body, as if patting her down for weapons. "Tell me if anything hurts."

"Everything hurts."

"You know what I mean." He continued to press at her body. "No signs of anything broken. You must have hit the railing first. But you're still going to have some major bruises. And you've got blood on your teeth."

Lisa swirled her tongue over a loose flap of flesh in her mouth. "I think I bit the inside of my cheek."

"What were you doing? Were you trying to get to the bathroom? Why didn't you turn on the light?"

"No ... I don't know ... I was having this incredible dream."

"You mean you were—"

Breaking glass interrupted him. Somewhere on the first floor.

David raised a finger to his lips. Lisa quietly pushed herself up to sitting and rotated her body to face the bottom of the stairwell. Her eyes drilled into the shadows, searching for the cause of the disturbance.

All was still and quiet.

David leaned in to her ear. "Don't move," he whispered. "I'll be right back."

He dashed up the stairs and disappeared into the hallway. Though he was trying to make no sound, Lisa could track his steps as he moved down the hall. There was a familiar squeal of the bedroom door hinge, followed by a moment of silence, then his footfalls in the hall again.

When he reappeared at the top of the stairwell, he held something in his hand. A boxy black handgun.

"Are you crazy?" Lisa whispered. "Where'd you get that?"

"I keep it in the nightstand. It's a Glock."

"I know," she hissed. "A Glock 19. Put it back."

David's eyebrows arched.

"One of my foster-dads was a gun nut," Lisa explained. "But you're asking for trouble. Let's go back upstairs and call the police."

He gave her a sharp look and raised a finger to his mouth again. He stepped past her on the staircase and trotted to the first floor where he disappeared into the gloom of the living area.

Lisa chewed her lower lip. She no longer tasted blood, but the muscles on the left side of her body throbbed. She caught the barest sounds of David's footsteps and tracked them through the house. He went through the living room and into the dining room. Then nothing. Seconds ticked by. The muscles in her stomach churned, as if they were trying to choke her innards.

Should she call out to David? Or would that only announce his presence to any intruders?

More silence. More quiet moments oozing like slugs. Indecision ate away at her.

"David?" she finally whispered into the dark.

"Oh, shit," came his reply. There was a burst of illumination as he turned on the kitchen light.

"You better come down here," David said with a heavy sigh.

Lisa grabbed the handrail and hoisted herself upright. Pain jabbed at her torso and thighs, but she was able to hobble down the stairs and into the living room. David stood in the arched doorway that opened to the kitchen, light streaming from behind him. In one hand, he held the Glock. In the other, a panting pug dog with black fur. Mr. Beverly.

"Did you leave the back door ajar?" he asked. "This guy got in and knocked over a glass on one of the stools."

Lisa sighed, sending a wave of pain through her ribs. "No, I don't... I mean ... I don't think I did."

David set the gun on the kitchen counter. He joined her in the living room and leaned forward, pushing the pug into her face. "Someone wants to say hi."

Lisa smiled and patted the dog's furry head. "You scared us, you little fuzzball. Tim and Tom must be worried."

David nodded to the back door. "We've both had a lot on our minds lately. Maybe somebody forgot to close the door. If the worst that comes out of it is this guy getting in, we're fine."

"I guess."

"How are you feeling? Can you get upstairs?"

"I'll live," Lisa said, rubbing her shoulder and neck. "I just don't understand how I got to the stairs. I remember lying in bed, then being in the middle of this bizarre, incredible dream."

"Don't worry about it. You've been under a lot of stress. From now on, I'll just chain you to the bed at night so you won't be able to wander off. I was planning on doing that, anyway."

Lisa smirked. "Ha ha. You talk pretty tough for a guy holding a tiny dog."

David's gaze lingered on her face, his eyes beaming with affection. "I'll clean up the glass in a bit. You going to be okay while I return this guy next door?"

"Yeah, sure, go on. I'll take some painkillers and drag myself to bed. Maybe I can still get some sleep."

As Mr. Beverly squirmed in his hands, David leaned in and kissed Lisa on the forehead. Then he walked into the kitchen and nudged the back door open with his foot. Shadows grayed his form when he stepped out to the porch. He turned back to the open door. "Love you, babe," he said.

"Love you more."

"Love you most."

David closed the door and was immediately swallowed by the night. Lisa rose from her perch on the sofa and walked up the stairs, leaving the kitchen light on for David's return. On the second floor, she went into the bathroom and turned on the overhead florescent bulb. She stripped off her pajama top and examined herself in the mirror. A row of reddish bruises ran down the left side of her ribs. She opened her mouth and peered at her reflection. A bloody gash on the inside of her cheek marked where teeth had scraped flesh.

She opened the medicine cabinet and removed a bottle of prescription-strength painkillers. She swallowed two pills and stepped into the hallway.

As she headed back to the bedroom, she noticed the open door of her office. A wide beam of moonlight was coming in through the window, spilling across the floor. She walked to the doorway and looked inside. It was as she'd last seen it, everything where it should be.

The photographs on the top shelf of the bookcase drew her eye. She walked to them and looked at the image of her mother. The jarring expression on the woman's face reminded Lisa of the parole hearing tomorrow.

"Don't worry, Mom," Lisa said to the picture. "He's not going to go free. And if he does …"

Margarita Kallman maintained her look of madness, staring at sights only she could see.

Lisa ran her hand along the top shelf of the bookcase. Where was the figurine that had been broken during the move? She was certain she'd left it next to her mother's photo. She walked to the wall, flipped on the overhead light, and returned to the bookshelf.

The ceramic statuette was gone.

Lisa furrowed her brow. Had David taken it? Why would he?

Then perhaps someone else had been in the room? Maybe someone from the party? She recalled seeing David's secretary and her friend with the ruby earrings returning from a trip to the upstairs bathroom.

But why would either of them take a personal artifact of little monetary value?

The painkillers began tickling the base of her skull and the urgency of the questions faded. She turned off the light, walked to the bedroom, and settled onto the mattress. Her heavy eyelids fell shut and she drifted off to sleep, casting any concerns about the missing figurine into the world of her dreams.

Chapter Ten

Jeremiah O'Brien sat at a desk in a windowless room with tan walls. The too-small pants he wore cramped his groin. The collars of the tweed jacket he'd forced his arms into scratched his neck. His hands fidgeted in his lap, defying his fervent desire to appear calm and in control.

A dozen feet away, members of the Ohio Parole Board settled into leather office chairs set before a wide conference table. Most of the group of five women and four men peered at laptops or paper printouts. The rest leaned back in their seats and examined Jeremiah with narrowed eyes.

Jeremiah's lawyer, a mustached Black man named Darius Clarkesdale, sat next to his client. He busily pecked thick fingers at his phone screen and muttered complaints about having to reschedule meetings.

More than a dozen people filled three rows of orange plastic chairs in the public seating area. Jeremiah faced away from them, but he could feel the heat from their collective gaze burning into the back of his skull.

Against the wall to his right stood the two guards who'd rousted Jeremiah from his cell in the morning and driven him to the downtown Hall of Justice. The older man looked to be in his early fifties, the softness of his corpulent body at odds with the grimace carved into his face. The second guard was in every way the opposite: young, rail thin, with milky white skin, and worried, expressive eyes.

"Good morning, everyone." A trim, middle-aged woman in a plum-colored pantsuit stood at the middle of the conference table. "My name is Dr. Adhikari and I am the chairperson of the Ohio Parole Board. I will be leading our conversation today."

In the space behind Jeremiah, chairs groaned as people shifted in their seats.

Dr. Adhikari turned to him, her serene expression offering neither condemnation nor forgiveness. She nodded. "Mr. O'Brien."

He tried to talk, but his throat was impossibly dry. He coughed into his fist and drew what he hoped was a calming breath. "Yes ma'am," he croaked. "I want to thank you for giving me this opportunity to talk, ma'am."

"We are very interested in what you have to say." The chairperson sat in a large office chair and waited as the other board members introduced themselves. When they finished, she declared that the state of Ohio had received Jeremiah's request for a hearing and because he'd served almost twenty years of his sentence, it had been granted. Her eyes, cement colored orbs that reminded Jeremiah of ball bearings, again rolled towards him. "I understand you have several reasons why you believe the state should parole you?"

"Yes ma'am, thank you ma'am. I feel I've done real good in prison, you know? I volunteered in the prison library. And I set up a program for a lot of the fellows who were illiterate. To teach them how to read."

He paused, struggling to interpret the expressions of the parole board members before him. Their slitted eyes and flattened lips told him nothing.

"And, uh, I've been working with the chaplain. He and I have gotten to be real good buddies. I guess he's already talked to you."

Dr. Adhikari's head lolled in a barely perceptible nod.

Jeremiah clasped his palms together, feeling the cool sweat. "I haven't gotten in an ounce of trouble since I've been in the joint, you know? And that ain't easy in a place like that. Even if you don't want trouble, it's got a way of finding you. Especially when you've got the record I do."

A cough came from the back of the room. A high-pitched voice shouted, "Praise Jesus! Guide them with your wisdom, Lord!"

Jeremiah froze. Beside him, Darius Clarkesdale whispered an expletive.

From the group of board members, a small white-haired woman stood and glared into the public seating area. "Please keep your comments to yourself, ma'am," the elderly woman said. "Or we will ask you to leave."

Jeremiah waited for the board member to sit back down, then he continued speaking. "Anyway, ma'am, I mean sirs and ma'ams, I've been in prison a long time, you know? I'm getting to be almost an old man. I feel like an old man already and I'm only forty-seven. I don't want to hurt anybody. I don't got it in me to hurt anybody. I just want to live a quiet life, that's all. Get a little apartment. Get a good job. Be able to walk over to the lake on Sundays and skip rocks on the water. Like I did when I was a little boy."

Dr. Adhikari tilted her head to one side. "Do you still deny your guilt?"

Again, the squawking voice from the back. "Show them his innocence, Lord!"

The white-haired board member shot up. "Ma'am, I will not say it again."

Jeremiah looked at his hands on the table. "Look, I admit I did touch those girls. I've always had the sickness, you know, and I—"

Dr. Adhikari interrupted. "You're not in prison because of those girls, Mr. O'Brien. You already served your sentence for those crimes."

His jaw clenched. He closed his eyes, trying to hide the moisture welling up at the edges. It had been so long. Maybe if he just went along with it, they would let him out. Maybe if he just pretended …

But he had that damn pride.

"You gotta understand. I didn't kill that man! I don't know what happened to him. I've never killed anyone." He tasted the salt of the tears flowing down his cheeks.

Dr. Adhikari's lips pressed together. "Police found shoe prints outside the window of the bedroom where the murder took place, Mr. O'Brien. They matched those prints to boots found in the home you shared with your mother. The mud from the Kallman residence was still on them."

"And I'll say it again," Jeremiah croaked. "I don't know how that all happened. I—"

"Jesus, free this man!"

Jeremiah spun around. The shouting woman perched on a chair in the back of the public seating area. She looked to be in her mid-seventies, though Jeremiah knew she was a decade younger. She wore a purple frock, frayed at the edges. Her silver hair flailed off her scalp in every direction. Her trembling, gnarled hands gripped a Bible.

"Mother," Jeremiah said through gritted teeth. "Can you be quiet? You're not helping."

"Officers," Dr. Adhikari said, "please escort this woman out of the building."

A man in an olive uniform approached Jeremiah's mother and gestured for her to stand. She complied while still jabbering about Jesus Christ and the devil's temptations. Even after she was led through the doors to the outside hallway, her prayers and yelps could be heard in the conference room.

"Back to the matter at hand," Dr. Adhikari said. "My understanding, Mr. O'Brien, is that you were claiming to be innocent of the crime for which you are currently serving a life sentence?"

He wiped his face and met the woman's gaze. She reminded him of teachers he'd known in his youth, women and men who judged their students with pursed lips and irritated sighs.

"Yes, ma'am," he said quietly.

Dr. Adhikari looked at the other board members. "Does anyone have further questions for Mr. O'Brien?" After receiving a litany of "nos," she turned to Jeremiah. "Your presence is no longer needed here, Mr. O'Brien.

The officers will escort you back to the penitentiary and you will be informed when we have made a decision."

Darius Clarkesdale rose from his seat and gave a curt nod. "I'll be in touch." He walked over to the public seating area and folded himself into a chair.

The COs from the prison approached Jeremiah and the older one signaled for him to stand. They handcuffed his wrists and led him towards the door. As he shuffled along, he looked into the public seating area. The faces were unfamiliar. He guessed most of them to be reporters or legal scholars interested in his case.

Then he saw her. The pretty redhead in the back row. She leaned into the chest of a tall young man next to her, almost using his body as a shield.

Was it her? It had to be. The daughter of Derek Kallman, the man he'd been convicted of murdering. He'd never seen her in person, only in photos from newspaper articles. When she was a child, she hadn't come to his trial and her testimony had been taken in private.

She looked at him, her flitting eyes laden with anxiety. But there was another emotion, something hard. He realized she was here to watch him beg for his freedom. She'd come to gape as the justice system turned its screws into him, like he was a victim of some horrible automobile accident bleeding on the side of the freeway.

As the guards shoved him through the doorway, Jeremiah locked eyes with Lisa Kallman. "Remember," he hissed. "Remember to tell the truth!"

Chapter Eleven

The truth?

This maniac thinks he can talk to me about the truth?

Lisa watched from the seating area as the two corrections officers hustled O'Brien out of the room. She'd taken only a few seconds to study the convict's face, but that was all the time she'd needed for his features to burn into her retinas. Yellow bags swelled under his eyes. The corners of his mouth curved down as if affixed in a permanent frown. His hair, trimmed close to his skull, was predominantly gray, making him look a decade older than he was.

He looked tired. Average. Unremarkable.

What had she expected? A monster? If she passed this man on the street, she would not give him a moment's notice.

But Lisa knew a person's face could belie what lay underneath. That *average* man had violently slaughtered her father twenty years ago, driving her mother insane.

She shuddered, rage and grief stabbing at her chest. David turned and gave her a sympathetic look.

But what had O'Brien meant with those final words? *Tell the truth?*

It had to be a ploy, a last-ditch attempt at swaying the parole board with the feint of innocence. She prayed it would fail.

"Miss Kallman?"

Lisa twitched in her seat. The head of the parole board, Dr. Adhikari, was looking at her.

"Yes?"

"May we ask you a few questions?"

"Of course. Do you ... do you want me to come up there?"

"If you don't mind."

Lisa stood, walked to the center of the room, and sat on the chair O'Brien had just vacated. Her nerves calmed when she saw the soft, almost maternal look in Dr. Adhikari's eyes.

"You're quite safe here, Miss Kallman," the woman said. "We just want to talk to you about the crime in question."

"Of course."

Dr. Adhikari removed a pen from her jacket and began tapping it against the laminate finish of the conference table.

"This is never easy to ask, Miss Kallman, but do you have any recollection of the night your father was murdered?"

Lisa took a breath. "I remember parts of it. I don't remember the crime even though I was there. My therapist, Dr. Stein says—"

"Dr. Gretchen Stein?" interrupted a voice. It was the white-haired board member who'd admonished O'Brien's mother. "The one who wrote the book?"

Lisa smiled. It had been several years since she'd been reminded of her therapist's fame. "Yes, that's her."

"I read it," the woman said. "Very compelling."

"I'll tell her you said so," Lisa said. "Anyway, Dr. Stein says I've blocked out the murder itself. She feels that when the human mind undergoes an event that is especially traumatic, it can be wiped from memory. Or buried somewhere deep in the psyche, to prevent the injury that may come with remembering."

"Yes," Dr. Adhikari said, her pen tapping on the table in an easy rhythm. "We've seen such situations before. Is there anything you do remember?"

Lisa exhaled. "I remember most of that day up until I went to bed. I remember my mom and dad unpacking. They were so happy to be in a bigger house. But I was nervous. I missed our old place. And I remember everything after the police and ambulances arrived. I was sitting in the back of a police car with ..." Lisa turned in her chair and looked into the public seating area, her gaze settling on a short, middle-aged man in a brown jacket.

"With him," she said, smiling at the man. He gave her a gentle nod in return.

"You remember Detective McCuddy?" Dr. Adhikari asked.

"Yes. He said that my life was going to be very different from then on. And he was right. But he also told me that no matter how lonely I got or how bad things seemed, there was so much good in the world. And I would always be safe because he was giving me ..." she paused, a frown crossing her face, "... a talisman. He gave me a little statue. The Archangel St. Michael."

Dr. Adhikari stopped her tapping. "The angel whom God chose to lead his armies?"

"Yes. Detective McCuddy said it would watch over me."

A spell of silence settled over the room, interrupted only by the creaks of chairs.

"And your mother?" Dr. Adhikari said. "How has she fared after the crime?"

"She never recovered. She never talks. She just sits … and stares. She's not part of this world anymore."

The chairperson leaned forward and turned her head to the left and right, scanning the faces of her fellow board members. None spoke, but they all appeared to communicate somehow. Lisa wondered if they'd arrived at a silent consensus.

"I don't think we need to take up any more of your time, Miss Kallman. We thank you for being so candid about a very difficult memory."

"Thank you. It was good to talk."

Dr. Adhikari stood and announced the end of the hearing. Board members pushed their chairs back from the conference table and gathered their belongings while talking quietly amongst themselves. Most of the public observers rose and moved towards the exit.

Lisa walked back to David. He had a wide grin on his face. "You did great, babe."

She smiled and looked around the room. Detective McCuddy stood near the doors, an expectant glimmer in his eye.

"Come on." Lisa tugged on David's arm. "There's someone I want you to meet."

Chapter Twelve

"It's been too long, lass."

Clad in a brown leather jacket with a label poking out behind his neck, Detective Devin McCuddy stood in the hallway outside the conference room.

"It has." She moved in to hug him and the familiar scent of a musky aftershave wafted into her nose. "I haven't seen you since my graduation."

They separated, and McCuddy looked up at David. "And who's this sturdy fellow? You haven't finally found a boyfriend, have you?"

Lisa's cheeks warmed. "This is David Hague. He's not my boyfriend ... I mean, he's also my fiancé. David, this is Mr. McCuddy."

The two men shook hands, and David looked appreciatively at the detective. "I understand you were very supportive of Lisa. That night and through the years."

"Aye, even as a wee lass, she was the kind that captured your heart. I always made sure to check in and keep an eye on her. Not that she's ever needed it." McCuddy paused and gazed at Lisa. "You've done very well for yourself. I could not be prouder."

Lisa felt herself blush again, then she noticed a security guard staring at them. Loitering, it seemed, was frowned upon. "Maybe we should get moving," she whispered, and the group began strolling down the corridor.

As they walked, Lisa glanced at McCuddy. Much about his face remained unchanged from the first night she'd met him. His gentle eyes were buffered by the same fleshy bulges. He still beamed a smile that seemed more wistful than happy, as if the toils of his occupation kept him from ever being truly at peace with the world. But now his brown hair had gone gray and thinned at the top. His stubbled chin no longer cut at a sharp angle, but sagged, resembling a bullfrog.

A gold crucifix on a chain rested against the detective's chest. In all the years she'd known him, she'd never seen him without it. The sign of a good Irish Catholic.

David draped an arm around her shoulder and looked over at McCuddy. "What do you think will happen now, sir? Regarding O'Brien? Will he get parole?"

McCuddy puffed out his cheeks and exhaled. "It's difficult to say, isn't it? The board will probably make their decision today, but they won't announce anything for several weeks. They know that if they release an infamous murderer, they'll face an angry public. So they may take some time to think on how to handle that. Get their ducks in a row, so to speak."

A scowl tipped across David's face. "I can't see how they could do it, sir. Let him out, that is. He's a sicko and a menace to the community."

McCuddy let the comment hang in the air, unanswered. Then he cast a paternal look at Lisa. "Don't you worry, lass. Whatever happens, you'll be safe."

The comment hit her like an ice pick to the gut. "Oh my God," she exclaimed.

The bulges around McCuddy's eyes drew back. "What's that, dear? Did I upset you?"

"No. It's just that ... I feel so terrible about this, but the statue, the St. Michael ... his wings broke during the move into our new house. And now he's gone. I've looked everywhere and I can't find him."

McCuddy's look of concern softened into amusement. "Dear Lord, I thought something dreadful had happened. Here you're all upset about that tiny trinket? It hasn't any value."

"But you gave it to me," Lisa said petulantly. "It was special."

He chuckled. "I bought a half dozen of those in a curio shop when I visited Italy, my dear. They were just gaudy little souvenirs. I gave it to you that night in the hopes that it might make you feel better."

"It worked," she said, upset at his refusal to take the loss seriously. "I always felt like it was protecting me."

"You don't need a little statue protecting you anymore, my dear. You've learned how to take care of yourself. Besides, you've got this one watching over you." McCuddy raised a bushy eyebrow towards David.

The trio arrived at the elevator and took it down one floor. They exited the Hall of Justice and crossed the street to a multilevel parking structure. David's Mercedes was parked at the far side of the street level. McCuddy pointed to his vehicle in the up-front area reserved for law enforcement.

As they prepared to separate, Lisa looked at McCuddy. "We just moved into a new house in the Old West End. You should come by. We could make you dinner."

McCuddy gave a soft laugh. "That sounds wonderful. Give me a call." He retrieved a business card from his jacket pocket and handed it to her. The familiar pensive smile crossed his face. "It's so good to see you. To see whom you've become. There's nothing that can happen because of this hearing that will change that."

Lisa leaned in and pulled the older man close. "I owe you so much, Devin." Then she stood back and let David shake the detective's hand. McCuddy gave a wink, turned and ambled towards a sky-blue Prius.

"He seems like a cool guy," David said.

"He was the one constant in my life for all those years. Whether I was at the orphanage or in a foster home, he'd always come by to check up on me."

David nodded and peered into the shadows of the garage. He gestured at his Mercedes parked against the back wall and they hastened towards it, their footsteps clattering against the concrete.

"The Lord can't protect you!"

The trebly squawk that came from behind them was instantly recognizable. Lisa and David turned and saw Jeremiah O'Brien's mother in her tattered dress, standing in the gloom. She held her Bible out in front of her, as if using its holy powers to ward off vampires.

"Oh, Christ," David muttered.

Lisa narrowed her eyes at the woman. "Excuse me?"

O'Brien's mother murmured something unintelligible and looked down at the ground, her head moving from side to side. Then she locked her gaze on Lisa. "I can see it just by looking at you. Plain as the nose on your face. You're cursed!"

David stomped forward. "Beat it, lady. I could nail you with a harassment charge without even trying."

The woman stayed put and her nostrils flared into perfect black ovals. "What did you say to those people about my boy? He never did nothin' to you."

Lisa spat her reply. "I didn't have to say anything about him. They know what he did. They found the proof when I was a child."

The old woman went back to babbling and shaking her head. She opened her Bible and began flipping through it, turning pages in groups. At various points, she paused and recited a passage, the fingers of one hand trailing the words in the air as she spoke.

David backed up, relaxing his shoulders. "Just get out of here, you crazy bitch."

A few passersby in the garage were looking over, curious about the developing situation.

"*No!*" the woman screamed. She marched forward in three blocky, bow-legged steps, stopping close to Lisa. "You're damned, and you want to take my boy to hell with you!"

David lunged at the woman. She stumbled backwards, almost toppling to the ground.

"Hey!" A uniformed police officer rushed over. "What the hell is going on here?"

David pointed at the woman. "This old hag just told my girlfriend to go to hell."

"Gee, that does give you the right to commit assault," the cop said, his voice dripping with sarcasm.

David took a breath. "Look ... this is a complicated situation."

"Her son murdered my father twenty years ago," Lisa said.

The cop's angry expression turned to puzzlement. "You're Lisa Kallman?" He looked at the woman. "This is Jeremiah O'Brien's mother?"

Lisa nodded, as the woman skimmed through the Bible once more.

The cop holstered his baton and rubbed his chin. "I think it might be best if you two just get in your car and leave. If you have a problem with anyone in the future, remember that it's a crime to hit people."

David rubbed his palms together. "Thank you, sir." He led Lisa to the passenger side of the Mercedes and opened the door. She got inside and watched in the rearview mirror as the officer escorted the old woman to the front of the garage. After getting in the driver's side, David gunned the engine and drove towards the exit.

"Well," he said once they were out of the confines of the building. "That almost went better than expected."

"At least it explains a few things," Lisa said. "I'm starting to understand why O'Brien turned out the way he did. I mean, if that woman was his mother."

David frowned. "I don't buy that. Plenty of people have lousy parents but don't become child molesters or murderers. There's such a thing as plain old evil in the world, babe. And O'Brien certainly qualifies."

Lisa gasped, surprised at the edge in her fiancé's voice. What right did he have to be angry? This was her tragedy, not his. But she let his words go unanswered, and the fingers of her right hand trailed against her cheek. After several moments, she said, "There's one thing I don't understand."

"What's that, babe?"

"O'Brien's mother said I'm damned. What do you think she meant?"

"She's just a crazy old lady. She blames you for putting her son in prison. She refuses to admit what he did."

"That's not what it sounded like to me. It sounded like—"

"Look, babe," David interrupted. "Don't worry about it. You did a great job in front of the parole board today. If they have any sense, they'll keep O'Brien locked up until he's dead and then some."

She continued to brush her cheek as she stared out the window. Slowly, the gray concrete of downtown Toledo gave way to the colorful homes of the Old West End.

But the neighborhood's quaint charm could not quiet the unease that percolated in Lisa's gut. As her mind spun a web of thoughts, she stayed quiet for the rest of the drive home.

Chapter Thirteen

A HIGH-PITCHED SQUEAK FILLED the room when Lisa shifted in her seat. The armchair's leather upholstery felt cold against her hands, which she'd nervously jammed under her knees.

Several feet away, Dr. Gretchen Stein perched before an ultramodern desk made out of glass partitions fitted into a metal frame. The middle-aged psychologist had stayed silent as Lisa had recounted her experience at Jeremiah O'Brien's parole hearing, but now she leaned forward and looked intently at Lisa.

"You understand why I couldn't be there?" Dr. Stein asked in a voice that held contradictory traces of professional authority and maternal affection.

"Because I need to stand on my own two feet," Lisa replied, barely restraining her irritation.

"Exactly. You've become a very capable young woman."

"That's what everyone keeps telling me."

Dr. Stein leaned back in her chair, brought her fingertips together and pressed them against her thin lips. Had she been a balding, white-bearded man, the pose would've cast her in the spitting image of an early 20th-century psychoanalyst. Instead, she was a small, portly, gray-haired woman dressed in a sensible teal green pantsuit. She offered no reply to Lisa's comment, seemingly letting the silence speak volumes.

Avoiding Dr. Stein's gaze, Lisa picked a mug of coffee off the desk. She took a sip and looked around the office, noting the extensive renovations since her visit several months ago. Previously, the rectangular room had been painted beige and filled with bland IKEA furniture. Now it resembled the probing chamber of a UFO. Shiny, black plastic paneling covered the walls. Several art déco lamps sat in corners or on end tables. A metallic bookshelf held a blinking stereo system and rows of dictionary-thick academic tomes.

Most conspicuous was the ceiling; it glowed blue, reflecting muted light from tracks of fluorescent bulbs. Lisa knew from her academic studies that the color was supposed to carry a calming effect. In this case, it only heightened the sensation of being in a bad science-fiction film.

The therapist resumed speaking. "Facing O'Brien … that was an important step. It gave you an opportunity to see that he has no power over you."

"You're right. He seemed so weak. There was nothing frightening about him. He was almost frail."

Dr. Stein nodded. "He's doubtless changed since the night he killed your father, especially being in the prison environment. His brain has slowed, his various appetites have dwindled. As you know, when we get older, we lose the neurotransmitters that energize and deliver pleasure to our brains. Our hunger for the bounty of life diminishes. Now he seeks the familiar and expected. There's a reason most murderers are young men."

Lisa fought the urge to bite her lower lip, fearful the therapist would analyze the tic's significance. Instead, she said, "I remember when I was a teenager and I started having nightmares about him. You told me I had to think of him as just a man. Not a demon, not a monster. To be honest, I thought you had no idea what you were talking about. But at the parole hearing, he actually cried when he begged them to let him out. It was sad. And pathetic."

"We have no idea what happened in his life to make him the way he was."

"We might. After the parole hearing, his mother harassed David and me in the parking lot. She was a real loon, some kind of religious nut." Lisa paused, considering whether to mention that the interaction had almost turned violent. She decided against it.

Dr. Stein's clucked her tongue. "Religious extremists often ruin their children's' lives. We'd be better off if Child Protective Services had the power to remove youths from such homes."

Lisa sunk into the armchair. "If O'Brien gets out ... what do you think he will do?"

"You know I can't answer that question. We have no control over the behavior of others, only ourselves. Do you feel you're prepared if he is released?"

"I guess so. We're armed. David has a handgun. He got it out a few nights ago when we thought someone had broken into the house."

Dr. Stein's jaw tightened. "I don't approve of handguns. If our society wasn't so obsessed with firearms, situations like what happened to you as a child would be much more infrequent."

"O'Brien didn't use a gun. When he killed my father, I mean."

"However," Dr. Stein said, ignoring Lisa's comment, "I trust you to employ good judgment. You are an intelligent young woman in the prime of your life. You've survived a highly irregular childhood. You've earned two academic degrees. You're going to be married, and you're embarking on a career helping others who survived trauma. A choice I'd like to think I had some influence on."

"Of course," Lisa said with a smile. "I owe you so much, Gretchen."

This was true. When Lisa had first come under Dr. Stein's care, weeks after the death of her father, she'd been mute, staring out at the world with darting eyes, intent on finding a bogeyman behind every corner. With the psychologist's guidance, Lisa had learned to confront her fears, to see the world as it was, not the waking nightmare she believed it to be. During the ensuing years of therapy, she'd blossomed into a teenager and then a young woman, gaining confidence and poise.

Dr. Stein pushed back from the glass desk and stood from her chair. "I believe we're done for today."

"Yes. And I do need to get going. I told David I'd be back for dinner by seven."

Lisa set down her coffee and walked over to embrace Dr. Stein. The small woman gave her a curt hug and stepped back. "I'll see you again in a month, no?"

"I'll call your secretary and schedule it," Lisa said. "Goodbye, Gretchen."

As she padded across the soft carpet towards the exit, an item on a corner table caught her eye. She walked over and picked up a book. On the cover was a picture of herself as a child of seven, a fearful look on her face. The title read *Out of the Shadows: One Child's Journey Through the Ultimate Tragedy*. Dr. Stein's name was shown prominently as the author.

Lisa glanced at her therapist. "Is this a new printing?" she asked. "I've never seen this picture before."

"Yes," Dr. Stein said. "It's a new paperback edition. They asked me to write an updated introduction. I'm sorry, I must have forgotten to tell you about it."

Lisa flipped the paperback over. On the back was a synopsis of both the book and her life. The murder of her father. The mental disintegration of her mother. Years in orphanages and foster care. And Lisa's salvation through the determined efforts of her therapist.

She set the book down.

Dr. Stein smiled. "I'm going to LA in a week to do some radio interviews and promotion. And there's some possibility of a television special."

Lisa clenched her teeth, blocking the churning emotions from rising to her face. Instead, she forced a weak smile.

"I hope everything goes well," she said before walking out the door.

Chapter Fourteen

Katrina Chen moaned as the man above her grabbed the headboard and pulled his body forward. Her hands stroked his shoulders, brushing down the sides of his naked torso and coming to rest on his butt. She felt his body roll back, as if being drawn out by the tides of an invisible sea. Then he thrust into her again.

They were in a small bedroom, two bodies tightly coiled underneath a soft yellow sheet. A trail of discarded clothes ran from the door to the bed. Two half finished glasses of wine sat on an oak dresser. An empty bottle lay on the floor near a corner.

The man leaned down and nuzzled the flesh under her ear, his heavy bursts of breath warming her skin. Then he arched his back, removed his hand from the headboard, and wrapped it around her throat. He smiled when she moaned her approval. But those moans quieted in the swell of panic when his fingers tightened into a vice grip. The bed rocked furiously against the floor, clacking in time with the man's plunging hips. He released his hold and his face flushed. He groaned, cried out, and collapsed onto her body.

"Liked that, did you?" asked Katrina. She ran a hand alongside her breasts to her throat where she could feel bruises already starting to form.

"That was fucking great," David Hague replied. "I mean literally fucking great." He laughed at his pun and rolled away from her, sweeping most of the sheets off the single size bed.

She stared at the ceiling, her pulse quieting in her temples. She was in an all-too-familiar situation: post-coitus with a man she barely knew. She couldn't stop her mind from replaying the events that had led up to this moment.

When David's text message requesting an estimate for feng shui services had appeared the previous weekend, she'd informed him she would need to examine the property and they'd agreed on the coming Monday afternoon. When she'd arrived at the house, she'd not been surprised to find him alone. He'd invited her to settle onto one of the garish plaid couches in the living room, and they'd commenced into a discussion of the feng shui practice, life in Toledo, and their respective college experiences. After a half hour, David had opened a bottle of wine. Soon his quick glances had turned into steady eye contact, and his easy smile had beamed a penetrating charm. They'd finished the bottle and started on a second. He'd asked if she would need to see the upstairs, and Katrina had said yes, knowing full well what she was agreeing to. Within minutes, they were in the guest bedroom, frantically tearing off their clothes, eagerly groping each other's bodies.

David's aggressiveness in bed had caught her off guard. She'd experienced her share of lovers, some of whom were excited by choking or spanking, but usually that kind of role-play was agreed upon in advance. He'd not asked for consent, and for a moment, as his grip had closed against her throat, she'd wondered whether the situation was turning into something far more sinister. But now, as he lay beside her, his chest rising and falling with slow breaths, his flaccid penis still wrapped in a condom, the danger seemed all but gone.

"You like it rough," she said. "Does Lisa let you play hard?"

He repositioned himself on the edge of the bed. "That's none of your business. Don't bring her into this."

"I presume you two don't have an open relationship?"

He removed the condom and grabbed a pair of boxer shorts. As he stepped into them, Katrina caught sight of his front reflected in a full-length oval mirror mounted on a stand across the room. His face was twisted in annoyance. "You knew what was going on here," he said. "We negotiated all this when you were giving me eyes at the party. Do I really look like I give a shit about fung shu?"

"Feng shui," Katrina corrected him, masking the sting of his words.

"Whatever. The point is this stays between us."

Her body tensed with anger. "You take a lot of chances for a guy worried about keeping secrets. We're in your house. Your girlfriend, sorry, *fiancée*, could come home anytime."

David picked a wine glass off the dresser and swallowed what was left. "I know where Lisa is. I know where she goes. She won't be home for another hour."

"Still ..."

His eyes drilled into her. "Let me make this perfectly clear. If Lisa finds out about this, you will regret it, you understand? I'll make you wish you were never born."

She held his gaze for a moment, then a beat more, until the simmering intensity in his pupils threatened to scald her. He towered above the bed, his muscles taut, while she lay naked and soft.

"Whatever," she muttered under her breath.

David flashed a smirk, his eyes glinting with satisfaction. He picked Katrina's black blouse and white cigarette pants off the floor and tossed them on her lap. "I've got to take a shower. You better get dressed." He scooped up his T-shirt and jeans, and walked into the hallway. Moments later, the wall pipes hissed with running water.

Well, this was a mistake, Katrina thought. At the party, she'd been unwilling to concede to herself the full power of David's magnetism. But he was right; she had been looking at him and giving him signs. And she'd known what possibilities were in the air when she'd arrived at his house that afternoon. In particular, which possibilities she hoped to explore.

David, however, had turned out to be a waste, a selfish lover. Why had she even bothered to fake those moans? But she knew the answer. As much as she hated to admit it, there was still a part of her that thought if she could get men to want her, to lust after her, she would feel some kind of power. As she sat on the bed and pulled her pants over her thighs, her cheeks grew flush with anger and shame.

In the end, a guy like David was pretty easy to figure out. Classic Madonna-whore complex. Sweet, delicate Lisa was his Madonna. Which meant Katrina was …

Her faux ruby earrings lay on the table beside the bed. The gems had earned high praise at the party, and she'd worn them again to today's rendezvous with David, but she'd removed them when they'd begun to fuck. Now she reached over and picked one earring off the table, preparing to attach it to her ear.

She stopped when she recalled that Lisa had liked the rubies. The fiancée of the man she'd just slept with had complimented her on the beauty of her jewelry. The poor woman had lost her father to a madman, and now she was about to marry Mr. Hyde. Life could be so unfair.

Sitting on the bed, Katrina raised the earring a few inches above the top of the headboard. She opened her hand, and the gem fell, landing somewhere in the crevice between the bed and wall.

"Oops," she said to herself.

The shower stopped. Within seconds, she heard David rapping the lyrics to a popular hip-hop song. In her mind's eye, she could see him performing for the mirror as he dressed and groomed.

She stepped off the bed and picked a pair of white pumps with red zebra stripes off the floor. As she pulled the shoes on, she looked at the digital clock on the nightstand and saw it was 6:26 p.m. She walked into the hallway as a clothed David exited the bathroom. He mumbled something vaguely apologetic and moved to let her pass.

"Don't worry, I can let myself out," Katrina said. As she descended the stairs, she heard David's soft footsteps behind her. When they were both near the front entrance, he stepped around her and opened the door. An act of chivalry, no doubt.

David looked contrite. "Look, I didn't mean to get so melodramatic back there."

Katrina said nothing.

"So, uh, if we're clear about everything, maybe we could do this again sometime?"

She rolled her eyes. "Yeah. Like that's going to happen." She walked onto the front porch and down the steps.

When she reached the sidewalk, she turned back and saw David standing in the open doorway. He peered out into the neighborhood, alert for curious neighbors. Seeing no one, he cast a steely glance her way.

"Just remember what I said."

Chapter Fifteen

As the last rays of the setting sun warmed the houses on the east side of the street, Katrina walked to her car. She'd parked several blocks away from David's house, partly because space was limited, and partly because parking too close didn't seem like a good idea. What was the name of the street she'd parked on? Something with an "F". Fullbrook.

While she strolled, she weighed David's threat. In all likelihood, it was empty. He was too Abercrombie & Fitch to actually turn violent. Boys like him were all talk.

Still, there had been that moment when they were in bed together, and his fingers wrapped around her neck ...

Questions burned in her mind. How had someone like Lisa ended up with a man like David? Was the redhead truly oblivious to this aspect of her fiancé's personality? If so, how had he kept his dark side so hidden?

It wouldn't stay a secret for much longer, Katrina mused. Once the wedding rings slipped on their fingers, the mask would come off.

Men—they were all bastards. Of course, they only got away with their crimes because some women let them, even enabled them. Katrina knew her desires often led her into dangerous situations, but at least she went in with her eyes open. Women like Lisa were too blind or naïve to see what they were getting into.

Katrina felt a renewed sense of shame for her actions. But what more could she do? Maybe the earring would fix it.

She turned onto Fullbrook Street, now only a few minutes from her car. The sun had dropped below the visible horizon, and the sky was a beautiful gradient of dark blue smearing to gray. She examined the houses passing alongside her as she walked. They were old; not her thing, but still beautiful. If houses were people, these would be friendly grandparents, settled in their rocking chairs, but eager to pull toddlers onto their laps and entertain them with stories. And the stately mansions were obviously cared for. The front gardens were well tended, the exteriors recently painted, the windows shined and spotless.

She came to an abrupt stop. Before her was the burned Victorian she and Sharon had discovered on the night of the housewarming party. She hadn't noticed it when she'd parked earlier.

The house stood blackened and scarred, bereft of the familial charm of the surrounding homes. Broken window frames cut into a charcoal scabbed exterior. Wet leaves filled the gutters, rotting into muck. Fluttering yellow caution tape marked the perimeter of the property, making clear none should enter.

Despite its damaged state, Katrina was drawn in by the house's character. While the other Victorians on the block were staid and conventional, this one took risks. It was not merely a collection of predictable angles and slants, rather its form twisted and turned like an impassioned dancer giving shape to deep and dark anxieties. And the single turret that rose along the right side of the structure seemed to reach defiantly towards the dimming sky.

She caught sight of her car at the end of the block and resumed walking. Then she heard it, a plaintive whimper. An animal? Or a child? She squinted, her eyes scouring the burned house's lawn, quickly spotting two tiny circles staring back at her. Her sense of the space around those twin dots expanded to reveal the face of a small dog, one she immediately recognized. The black pug named Mr. Beverly lay on his side in a patch of weeds at one edge of the yard.

"Hey little guy," Katrina called out. Why was a pet who'd seemed so well cared for when she'd first seen him now running loose?

The dog made another sound—a half sigh, half moan—then righted himself and began limping towards the rear of the house.

"Oh no. Are you hurt, baby?"

The pug ignored her and continued walking with its wounded gait.

Katrina fretted. She couldn't let the injured animal wander loose. Should she go back to David? That didn't seem smart. She recalled the dog's owners were neighbors of his, but in which house? And how would she explain what she was doing in their neighborhood at—Katrina checked her watch—6:42 in the evening?

Mr. Beverly turned and disappeared behind the dilapidated mansion.

"Shit, shit, shit." She looked around. The sidewalks on both sides of the street were empty. Through the windows of neighboring houses, she could see people preparing dinner or eating. It seemed unlikely any of them would want to suspend their activities to go looking for a dog.

She ducked under the yellow tape and approached the turreted side of the house. Her high heels sunk into the soft earth, making it difficult to walk, but she couldn't go barefoot. She slowly made her way past the swell of the turret and along the house's exterior wall, eventually rounding the back corner. Here, the mansion abutted a six-foot gap that ran parallel with a dark-stained wooden fence. The slats only rose eight feet in the air, and she could see the thicket of trees and the rooftop of another stately Victorian on the other side.

A waxing gibbous moon hung in the western sky, teardrops of its light illuminating the corridor between the house and the fence. Katrina ran her gaze over crowded thistle bushes and patches of dried grass, before spotting Mr. Beverly about twenty feet away. The dog sat on his hind legs and looked up at her with mournful, liquid eyes.

"Okay, baby. Don't go anywhere. Mommy's coming."

As if on cue, Mr. Beverly stood and began walking away. After a few limping steps, he turned towards a small stairwell that went down to the mansion's foundation. He approached the first step, sniffed it, and clumsily hopped downward.

"Oh, come on!" Katrina muttered. Still wobbly on her heels, she put one hand against the soot-covered house. Using the wall for support, she gingerly made her way to the stairwell and peered down into it. The stairwell went down several steps to a basement door that hung half open on its hinges. Mr. Beverly was nowhere to be seen.

She paused. She loved animals, but this was getting ridiculous. Again, she considered tracking down the dog's owners, but was still nervous about having to explain her presence in the neighborhood. Maybe she could find the dog and call the city's animal control department, who would then return him to his owners? She pulled her cell phone from her purse, switched on the flashlight and aimed the beam at the stairs. Her heels clacked against concrete as she descended the steps one by one. At the bottom, she pulled open the rotting, blackened door.

Light dripped in through basement windows and revealed what had once been a laundry room. On the left, a folded ironing table hung from the wall. On the right was a trio of rusty metal sinks. Corroded pipes slithered up the wall into slots in the ceiling.

The room smelled of musty wood. And something else. Decaying garbage or baked rubber.

Mr. Beverly sat in the shadows of the middle sink, panting.

Pushing away spider webs, Katrina went to the metal fixture and leaned down, looking underneath. The wounded animal might be dangerous, and she fought her urge to reach out and stroke his chin.

"What am I going to do with you? You seem to be making a lot of trouble for both of us."

The dog looked up at her with sad, wet eyes. Reflected in the twin circles were blurry images of the basement doorway, the concrete stairs, and the outside fence. Katrina watched a dark shape rise up behind her, a moment before she felt a hand wrap around her throat.

Chapter Sixteen

Lisa clenched the steering wheel and struggled to quell the expletives yearning to burst from her lips. Crosstown traffic had slowed her drive home from her therapy appointment, and when she'd arrived at the Old West End, she'd discovered a temporary sign announcing that the north sides of all streets were blocked off for a cleaning the next day. Finding parking anywhere near her house would be impossible.

She felt her shoulders tighten in annoyance: she always hated being late. David had been so supportive recently, especially during the parole hearing. After their fight, she'd had doubts about their relationship, and a sinking feeling that a distance was growing between them. But that had all been in her head. Their relationship was stronger than ever.

"Yes!" she shouted when she spied an open spot between two trucks. She pulled into the tight space, killed the engine and looked around the inside of the SUV for anything to take to the house. Various objects littered the passenger seat, including two pairs of sunglasses, a pile of work pamphlets, and a bag of peanuts. Her purse lay on the floor mat of the passenger side. Hooked around the rear-view mirror was a parking pass good for two hours in the garage underneath Dr. Stein's office complex.

Dr. Stein. Lisa thought about the meeting, particularly her irritation upon learning of the latest reprint of *Out of the Shadows*.

The book had been published when she'd turned eighteen. It had been praised by readers and given almost universally positive reviews by the media. For the several years after its release, Lisa had received consolatory emails and letters from people who'd also suffered the loss of a parent or loved one. And the book had done well for Dr. Stein; the therapist had appeared on several national television shows, raising her professional stature.

By the time Lisa had entered graduate school, sales of *Out of the Shadows* had tapered off. In response, the publishers had released a second edition augmented with a new introduction and an epilogue that updated readers on general details of Lisa's life. The new version had temporarily revived interest in her story before it too faded from popular consciousness.

So what was the point of releasing it yet again?

She grabbed her purse and stepped out onto the sidewalk. A purple dusk was slowly fading into night and a gloom had settled onto the houses around her. Because of the dimness, it took her a few seconds to realize she was standing in front of the burned out Victorian she and David had spied more than a week ago. Monster Mansion.

When she'd seen the house before, in the sunlight of a lazy Sunday afternoon, she'd found it insignificant and harmless. Now, something was different. The building's two sections—the main body that rose up to an angular roof, and the cylindrical turret topped off with an upside-down cone—looked like a pair of bitter, blackened warlocks. Twin malcontents who wished only violence and despair on the world.

Lisa smirked, aware of the runaway quality of her thoughts. It was funny how the mind could take something as innocuous as an empty building and give it personality and intent. Like seeing faces in the clouds.

She gasped. Something moved in the windows in the top story of the turret. A human-sized shape flashing behind the shards of glass that clung to fire-scarred grilles.

Could there be squatters inside? Homeless people who'd taken up residence in the condemned building? It seemed unlikely. Even the chilly open air of Toledo's fall nights would be preferable to entering a home that looked so structurally unsound. More likely it had been a trick of the light, or maybe some kind of animal. She dismissed the percept and turned to walk home.

Ten steps later, she heard it. A distant, guttural voice that sounded like someone talking with their mouth full.

"Open the door, Lisa. I want to get out."

She whirled back towards the house. Somehow she knew the voice had come from that direction, though every word had echoed as if it were bouncing in her skull. She scanned the exterior, searching for anything visible through windows cloudy with soot. She envisioned a monstrous creature looking out at the street, the grin stretched across its face revealing rows of pointed shark teeth.

But the windows were empty. There was nothing to see.

Her heart surged. Sweat dampened her palms. It wasn't just the voice—there was something else. Why did those words seem so familiar? Why did the voice *sound* so familiar?

At the end of the block, an engine revved. A pair of headlights burst to life, the yellow beams assaulting her eyes. A sports car took off down the street and, as it passed, teenage voices shouted something unintelligible. The vehicle reached the corner and turned in a squeal of tires.

The intrusion broke the moment's eerie mood. Her heartbeat began to slow and the tremor that had overtaken her body faded. She realized she'd temporarily left the physical world and fallen into the interior of her mind, a dark domain where a seven-year-old girl lived forever in terror. But now she was back on the solid ground of reality.

But what had happened? Was the stress of her life causing her mind to play tricks on her? Maybe the voice came from a horror movie she'd seen as a kid, churned up in her subconscious by a walk past a scary-looking house. It was plausible. After all, less than a week ago, she'd been in a room with the man who'd murdered her father. And she'd just spent an hour discussing her mental state with her therapist.

All that activity was bound to shake loose some detritus of emotion.

It was stress. It had to be.

Still, as she made her way home, she found herself falling into a quick jog. The farther she got from the burned house, the better.

Part Two

Chapter Seventeen

The administrators of the Grand March Correctional Facility kept the temperature of the visiting area cool, but Jeremiah suspected it was his frazzled nerves that sent a shudder down his spine when he parked himself on a metal chair bolted to the floor. With hands trembling in their handcuffs, he lifted a phone handset to his ear. He'd been dreading this meeting for days.

On the other side of a Plexiglas partition, Darius Clarkesdale huffed a curt greeting. The mustached lawyer's eyes stayed low, never rising to meet his client.

Jeremiah's gut rolled in his belly. Unlike his mother, he did not believe in omens, but this did not bode well.

The 20' x 30' visiting area was busy. Of the twelve seats available at the long metal table, eight now held prisoners who stared at their guests in an adjoining room on the other side of the Plexiglas. Two corrections officers, armed with batons and canisters of pepper spray, stood by the room's only entrance. One of the men, short and fat, had been nicknamed "Angry Elvis" by the prisoners because of his greased back pompadour and persistent scowl. The second guard was the fair-skinned young man with nervous, darting eyes who'd escorted Jeremiah to his parole hearing the previous week.

Jeremiah turned back to the transparent partition and saw the glint of the laminated yellow visitor's badge pinned to Clarkesdale's jacket. The lawyer's stilted monotone crackled through the phone as he delivered a jargon-laden summary of the status of Jeremiah's clemency case. *Undeclared political calculations will doubtless be factored into the determination ... board must consider questions of public safety ... a particularly positive disposition at this juncture unlikely ...* The phrases seemed designed to frustrate any attempt at discerning their true meaning.

As Clarkesdale droned on, Jeremiah's mind drifted back to his first lawyer, a nervous woman from the public defender's office who'd defended him against charges of child molestation. Her incoherent closing argument had earned him a four-year sentence at a high security prison near Dayton, a hellhole where he'd been routinely assaulted by larger, gang affiliated inmates. But she'd been Perry Mason compared to the furtive man with tiny eyes who'd insisted that taking the plea deal offered during the Derek Kallman murder trial was the only way to avoid the death penalty. When Jeremiah had asserted his innocence, the attorney had wearily replied, "All my clients are innocent."

The temperature in the visiting room seemed to drop another five degrees and Jeremiah found himself catching snatches of other conversations around him. A Latino prisoner spat a cascade of Spanish at a teary-eyed elderly woman opposite him. A slender convict with bushy blond hair complained about prison food to an older, well-dressed man holding a cane. Two seats over from Jeremiah, a tattooed skinhead with a long red beard hurled accusations of infidelity at a fleshy blonde bimbo.

Clarkesdale stared through the partition, his eyebrows raised. The lawyer had probably asked a question, but Jeremiah responded with his own, the only one that interested him

"If I'm denied parole, then what?"

"You'll have an option to appeal within sixty days of the Notice of Action advising you of the board's decision. That appeal will go to the National Appeals Board. But if they reject it, you're out of options."

The handcuffs bit into Jeremiah's wrists. Pins and needles began to radiate from his fingertips. "So when do I get the Notice of Action?"

Clarkesdale didn't actually shrug, but he might as well have. "It should come in soon. It has to appear within a month, and it's been a week already."

Jeremiah paused, shifting the phone from one hand to the other. "What are my odds here?"

"I'm not going to lie to you, Mr. O'Brien. From what I saw, after the board talked to Ms. Kallman, their minds were made up. And not in your favor."

The phone cord stretched taut as Jeremiah leaned back in his seat. How many more years would he have to rot in this concrete hellhole? Just days ago, freedom had seemed so close he could taste it. And now …

The bearded skinhead two seats down began to shout. He pounded his shackled fists against the transparent partition while denouncing the woman across from him for her whoredom.

Jeremiah knew the guards would react quickly, perhaps violently. He set the handset on the table and turned in his chair to monitor the situation.

Angry Elvis marched up behind the skinhead. There was a clang as the heavyset CO swung his baton against the back of the bearded prisoner's metal chair. "Flannery, shut the hell up!"

The prisoner grew still as the cords of muscle in his neck pulled tight. Then he quickly ducked down, yanked up the hem of his pant leg, and removed a pointed strip of metal from a cloth holster tied to his ankle. As Jeremiah gaped, the man spun in his seat and jammed the shiv into Angry Elvis's neck.

The officer stumbled backward and dropped his baton. Flannery stood and jackhammered his weapon several more times into the guard's jugular. A geyser of blood arched through the air, spattering against the Plexiglas partition. Angry Elvis dropped to his knees, clawing at the blade now lodged in his throat.

As the other prisoners hooted and hollered, Jeremiah scanned the room for the younger CO. The pale boy stood by the locked door, seemingly frozen in place. After several seconds, he reached for his pepper spray, but it was too late. Flannery crossed the room and smashed his beefy forehead into the boy's nose. The officer crumpled to the floor.

A shrill alarm sounded in the room, drilling into Jeremiah's ears.

Flannery now towered above the prostrate guard who curled on the floor. The prisoner lifted his foot above the boy's neck, ready to stomp.

Jeremiah shot across the room, hooked his handcuffs over Flannery's head, and yanked the chain into the man's throat. The skinhead growled and spun to one side, sandwiching Jeremiah against the concrete wall. The air shot out of his lungs and his legs felt like pudding.

Flannery dropped his head under the handcuffs, then placed two meaty paws underneath Jeremiah's armpits, heaving him into the air. For a half second, Jeremiah felt like he was on a rollercoaster, his surroundings whizzing past him in a blur. He came down hard on the concrete, and a grenade of pain detonated across his back. Blots of red and white sparked in his vision field, through which he saw a grinning Flannery turn back to the young CO on the floor.

The door burst open and a dozen guards swarmed into the room. A barrage of barbed Taser darts shot into Flannery's chest, jolting him with electricity causing his legs to crumple. Several guards ran to Jeremiah and began pounding his torso and legs with their batons. His muscles screamed in agony under the blows, stifling his pleas for mercy. As suffocating waves of pain smothered him into unconsciousness, Jeremiah heard the young guard he'd saved begging the other guards to stop their beating. "No, he's the one who saved me!"

Chapter Eighteen

"What happened to you is not unusual," Dr. Stein said. "The experience of hearing unexplained voices has long been associated with periods of intense stress."

Letting her words settle in the air, she leaned back in her office chair. She was not surprised to be talking with Lisa Kallman for the second time in as many days. Indeed, her former patient had seemed tense during her previous visit, as if weighed down by an emotional turmoil that she would not admit to (or was not consciously aware of). When Lisa had called that morning and reported hearing a malevolent voice coming from the turret of an abandoned Victorian mansion, Dr. Stein had presumed classic paracusia—stress-caused auditory hallucinations.

"But they sounded so real," Lisa insisted. She sat with her back straight in the leather armchair, her taut muscles making her look like an antelope wary of approaching leopards. "And it was more than just a voice. I'd swear I saw someone moving around in there."

"Our senses are imperfect, Lisa. What they show us of the outside world is, at best, only an impression. The mind takes the information it receives from our eyes and ears and tries to consolidate it into a narrative. You simply saw what your brain wanted you to see."

Lisa's frown seemed to reflect equal parts anger and confusion. "But why?" she asked. "Why does my brain want me to see something like that?"

Dr. Stein set her fingertips together. "What is your greatest worry right now? You fear the man who murdered your father is going to be released from prison. He's going to 'get out.' I suspect that your psyche, when confronted with the disturbing imagery of this strange house, superimposed this anxiety onto your environment."

The tight line of Lisa's lips softened, but her eyes betrayed a continuing angst. "That makes sense," she said. "It does. But there was something else. I can't explain it, but something seemed so familiar about the whole experience. Like it had happened before."

Dr. Stein nodded. "Déjà vu is acknowledged as a genuine psychological phenomenon. Its causes are not completely understood, but it involves chemical activity in the brain. However, the fact that an event *seems* familiar does not mean that it *is* familiar. Again, your mind is playing tricks on you."

The young woman's shoulders relaxed and she dropped back in her chair, as if surrendering to the argument. "Everything you're saying corresponds with my own training. But I guess it's one thing to read about hallucinations or déjà vu in a textbook. It's not the same as actually experiencing them."

"Of course. Even people trained in the psychological sciences, like us, can be fooled by the mind. It's a cunning adversary."

Lisa inhaled and released a breath. "I just want this to be over. I just want to know they're not going to let O'Brien out."

"That's perfectly normal. This is one of the most stressful periods you've experienced in a great while. In all the years we've been talking, nothing has brought you to the proximity of your father's murder like this parole hearing. But you can't let one event absorb the focus of your life. You need to concentrate on your responsibilities. Think about planning for your marriage. What projects are your priorities at work?"

"We're having some of the kids over to the house on Saturday for a barbecue. I don't think David's really looking forward to it. He thinks they're going to break something."

Dr. Stein chuckled. "That's good. That's positive. You are helping the children live their lives."

Lisa looked down at the carpet. Dr. Stein let the silence linger for a moment, then spoke. "Do you feel better?"

"I guess so. I feel pretty silly coming here. Wasting your time like this."

"You shouldn't. These are exactly the kinds of events I need to be aware of. Don't let your brain outsmart you."

Flashing a soft smile, Lisa rose from the armchair. Dr. Stein stood and joined her, and they walked to the door. After a quick hug, her troubled former patient opened the door and rounded a corner into the reception area.

A tingling warmth settled in Dr. Stein's stomach and a wetness gathered in her eyes. She was proud of Lisa. The young woman had endured so much more than one person should. The terrible tragedy of her childhood. Then bouncing among various foster families, many of whom found the quiet, moody girl to be strange and unnerving. But as an adult, Lisa had prevailed by pursuing an academic degree and now, despite a few recent bumps on the road, seemed poised to live a happy, fulfilling life.

Dr. Stein checked her watch, remembering she'd been booked for a therapy session in a half hour. She returned to her desk and retrieved a folder containing handwritten notes on her next patient. Michael Osborne was a former police officer who'd been driven to a cocaine addiction by the stress of his work in the vice unit. Though he'd gotten clean, he still experienced occasional panic attacks and periods of depression. Working in tandem with a psychiatrist, Dr. Stein had recommended a specific dosage of antidepressants that seemed to be relieving the cop's anxiety.

She was several minutes into reviewing her notes when she set the papers on the table and began tapping her fingertips together. She scooted her chair over to the metallic bookshelf where she retrieved an old cassette player and a cardboard shoebox marked "Kallman, Initial Interviews." She removed the box's lid and stared at two-dozen cassette tapes, each marked with a time and date. After rolling back to her desk, she inserted a tape into the player and began fast forwarding, searching for a particular section. Finding what she was looking for, she let the tape play out. Her own voice fizzed through the small speaker.

"You said that you knew something was in the closet before your father was killed? How did you know this, Lisa?"

The tiny voice of a seven-year-old girl cut through the air. "I could hear him. I could hear him moving around. And he talked to me."

"What did he say?"

"He said, 'Open the door, Lisa. I want to get out. Let me out.'"

Dr. Stein clicked the pause button. She rewound the tape and replayed the section. Then once more. Each time, her brow furrowed when the girl said, "Open the door, Lisa. I want to get out."

Frowning, Dr. Stein opened the cassette player and pulled out the tape. She inserted two fingernails into the bottom and unspooled the magnetic strip. Once the loose coils had piled in her lap, she found a document-sized envelope in her desk drawer and slid the ruined cassette into the flap.

She left her office and walked down a hallway. At a midpoint, the metal handles of a garbage chute protruded from the wall.

Dr. Stein's face darkened when she pulled open the chute and dropped the envelope into the gap.

Chapter Nineteen

"I have no idea where Katrina is."

Standing in the kitchen of his new home, David Hague barked the words into his cell phone. His secretary, Sharon Hewsen, was on the other end. She'd been curt with him since the middle of the week, though he'd had no idea why. It had not bothered him. Women in his life often seemed to get upset over unintended or imagined offenses.

However, upon taking Sharon's call minutes ago, he'd gleaned the reasons for her ire. Apparently, Katrina had told Sharon over a week ago that she was planning to meet David at his house on Monday. That was the last Sharon had heard from her. Her employer—presuming the hard partying vixen had run off with a wealthy consort she'd met at a club—had fired the feng shui assistant in absentia.

"Well, boss," Sharon said dryly, clearly unconvinced by David's claims of ignorance, "if you see her around or have some recollection of where she might have gone, call me."

After a quickly muttered farewell, he ended the call. *This is a grade-A fuckity muck*, he thought. The whole thing with Katrina had obviously been a huge mistake. During his past relationships, he'd often had a girl or two on the side and they'd all practiced the fine art of discretion. When he'd phoned Katrina and invited her over, he'd presumed she'd understood the real purpose of the call. But she'd gone and blabbed to Sharon and now he was going to have to perform a tight wire act to make sure Lisa didn't find out.

He opened the refrigerator freezer and pulled out a bottle of vodka. He poured the clear liquid into a glass, mixed in vermouth and ice, and added a lemon peel. A smile bloomed across his face as he paused to admire his handiwork. A Martini. Just like James Bond. After two sips, the tension in his shoulders and neck began to ease.

The window above the sink framed the backyard where Lisa and two of her co-workers were holding a barbecue party for more than a dozen kids. The children, ranging in age from six to ten, sat on fold out chairs or the grassy lawn, fidgeting, reading or staring at the sky. They seemed to have little interest in talking with either each other or any adults.

Over the course of his two-year relationship with Lisa, David had interacted only occasionally with the kids she worked with. They always creeped him out. Their blank eyes always looked right through him, as if he was a nonentity. He wondered how many of these weekends he would have to endure when he married Lisa. Was he destined to see his home routinely overrun by these living vacancies—creatures so alien he could barely call them human?

He took another sip of his martini. *Aw hell, maybe these kids aren't so bad? Why not go outside and give them another chance?*

Glass in hand, he opened the kitchen door and stepped over a small girl sitting on the stoop, intently counting blades of grass. He nodded at Darlene, one of Lisa's co-workers standing guard by the fence, and headed towards the barbecue grill where Lisa was cooking hamburgers and chatting with Meg. As he walked, an airy breeze blew the smell of the neighbor's eucalyptus trees towards him.

"Hey babe." He leaned to kiss Lisa on the cheek. "Hi Meg."

Meg gave a broad smile. Lisa, eyeing his martini, turned up her nose. "Jesus, David, it's not even lunchtime."

"It's a freaking Saturday, babe."

"I don't care, hon. You can't be around the children with liquor. Either put it away or go inside the house."

He sighed. "I'll be inside watching TV." He turned around and his knee knocked against a small boy clad in red overalls and a yellow fisherman's hat. The child fell backwards onto the lawn.

"Babe, you practically crushed Patrick." Lisa leaned down to the boy. "You all right, buddy?"

Offering no reply, Patrick got up and scampered away, using a strange back-and-forth gait.

"Sorry, little dude," David called out. He looked at Lisa. "How am I supposed to keep track of these guys? They're like munchkins." He chuckled and took another sip of his martini.

Lisa glared at the glass. "David. No. Booze. In. The. Yard. Period."

He gritted his teeth. For the most part, Lisa was demure, shy, and ready to let him direct their lives. But when she was around her kids, she showed another side. Willful and obstinate. Protective. He didn't like it. And in the future, there might come a time when he would show her the error of her ways.

Now she just looked at him with an expectant eye. "Well? Toss the drink or move your butt, handsome."

"Ok, I'm going, I'm effing going." He went to the foot of the stairs, and then turned and surveyed his backyard filled with strange, broken children.

Weird little fuckers, he thought as he walked up the steps.

Chapter Twenty

Lisa shook her head and sighed as David walked into the house. She caught the flicker of a scowl when he turned to shut the door behind him.

"I don't know what I'm going to do with that boy," she said, glancing at Meg.

"But he's sooo cute."

Lisa let her jaw drop, pretending to be shocked. "Why Megan Ford," she intoned in a Scarlett O'Hara accent. "Are you lusting after my fiancé?"

"Totally."

They both laughed. Lisa flipped a few burgers and paused to do a head count. Arrangements had been made for fourteen children to come to the barbeque. All of them now filled the grassy area, playing together or examining rocks, potato bugs, and other curiosities of the environment.

Lisa felt her phone vibrate: a text from Dr. Stein.

`I'm glad we had a chance to talk yesterday. Feel free to bring up any further concerns you have.`

Thanks mom. Lisa rolled her eyes. Now was not the time for a chat.

A seven-foot-high white fence with a locked gate enclosed the yard. In one corner, Patrick was running in circles around a small lemon tree. Lisa waved at Darlene to get the middle-aged woman's attention. "Keep an eye on Patrick. He's wandering." Darlene gave a thumbs-up.

Content her co-workers had things well in hand, Lisa continued grilling hamburgers for several more minutes, flipping them over until both sides were browned. Darlene lined the children up and took their orders for ketchup, mustard and pickles while Meg handed out bags of potato chips. With the food preparation complete, Lisa ran into the kitchen to wash her hands. David was sitting on a couch in the living room, drinking his martini and watching a football game. He ignored her, apparently still steaming from their interaction in the yard.

When she returned outside, she surveyed the scene. The children sat on the grass eating their food, with Meg and Darlene watching over them. Lisa walked up to a serving cart next to the barbecue grill. One hamburger lay on a plate.

"Who didn't want to eat?" Lisa asked Meg.

"What?"

Her gut tightened. She'd made fourteen hamburgers, one for each child. But there were only thirteen boys and girls seated on the grass. She ran through her roll call in her head. Jefferson, Kumiko, Waldo, Danny ... she didn't need to go through the full list before she realized who was missing.

"*Patrick*," she exclaimed. "Where's Patrick?" She looked at the lemon tree where she'd last seen the child. He wasn't there.

Meg stammered. "I didn't ... he's got to be around here somewhere."

Lisa turned and ran into the house. She shouted at David. "Have you seen Patrick?"

"Who's Patrick?"

"He's got the red overalls. And the hat, he—"

"Nobody's come inside the house."

His words hit like an electrical jolt. She ran back outside and looked at Meg and Darlene, whose panicked expressions made clear they hadn't found the boy.

It had been only minutes since Patrick had been in the yard. He couldn't have gone far.

"I'm going to check the front of the house," Lisa shouted to her co-workers. She unlocked the gate of the fence and ran to the sidewalk. Straining her eyes, she looked up and down both sides of the street for any sign of the child.

"Patrick!" If he'd made it this far, what direction would he have gone?

She jogged along the sidewalk, calling out the boy's name. Curious neighbors drew back their drapes and pressed their faces to windows. At the end of the block, she still hadn't seen him. Again, she faced a decision. Would he have gone left, heading south towards the Maumee River, or right towards Central Avenue? She continued calling for him, making no effort to hide the fear quavering her voice.

"You looking for a little kid?" a male voice shouted. A passing car had come to a stop in the middle lane and the driver was waving at her.

"Yes! He's got a yellow hat and red overalls."

"We saw him. He was walking a couple of blocks north of here. We were wondering why he was alone."

Lisa turned and ran north, all the while scanning the surrounding area. Young couples walked dogs. Joggers panted through early afternoon runs. A few parents pushed strollers or led toddlers by the hand. But there was no sign of a wandering six-year-old boy in a yellow fisherman's hat.

She crossed one street, ran the length of a block, crossed a second street, and ran up to the corner of a third. There, she stopped, her chest heaving as she gulped down air. It seemed hopeless. With each block, the paths Patrick might have taken grew exponentially. It was time to call in reinforcements. David and Meg could help her search.

She reached into her back pocket and found it was empty. Her phone was on the serving cart back at the house.

She turned and looked down a quiet suburban street. There it was, three houses down on the north side. The burned house. Monster Mansion.

Surely Patrick had not gone there. Why would he?

Still, she found herself jogging over to the decrepit building. As it swelled closer, she sensed the same menacing aura as when she'd parked her car in front of it several nights ago. The night when she'd heard the voice.

She stopped on the sidewalk in front of the house and scanned the yard. The yellow warning tape rippled in the wind, like a row of flickering candles. Beyond it was a yard of mostly dead earth blotched with swatches of weeds.

Then she saw it: a yellow fisherman's hat sitting in the dried grass near the porch.

Patrick had been here. And he was now inside.

How could this be? How could he have even known about the house? It was as if ...

Brushing her fingers against her cheek, she contemplated what to do. The smart move would be to run back home, grab David and the others, and return to explore the house as a group. Or call the police and let them do it. But was that fear talking? Patrick had vanished from her yard in mere seconds. In the time it would take to get back to her house, God knows where he could be. And she would lose a child entrusted to her care. She would be casting him to his fate, just as she'd been cast to hers so many years ago.

And she would die before she let that happen.

Chapter Twenty-one

The caution tape writhed in the air like a trail of serpents. Lisa ducked under the yellow strand, feeling the temperature cool when she stepped into the yard. Goose bumps dotted her forearm and a sense of dread stilled the breath in her throat. It was suddenly clear why the few patches of grass were brittle and tan. Nothing living could thrive here.

She padded across the dirt and climbed the porch steps. Though the front deck was grayed with soot and littered with broken glass, she envisioned how, in better days, family elders might have sat in rocking chairs and watched children chasing balls and pups around the yard.

But now was not the time for such imaginings; she had a child to find. She walked across the deck, shards of glass crunching under her sneakers, and arrived at the tall, windowless front door.

Now what? Should she knock? Would the demons and warlocks living within the house graciously reward her decorum and return the missing child without complaint?

Not likely.

She reached for the knob and saw that heat from the fire had split its bronze skin. Once the orb was in her grasp, it felt like rows of tiny teeth were biting into her palm.

The door easily rolled into the house and Lisa stepped into a mid-sized foyer. The room was dustier than the porch, with a ragged coat of lime green paint on the walls and muddy splotches on the floor. No doubt where the ghosts wiled away the hours while awaiting the arrival of new guests to torment.

She crossed the foyer, stepping carefully to avoid pellets of rat shit, and went through a doorway into what had likely been a dining area. Shadows mired the room, but enough natural light slipped through the cracks in the boarded windows that she could see the interior. The ceiling was dark and charred in spots; the walls bowed and splintered. The floor was less damaged, though the tongue and groove oak boards still showed the occasional scar of flame. The fire, she guessed, had come from above.

A wide arched doorway stood in one corner. Just beyond it, a circular staircase wound its way up the turret to the higher floors.

The chill Lisa had felt in the yard had never left her body. She wrapped her hands around her arms, rubbing warmth into her skin.

"Patrick?" she called out. "Are you here?"

There was no response, though the whole frame of the house seemed to moan.

Well, I knew this wasn't going to be easy. She turned to a door cut into the dining room wall. Past the doorframe were exposed pipes and rows of skeletal cabinets and cupboards. A kitchen, obviously. But with no sign of Patrick.

Where would he have gone? How would the deformed house and its shadowed corners appear to his mind? He'd seek something familiar, something to give him a sense of order. Perhaps a bedroom, like he had at home.

Lisa walked across the living room and passed through the doorway to the turreted stairs. In the rounded chamber, a handrail was mounted on beveled balusters that ran along the side of the circular staircase.

She pressed her shoe onto the first step and, after determining it was solid enough, began climbing to the second floor.

The few streams of sunlight burrowing through cracks in the walls were enough to travel by. The wooden staircase creaked with each step, but held firm.

She reached the second floor and stepped onto a wide platform that stretched out over the dining room below. The windows on the left side were boarded with plywood slats. To the right, a hallway parted the middle of a wide wall.

A fetid smell drifted into her nostrils. Garbage. Or maybe a recently dead raccoon. Lisa shuddered. The house would be such a lonely, terrible place to die.

She walked to the entrance of the hallway. Four closed doors staggered down the corridor, two on each side. A few sections of the floor were burned away, gaps abutted by charred wood.

"Patrick? Are you here?"

The shadows seemed to eat her timid voice.

She carefully opened the first door and peered into a small room. Despite the looming shadows, she could see the space was empty, its blackened windows warped with heat. She moved to the second room across the hall. It contained what had once been a bedframe, now reduced to a jagged carcass of browned metal rims and springs.

A blackened metal filing cabinet and the burned remains of a wooden desk filled separate corners of the third room. Perhaps it had been an office. With no sign of Patrick, she stepped back into the hallway.

She froze. It had been only a creak—two pieces of wood softly grating against each other—but it sounded like a person shifting their weight on floorboards above her. She strained her ears, but no other sound followed.

This was what she'd been avoiding. The third floor was where she'd seen the figure only a half week ago. The third floor had the voice.

She darted out of the hallway and jogged back to the stairs. When she got to the spiraling staircase, she contemplated running down the steps, out of the house and getting David or Meg or even calling McCuddy. But she remembered what Dr. Stein said. There was no figure; there was no voice. Only her subconscious playing tricks on her. The argument had sounded so convincing at the therapist's office. It was time to put the theory to the test.

Lisa took several steps up the stairs. *There's nothing here*, she told herself. *Nothing*. But she was not surprised when she heard the voice. Slow and sloppy, a mucus filled gurgle. It sounded muffled, distant. Not talking to her.

"*That's real good, Patrick. You're doing a great job.*"

She ran up the steps. "Patrick! I'm coming!"

"*Nice work, Patrick. You're a real van Gogh.*"

She arrived on the third floor. It had low ceilings and a looming hallway in the middle of a wall.

Scuffling sounds from close by. She ran into the hallway, towards the noise. An open doorway stood at the far end. Through the portal she saw Patrick, kneeling on the floor, an artist's paintbrush in his hand.

"Patrick!" she shouted. He did not acknowledge her. She ran to the doorway.

The light pouring in through two dormer windows revealed an attic space enclosed by short walls with gables that rose to a pitched ceiling. In the center of the room, Patrick squatted and painted a large smiley face on the wooden floor, his paintbrush wet with red.

Next to the child, a naked woman's corpse lay face up, tattooed arms and legs splayed out. Lisa instantly recognized the Asian girl from the party. The one who did feng shui. Katrina.

Her eyes were gone from their sockets. In their place were empty caverns bleeding crimson tears which Patrick was using as paint.

Lisa staggered through the doorway, her gaze darting across the empty room. She ran to the child and scooped him into her arms. He cried out and dropped his paintbrush. She threw him over her shoulder and bolted out of the attic to the stairwell. Down past the second floor, then onto the first. And, as the gurgling laughter rose up around her, she ran out of the house.

Chapter Twenty-two

"It's plain as day, lass," Detective Devin McCuddy said. "There is no body in that house."

Lisa sank into the corner of the green plaid couch, a throw pillow on her lap. David held a protective arm around her while Meg perched on the couch's arm. The Irish detective was the only other person in the room, standing in front of them with a grim expression etched on his face.

Eight hours had passed since Lisa had fled the ruined house with Patrick in her arms. After sprinting home, she'd phoned McCuddy who—despite finding her assertions implausible—requested a pair of police officers to search through the abandoned Victorian. The uniformed cops had spent several hours examining the building and its surroundings, finding nothing of interest.

McCuddy scratched his bristled chin and continued talking. "If there had been a corpse in there, especially in the condition you describe, we would have found some kind of biological evidence. You said the boy was ... painting with the woman's blood. That sort of thing would be very hard to hide. But there was nothing in that room. The whole place is just a burned-out husk."

Lisa stared into her palms. She knew what she'd seen. "Did you talk to Patrick?"

"I did. It's difficult to get much information out of the boy. He knows he was in the house, but can't, or won't, say much beyond that. His mother was there when I talked to him, and I have to tell you, lass, she's quite upset. She's going to remove him from your program."

Lisa sniffled and rubbed her eyes. David pulled her closer.

McCuddy shifted his weight, causing the floorboards to squeak. His weary expression evinced a growing discomfort with the conversation. "I did some calling around. The Chen woman hasn't shown up to work for several days. But I talked to some of her friends and relatives, and that sort of behavior isn't uncommon for her. Some people like to disappear to Vegas for a spell. But it doesn't mean they're missing."

"I'm not saying she's missing," Lisa replied. "I'm saying she's dead."

Lines folded McCuddy's brow. "I know this has been a difficult time for you lately. I want you to know I'll do anything I can to—"

"I'm not crazy!" she shouted.

McCuddy leaned down, his hands on his knees. "Nobody is saying you are, my dear. Good lord, I've known you for such a long time. If you were going to snap, it would've happened years ago. You're made of very stern stuff now, life has seen to that. But we all experience a few cracks in our armor from time to time."

Lisa grabbed a tissue from a box on the coffee table and wiped her eyes. She despised being seen this way. Hysterical. Delusional. Weak. And she hated that nobody believed her. Both David and Meg had been relieved when she'd returned with Patrick, but they'd made no effort to hide their incredulous looks when she'd recounted her experience in the house.

McCuddy took a few steps to the door, then turned back to Lisa. "My dear, you did a good thing today. You found your lost lamb." He paused and pinched the flesh under his chin. "And I do have some information that will interest you. Sources I can trust tell me the parole board is going to deny O'Brien's request. He's staying in prison."

She offered no reaction to the news. McCuddy sighed, gave a polite nod to David and Meg and let himself out.

Once the detective was gone, Meg leaned over and put a hand on Lisa's shoulder. "You going to be okay?"

Lisa wanted to scream in response. She wanted to curse Meg and David for their disbelief, their lack of faith. She knew what they were thinking: *Poor Lisa. Her father was horribly killed years ago, and she's never been right in the head.* Well, damn them both to hell.

"I'll be fine," she said, avoiding her friend's gaze. "It's late. You should get home."

Meg nodded, retrieving her jacket off the coat rack. "I'll see you at work on Monday," she said. "We can see how things are then." After waiting for a response, and receiving none, she pulled the front door open and left the house.

Lisa silently cursed herself as the door clicked shut. McCuddy and Meg were friends, yet she was treating them like enemies, like they were somehow responsible for the day's nightmarish turn. Could she really blame them for questioning her sanity when she was doing the very same thing?

David shifted on the couch. "How you feelin', babe?"

"Been better."

"Yeah, I know. It's been a rough day. I'm going to make a drink. You want one? You could probably use it."

"No. I think I'm going to take a sleeping pill and go to bed." She stood and walked to the stairs.

"I'll see you up there," David called out from the kitchen.

She entered the bathroom and flipped open the medicine cabinet, grabbing a bottle of sleeping pills before washing two down with a sip of water.

Her reflection came into view when she swung the cabinet door shut. Creases trailed out from the sides of her bloodshot eyes. She could almost forgive anyone who thought she'd gone mad.

Had she? The sight of Katrina Chen's splayed and naked body flared in her mind. It seemed impossible the image could be so clear and detailed, but not real.

Of course, hadn't Dr. Stein described that exact phenomenon days ago when she'd argued Lisa's subconscious was taking control of her senses? If that was true, how could she know what was real and what was invented by her mind? What about this very moment? Was she in her own house? Did David, Meg, and Detective McCuddy even exist?

She recalled a horror movie she'd watched as a teenager. At the beginning of the story, a female protagonist suffered a violent accident. As the film continued, the events in the woman's life became increasingly surreal. Eventually, it was revealed she'd been fatally injured in the accident, and the rest of the film had taken place in her mind moments before her death. As the woman had succumbed to her wounds, time had slowed and the chaotic firing of her neurons had brought to life a complex and jumbled narrative.

A strange thought rose in Lisa's head. *Am I living in such a film myself?* Perhaps she was a seven-year-old girl lying in her new bed, about to be murdered?

When will the axe fall? When will the nightmare end?

A wave of drug-induced lethargy passed through her body, sapping the urgency of her ruminations. She went to the darkened bedroom, rolled onto the bed, and slid under the soft sheets. As she lay on her side, she drowsily anticipated the warmth of slumber.

She was still awake a few minutes later when she heard David come into the bedroom and lay down beside her. She felt his lips touch her cheek. "Night, babe," he said. "Love you."

"Love you back," she murmured. She lay under the sheets for a half minute while fading into unconsciousness. Then she opened her eyes, turned over, and looked at David. "Honey?"

He groaned, indicating he was partially awake.

"What I don't get is why Katrina would even be in that house. What was she doing in this neighborhood? Did you ever see her walking around here after the party? I remember she talked about coming by to do that feng shui thing."

David opened his eyes. "I ... no. I never saw her. Frankly, I'd forgotten all about that conversation."

She pursed her lips, lost in thought, when a new wave of fatigue tickled the back of her neck. She rolled onto her side and closed her eyes.

The mattress moved as David shifted. "Maybe you should go see Dr. Stein tomorrow," he said.

She yawned. "It's Sunday. She doesn't work on Sunday. Besides, there's somebody else I want to visit." Her voice faded to a murmur, and within seconds, she was sound asleep.

Chapter Twenty-three

The aluminum splint taped across Timothy Baker's nose made him feel like he had a bird's beak growing out of his face. His nasal cartilage—broken during the attack by the bearded skinhead several days ago—flared with jolts of pain. A less intense ache nagged his upper back, which had flowered with green bruises. But those were both minor irritations compared to the sting from the stomach acid gnawing his gut 24/7, like ants devouring road kill.

The door to Timothy's locker hung open. His CO uniform lay neatly folded on a metal shelf. As he peeled off his flannel shirt and jeans, he stared at the reflection of his thin, fair-skinned body in the mirrors lining the far wall.

His job as a corrections officer had surpassed all his fears about a career in prison work. His fellow guards assured him the anxiety would pass, but he was a month in and it was only getting worse.

What the hell was he doing at Grand March?

He thought back to his first job, right out of high school, pumping gas at a Chevron station off I-280. He'd spent two years there, before switching to work for a distributor of cleaning supplies. There, he'd spent his days driving an electric order picker down the corridors of a warehouse, listening to tunes on his iPhone while he loaded pallets of chemicals into trucks. He still looked back fondly on those days.

Several months into his tenure there, two of his fellow employees left to work as COs in the prison system. When Timothy ran into them on the streets, they raved about their new profession. The money was good, they received benefit packages, and their family and community respected them.

During his second year working at the cleaning supply company, Timothy met a girl at a bar. Seven weeks later, Janine called to tell him she was pregnant. As he escorted her to medical appointments and birthing classes, he contemplated his future. And once his daughter was born, when he looked into her precious blue eyes, he knew he would need the means to take care of her. He applied to become a corrections officer the next day and was quickly accepted.

The job required a six-week training program. At the start, several of the instructors looked at Timothy's thin frame and argued he would flunk out. Their skepticism only fueled his determination to succeed. Three weeks into the program, all the students were tear gassed for an exercise. While his fellow recruits fell to the floor in wheezing, heaving piles, Timothy stood tall, his eyes clenched shut. On written tests, his scores were always near the top. And so, after completing the training, he began his new job.

But the training did not prepare him for what he saw in his first weeks as a CO. The prisoners treated each other like animals. During one shift, he and three other guards had come upon a gang rape in the laundry room. Day later, he'd stood in the prison hospital as the purple, bleeding body of a prisoner accused of snitching was rolled in on a gurney. As Timothy watched with wide eyes, the man coughed blood, convulsed, and died.

The worst had been the attack in the visiting area four days ago. Timothy's limbs had frozen as a bearded prisoner named Flannery repeatedly stabbed CO Sanchez in the throat. The skinhead would have killed Timothy too, if not for the actions of another prisoner in the room.

Other COs told him Jeremiah O'Brien was a pedophile and a murderer. But in Timothy's mind, the man was a hero.

Timothy now stood fully clad in his uniform, his baton hooked to his belt. All he had to do was make his way to the security gate where he could enter the prison.

If only he could will his feet to move.

A shuffling came from one of the shadowed nooks between the rows of lockers. Another CO coming off their shift, perhaps. Or, like him, starting one.

He looked down at his hands and realized he'd managed to stop their shaking. But it was a temporary fix. He had to get out of this job. If it meant going back to driving an order picker, fine. If it meant people on the street snickering as he walked by, it didn't matter. This place was hell. And he knew the things he'd see here would burn into his psyche, turning him into someone he did not want to be.

So why not quit? Right now?

Because as bad as life was at work, it was worse in the tiny apartment he shared with his new family. Janine, embittered about losing the best days of her youth to a crying child, took her rage out on him. Timothy knew that if he returned home without a paycheck, he'd face a barrage of screaming that would last into the night. He had to have a job lined up before he quit. Something that paid decent money and provided medical care for his daughter.

He closed the locker door and walked towards the exit. He was surprised to discover he was alone. Whoever he'd heard was no longer there.

For a second, a strange odor flitted under the bandages across his face and teased his nostrils. It reminded him of burning tires or the rot of the city dump.

But as quickly as it appeared, the smell vanished and he turned his focus to the shift ahead.

Chapter Twenty-four

The tires of Lisa's SUV spat rocks and dirt as she drove down a double-lane gravel road. At both sides of her vehicle, cornstalks taller than men sprung from damp earth, the vast fields arranged in neatly aligned rows. In the sky, cement-colored clouds threatened rain.

Lisa spied a turnoff marked by a sign comprised of three silver letters: MPH. She slowed her approach and turned onto a long driveway paved with smooth asphalt.

A guard shack stood beside a security gate fifty feet in. She rolled to the structure and lowered her window. An elderly Hispanic man in a blue uniform peered through an open window and smiled at her. "Miss Kallman. Good to see you."

"You too, Leo," Lisa replied. The man pushed a button and the arm of the gate slowly rose, letting her pass.

She drove another thirty yards down the driveway and arrived at an uncovered parking lot. Nearby, three white multi-story buildings lorded over a small campus of well-tended lawns and concrete walkways. A sign above the entrance of the largest building read "McArthur Psychiatric Hospital."

Lisa parked and walked into the main building. A reception desk stood in the center of a high-ceilinged room dominated by shades of blue and white. A woman in a shiny cream-colored blouse sat at the desk, staring at a computer monitor. Her blunt-cut bangs hung over her forehead.

The receptionist looked up when Lisa approached. "Can I help you?"

"My name is Lisa Kallman. I called ahead about seeing my mother."

The woman tapped several keys on her keyboard and murmured to herself. "Kallman ... Kallman ..." Lisa felt a growing sting of impatience.

"Lisa?"

She turned and saw a middle-aged Black woman in a light blue uniform. The nurse's eyes brightened. "I thought that was you. We haven't seen you in ages."

"Hello, Molly. Yes, I'm sorry, it's been a while." Lisa raised and tilted her fingers so the diamond on her engagement ring sparkled in the light. "I'm getting married." The announcement had nothing to do with the infrequency of her visits, but it was a convenient way to change the subject.

Molly beamed. "That's wonderful, dear." She caught the attention of the receptionist behind Lisa and mouthed the words, "It's okay." Returning her gaze to Lisa, she said, "You want to see your mother, no doubt. She's in the botanical garden. You remember how to get there?"

"Of course."

"Then run along, dear. It's good to see you again. And don't be such a stranger."

"I won't." Lisa moved away from the reception desk, eager to gain some distance from Nurse Molly. The woman's tone was pure sugar, but Lisa detected disapproval in her words. Doubtless, Nurse Molly thought Lisa was failing in her obligation to her mother.

The wide wall behind the reception desk was split at the center by an open hallway. Both security guards at the entrance had seen Lisa many times and they waved her through.

The corridor she stepped into reminded her of Dr. Stein's sterile office, though without the sci-fi accents. Notices about meal times and medicine distribution occasionally concealed beige paneling. The atmosphere was cold, antiseptic, and clean.

As she strolled, Lisa remembered her first visit to the sanitarium. It came a few months after the murder of her father. She'd been living in a state orphanage, and the experience had flooded her psyche with fear and disorientation. Only weekly visits by Detective McCuddy had provided any sense of continuity.

One day, the detective arrived at the orphanage to take her to her mother. She sat in the backseat of a police cruiser, listening to a CD of Celtic music as he made the long drive from Toledo to the sanitarium. Once inside the building, McCuddy took her hand and guided her down the long hallway, coming to a stop at a particular door.

Lisa had furtively entered the room and saw a figure lying under the sheets of a bed, staring up at the ceiling. She ran up and embraced her mother, but the woman showed no reaction. If not for her occasional arrhythmic blinking, or the rise and fall of her chest, she could have passed for dead.

Lisa had convulsed with grief, shrieking and begging for her mother's recognition. McCuddy kneeled and pulled Lisa to his chest. "I'm so sorry, dear lass," he said as he carried her out of the room.

Several months after the visit, McCuddy escorted Lisa to the sanitarium a second time. They walked to Margarita's room and again found her in bed, unresponsive to her surroundings. This time, Lisa said nothing and showed no concern. She was standing at the precipice of a self-retreat that would last for years.

As Lisa grew into a teenager and then a young woman, she visited her mother every six months or so. She'd sit by her bed, or push her around the corridors of the sanitarium in a wheelchair, passing whatever news might be of interest. Without fail, Margarita would silently gaze off into the distance. It was only when Lisa was in her early twenties, immersed in her own studies of psychology, that she asked doctors at the sanitarium to explain her mother's passive state. How could a body stay alive when the person inside had ceased to exist? The doctors had theories, but no definite answers. Who could fully explicate the black box that was the human mind?

Lisa reached the end of the hallway, arriving at a door made of tinted glass. Looking through it, she saw a room filled with flowers and greenery. She pushed open the door and stepped inside.

The botanical garden was the size of a high school auditorium. Tall plants, including weeping figs, bamboo palms and birds of paradise, sprung from wooden beds that ran along the perimeter. In the center of the room were rows of flowers and smaller plants, all accessible by concrete pathways.

A dozen or so people wandered about, a mix of patients and green-garbed employees of the sanitarium. Some patients wandered freely, others sat in wheelchairs pushed by orderlies.

Margarita Kallman was nowhere to be seen.

The clouded glass ceiling, three stories up, trapped in the heat that was starting to line Lisa's brow with sweat. Her tennis shoes scuffed against the floor as she moved down the center aisle. She eyed the strange plants and flowers, noticing there were no cacti, or any flora with sharp appendages, anything that could be used for self-harm.

She reached the far wall, where a limp figure slumped in a wheelchair faced a row of geraniums. Long bristles of white hair hung off the woman's head, going off in all directions. One of her arms dangled at her side, gently swaying like the pendulum of a grandfather clock.

Lisa took a deep breath and kneeled beside the woman.

"Hello Mom."

Margarita's left eye twitched. Lisa knew better than to mistake the reflex for any kind of recognition.

She put her hand on her mother's forearm, stalling its motion. "I'm sorry I haven't been here in a while. There's a lot going on in my life right now. In fact, I want to tell you about some of it."

Margarita quietly breathed in and out with mechanical regularity, showing no awareness of her daughter's presence.

An ember of frustration fired in Lisa's gut, and she strained to hold a friendly tone.

"I guess the good news is that I'm getting married. His name is David Hague. You've never met him, but he's a great guy. We just moved into a house together and he proposed during our housewarming party. Got down on one knee and everything."

Margarita's gaze shifted sideways, settling on a new focus point.

"The house is great too, Mom. It's big and kooky and has all these rooms. It's in the Old West End. We can stroll to Lake Erie. Did you and Dad ever walk around there?"

Margarita made a strange, wispy sound, like a dog sighing.

"But, I guess that's not the real reason I came here. The man ... Jeremiah O'Brien ... the man who killed Daddy ... he was up for parole. He's been in prison for twenty years now. He wanted them to let him out. There was a hearing downtown, and he went in front of all these people and cried and begged them to let him go. But the board wanted to talk to me. And I told them what he did to Daddy. What he did right in front of us. I told them what he did to you. And now they're not going to let him out."

A ball of heat expanded in her chest, pushing up bile that stung her throat. She searched the landscape of her mother's cracked and weathered face, desperate for some sign that the words were getting through. Margarita simply stared, her dark eyes revealing nothing.

The ball in Lisa's chest exploded. "Oh, Jesus Christ, Mom! Can't you hear me? You must be in there somewhere."

The aged woman remained still.

Lisa removed a tissue from her handbag and dabbed her eyes. "Anyway, I guess that's all I really had to say. I'll see you in six months."

She stood and walked down the pathway. A row of black hollyhocks had been set against the wall, their petals forming sneering smiles that mocked her dashed hopes for the visit.

Then, as she approached the turn onto the garden's middle pathway, she heard the rasped words.

"Not ... not him."

An electrical jolt shot through Lisa's chest. She hadn't heard her mother's voice in twenty years, but she recognized it instantly. She whirled in a half circle. Margarita was still facing the wall, arm swaying.

Lisa rushed back and kneeled beside the wheelchair. "Mom?"

This time, she saw her mother's lips move.

"It ... wasn't him."

Her voice was hoarse and breathy. She spoke with little expression, like a robot trying to pass as a human.

"What? What are you talking about, Mom? Who wasn't him?"

Margarita's head swiveled and Lisa found herself looking directly into a pair of liquid brown eyes. Eyes no longer dead, but full of passion. And anger.

"Don't you remember what happened?" came the hissed words.

The air left Lisa's lungs. Her mother's presence—her *real* presence—simultaneously alien and intimate, threatened to overwhelm her. She struggled to reply.

"W—what ... what do you mean, Mom? What? What happened? Tell me!"

For two seconds of eternity, Lisa stared into her mother's face, exploring the blotted and weathered skin. Then Margarita sighed and turned her head back towards the plants.

"What, Mom? What do you mean?" Lisa reached out and shook her mother's shoulders. The older woman's head lolled on her neck. Her eyes showed no sign of the fury that had burned in them only seconds earlier.

"Goddammit, Mom!" Lisa exclaimed. "What are you trying to say?"

"Lisa? Is everything okay?"

Nurse Molly stood in the aisle, a frown crossing her face.

"It's fine. It's just ..." She considered explaining that her mother had momentarily returned to life. But would Molly believe her? More to the point, did Lisa believe it herself? Could she trust her own senses to tell her what was happening?

She looked at the stern-faced nurse. "Goodbye, Molly. Thanks for everything you do for my mother." The words hung in the air as Lisa walked down the center row of plants towards the garden's exit.

Chapter Twenty-five

Jeremiah sat on a stained mattress set on a bedframe pushed against the wall. His new cell was small—12' x 12'—and built out of unforgiving concrete. A metal toilet in one corner glinted light from the fluorescent bulb attached to the ceiling. A locked steel door cut into the wall to his right.

The air was musty, heavy with a scent that reminded him of his mother's basement.

How long had he been in solitary confinement? It felt like days had passed since his altercation with the skinhead prisoner. But perhaps the slow ebb of time was merely an illusion. It was impossible to know when one languished in a chamber designed to deplete the human mind of its faculties.

One thing he was sure of: he'd saved the young CO's life. But the other guards had rewarded that heroism by tossing him into solitary, where he now sat with his flesh bruised and his bones aching.

The irony washed over him. Only a few weeks earlier, he'd been savoring the possibility of freedom. Perhaps he'd been naïve, but he'd truly believed he'd had a shot at parole. As a model prisoner, he'd tried to maintain some sense of decency in a sewer overrun by animals disguised as men. Only the hope of feeling the warm sun or a cool afternoon breeze had given him the strength to endure the past two decades of captivity.

It was the girl who had ruined everything; that was what Clarkesdale had reported. By speaking in front of the parole board, Lisa Kallman had stolen Jeremiah's chance at freedom. What had she said to turn them against him? What would it take for her to leave him alone?

He sunk his head into his hands and wept. He'd been cursed throughout his life. God had filled him with the urges to be with children in a way that was sick and wrong. When he'd been released from prison the first time, people had spat on him. It had been impossible to find work. His mother's constant recitation of her religious proclamations had almost driven him mad. And just when it seemed like it couldn't get worse, the police had come into his house and arrested him for the murder of Derek Kallman.

A distant *clack clack* cut into his awareness. Footsteps in the corridor, approaching his cell.

Was it time for a meal? It seemed like the guards had delivered a food tray only a couple of hours ago. But time had no meaning here.

A powerful stench wafted into his nostrils, something rank and foul. A key clicked into the lock and the door slowly opened.

Chapter Twenty-six

In the parking lot outside the sanitarium, Lisa slumped into the driver's seat of her SUV. Sprinkling rain dotted her windows. The clouds massing above looked dark and ominous.

She held her cell phone in a clenched fist while the fingers of her other hand drummed against the vinyl dashboard. Finally, she tapped a series of numbers on the screen and initiated a call.

Dr. Stein's voice sounded after one ring. "Lisa?"

"Gretchen, I know you don't like to be disturbed on Sunday. But I have to talk to you."

"That's fine. In fact, I was expecting you. I had a phone call from our friend Devin McCuddy last night. It sounds like you had an unusual afternoon yesterday. At a house on Fullbrook?"

Lisa paused. She'd considered telling Dr. Stein about the events in the old house, but knew the therapist would only reiterate her previous diagnosis: stress and hallucinations.

"I'm not calling about that. I visited my mother today."

"I'm not sure that was a good idea, Lisa. You appear to be fixating on certain ideas ... certain behaviors."

Lisa ignored the comment. "I have a question, Gretchen. And I need you to tell me the truth. Can you do that?"

The doctor's irritated sigh whispered through the phone. "Lisa, I have always been honest with you."

"When I first saw you, twenty years ago, did I say what happened to my father? Did I see who killed him?"

"Lisa, you shouldn't be trying to relive the past. You've made so much progress."

The rain grew heavier on the windshield. Lisa took a deep breath, hoping it would quell her simmering anger. "You said you would be honest here, Gretchen. There's something you're not telling me. What did I say I saw?"

"Lisa … you were a child. A terrified child."

Lisa heard the knife's edge creep into her voice. "Answer the question, Gretchen."

Another sigh, this one with a hint of resignation. "You had an incredible story. You spoke of some kind of monster in your closet. Classic childhood fears. You said that was what killed your father."

"And why didn't you believe me?"

"Why didn't I believe a fantastical story from a traumatized child? Listen to what you're asking. The police had your father's murderer in custody. Your mother was incapable of testifying. Should I have let you destroy the case with your babbling? Jeremiah O'Brien is the man who killed your father."

A bolt of lightning flashed in the distance, followed by a belch of thunder. "So you changed my memory?" Lisa said. "You made me forget what I saw?"

"Lisa … a human killed your father. A man of flesh and blood, not some monster created out of a frightened girl's imagination."

"You're wrong, Dr. Stein. You were wrong twenty years ago and you're wrong now. And there's something in that house!"

She ended the call and tossed her phone on the seat beside her. As more lightning flashed in the distant sky, she started the engine and raced out of the parking lot.

***

Miles away, in the home office of a luxury apartment in downtown Toledo, Dr. Stein sat in a padded leather chair. She set her cell phone in her lap and opened the top drawer of her desk. After rummaging through its contents, she pulled out a small digital voice recorder and pressed a red button.

"Subject: Lisa Kallman. Case review. Subject is clearly becoming disturbed. Despite years of continual progress, she seems to have begun a process of psychological unraveling. Subject is experiencing a break from reality, including auditory and visual hallucinations derived from childhood trauma. The recent parole hearing of her father's killer is almost certainly one source of agitation. But the subject has also become fixated on a decrepit house in her new neighborhood. For some reason, this locale seems to be pulling her into its orbit. There is something about that house ... something ..."

Dr. Stein clicked a button and ended the recording. She brought her fingers together and focused her gaze on the tips. For several moments, she sat in her chair, lost in thought. Then she grabbed a ring of keys off her desk and exited her apartment.

Chapter Twenty-seven

The door to Jeremiah's cell rolled open with a labored groan. A shadowed silhouette stood in the corridor. The darkened gloom hid the person's features, but not the shotgun they held in one hand, nor the backpack they'd hung off one shoulder.

Jeremiah gasped when the figure stepped into the cell. It was the young guard whose life he'd saved in the visiting area. The boy wore no expression, but appeared to be in poor health. His eyes sunk deep into his skull and the skin that draped over his frame looked thin and gray.

"My name is Timothy Baker," the guard said. "Do you want to get out of here?"

Jeremiah blinked. "Are they taking me out of solitary?"

Baker stepped closer. He held the shotgun by the stock, the barrel pointed at the floor. He stared impassively at Jeremiah. "We both know you're never going to get out of here by pleading your case to the parole board. If you want to live the life of a free man, come with me."

Excitement sparked in Jeremiah's gut. "What are you talking about?"

"One of the new guards, Hunt, has been assigned to a van carrying a prisoner into the courthouse downtown. I intercepted the assignment before he was notified and I have his uniform and ID card in the backpack. I can escort you to the vehicle pool and to Prisoner Transport. You can assume Hunt's identity and ride out in the back of the van. What happens after that is up to you."

Jeremiah teetered in his shoes. Could he believe what he was hearing? For several seconds, he considered whether this was all a hallucination dreamed up by a mind gone mad in isolation.

But Baker sure looked real. Jeremiah narrowed his eyes. "Are you crazy? This could cost you your job. Maybe even your freedom."

Baker sighed. "If it hadn't been for you, I'd be dead right now. I owe you my life. This job ... this job is too much for me to take. After I take you to the vehicle pool, I'll come back here. I'll lock myself in the cell and wait. When they come to feed you again, I'll say that you overpowered me."

"I ... Christ, I don't know what to think ..."

"You need to make a decision now. You can stay here until you're an old man, or grab your last chance at freedom."

Jeremiah's mind raced. A chance at the life he'd been yearning for, the life that Lisa Kallman had snatched from him, was once again possible. He knew that going with the young guard was fraught with risk. But he'd spent twenty years in this concrete hellhole playing by the rules, playing it safe. If he didn't act now, he could spend the rest of his life grieving for this lost opportunity.

"Give me the uniform."

Baker unhooked the backpack from his shoulder and dropped it to the floor. Jeremiah opened it and removed a light gray CO's uniform. Affixed to the breast pocket was a photo ID card for officer Oliver Hunt. The man in the picture was nearly Jeremiah's age and of unremarkable features. If no one looked closely, the ruse could work.

Jeremiah quickly swapped his clothes for the uniform. "I'm ready."

Baker held up the shotgun. "You'll want this. It's a pump action with one shell chambered. You've got seven shots before you're empty."

Stunned by the guard's trust, Jeremiah wrapped his hand around the weapon's grip. It gave him a sense of something he hadn't felt in decades. Power. The power to exact vengeance on those who'd wronged him.

They walked into the corridor and Baker pulled the door shut. Then the young guard led Jeremiah down a long corridor that ran past the closed cells holding Grand March's most dangerous prisoners.

A security camera above one door mechanically turned towards them. Baker pressed a button on the wall and spoke into a grill. "Baker and Hunt. Coming through."

Jeremiah tensed. Mere minutes into his escape, and the plan seemed destined to fail. Surely the guard on the other side of the wall would realize Baker had entered the confinement area alone.

The metal door slid open and Baker led Jeremiah through the doorway. As they walked through the portal, Jeremiah turned to the right and saw a sentry room cordoned behind wide Plexiglas windows. Inside, a portly guard stared at a computer screen filled with pornography. He was paying no attention to who was passing in or out of the security door.

Baker guided Jeremiah down a new corridor before they stepped into an elevator. Baker clicked a button marked "V."

As the rising elevator's hum filled the space, Jeremiah studied his liberator's face. Baker stared ahead, his shadowed eyes never blinking. He had the look of a man aware of his own damnation.

"I don't know how to thank—"

"Don't talk," Baker interrupted. The elevator door slid open, revealing an auditorium-sized room with high ceilings. In the distance, several dozen white vans parked in rows. A few COs and maintenance crewmembers wandered throughout the area. The smell of grease and gasoline soiled the dry air.

They walked towards one van. Jeremiah saw a dark-skinned guard sitting in the front seat, his window down, smoke from the cigarette between his lips curling into the air. He looked at Baker with a sneer. "What are you doing here? This isn't a place for children."

"I found Hunt for you," Baker said.

The guard in the van looked at Jeremiah. "Christ, you're not like Baker, are you? Green?"

Jeremiah, amazed his disguise was being so readily accepted, stifled a grin. "Nope, been in the business twenty years. Just new to Ohio, that's all. Still finding my way around here."

"You replacing Sanchez? Baker's the one who got him killed."

"Uh, well, I guess I am. It was awful to hear about that. That happened to one of my brothers in Mississippi."

The guard sighed, apparently content that "Hunt" met his expectations. He stubbed the tip of his cigarette against the center console. "I'm Bautista. You'll be riding in back with the prisoner. Let me lock you in."

Bautista hopped out of the van, and Jeremiah saw the guard was short—only a few inches over five feet—and had a black service revolver holstered on his hip. Sauntering towards the back of the van, Bautista motioned for Jeremiah to follow.

A numeric keypad was embedded under the handle of one of the two pull out doors at the van's rear. Bautista punched in a code and grunted at an electronic chirp. He removed a ring of keys from his pocket, inserted a key into the lock, and heaved open both doors.

Twin metal benches ran along each side of the van, their steel feet welded to the floor. Sitting on the left was a Hispanic man in a short-sleeved orange jumpsuit. His black hair was greased back to his skull and his visible flesh was covered with tattoos, including a single tear beside his left eye. The chain between the man's handcuffs wrapped through a hook on the bench, forcing his hands into his lap. Other manacles ensnared his ankles, connecting to a chain that ran to a bolt on the floor.

Bautista crossed his arms and nodded at the prisoner. "Meet Enrico Vasquez. He's serving two terms for sexual assault and is going downtown to be arraigned on new charges of methamphetamine distribution."

"Hello," Jeremiah said.

The prisoner scowled. "Fuck you, bitch!"

Bautista put a hand on Jeremiah's shoulder and smiled. "Hop in. I predict the two of you are going to be the best of friends."

Jeremiah looked over at Baker and offered a curt nod. The young CO stared into the distance, lost in thought. Jeremiah climbed into the van and sat facing the prisoner. He let the barrel of the shotgun rest on his left knee, his right hand wrapped around the grip. Hopefully Vasquez would get the subtle message: don't mess around.

Bautista swung the doors shut and the electronic security system reactivated with a beep. The engine grumbled to life, and the vehicle lurched forward.

For the next three minutes, the van moved slowly, stopping several times at what were presumably security checkpoints. Then the pace quickened and Jeremiah began tracking the shifting of gears. The transmission clanked from first to second, second to third, finally settling into fourth. In his mind's eye, he saw the van speeding over the interstate, headed to downtown Toledo.

The grin Jeremiah had been holding back burst across his face. For the first time in twenty years, he was beyond the walls of the prison as a free man.

Chapter Twenty-eight

Lisa caught sight of the digital clock on her dashboard display as she turned her SUV onto a side street in the Old West End. It was 4:05 p.m. Rain fell in sheets and parking looked scarce. She searched for several minutes before squeezing in between two family vans a few blocks from her house. She dashed into the pelting rain and was breathless and drenched when she charged through the front door of her house.

David settled back on the green plaid couch, watching a football game on TV. A half-empty martini glass sat on the coffee table. He looked over at her.

"Hey babe. How'd the visit with your mom go?"

During her drive back from the sanitarium, Lisa had contemplated the best answer for the question she knew David would ask. He'd been supportive enough when she'd told him about Katrina's body and the voice in the house, but she still had a sense he didn't quite believe her. How would he react if she declared that her mother—silent for so many years—was suddenly talking, prompting Lisa to question everything she believed about her father's murder?

"Fine," she said. "The usual." She placed her keys on a table near the door and removed her wet raincoat.

David smiled. "You want to watch the game? It's Detroit versus the Rams. I can fix you a cosmopolitan. I got that cherry mixer you like."

"No thanks. I'm tired. I think I'm going to take a nap."

He shrugged. "All right. I'm down here if you need me."

She trudged up the stairs to the bathroom. At first, a sleeping pill seemed like a good idea, but something about seeing David drinking what was obviously not his first martini for the day soured her on the idea. Instead, she blew her hair dry, gathered it into a ponytail, and walked into the bedroom where she lay on the bed.

Rain continued tapping on the roof, joined by occasional streaks of lightning that flashed through the window. Lisa shut her eyes, but she could still sense the brightness of each bolt of electricity as it crossed the sky. Frustrated, she rolled over and tried to shield her face with a pillow. Why hadn't she added thicker curtains to the windows to help shut out the light?

After a few restless minutes, it occurred to her that other rooms in the house might be better suited for afternoon naps. She got up, walked into the hall, and turned into the guest bedroom.

She'd cleaned and decorated the room the weekend she and David had moved into the house, seldom entering it since. The sole window was covered with a drop-down shade and the aperture was blessedly pointed away from the lightning storm.

Lisa walked over to the single-sized bed and drew back the covers. She was surprised to see the lime-green sheets were not the ones she'd put down. Apparently, David had changed the bedding. She lay on the soft mattress and pulled the sheets around her, pleasantly surprised at their comfort. Perhaps here she could find slumber.

Something nagged at her. While getting into the bed, she'd noticed a sparkle of light reflecting off an object on the floor. The percept had teetered at the edge of her awareness, taking several moments to fall into place. But now that it had, she was curious. She rolled off the bed, squatted beside the bedframe, and lowered her head.

A piece of red glass sat directly underneath the headboard. She plucked the glittering object off the carpet and saw that it was a ruby earring. One that seemed vaguely familiar.

It came to her in a flash. Katrina Chen had worn a pair of ruby earrings to the housewarming party weeks ago. Lisa had complimented the woman on the gem's beauty.

Holding the earring in her fist, Lisa strode out of the room and stomped down the stairs. David was still watching television, a fresh martini in his hand.

Lisa held up the ruby. "What the fuck is this?"

He turned in his seat. For the briefest of moments, a look of recognition seemed to cross his face. Then his lawyer's instincts kicked in. "What?"

"I just found this in the spare bedroom. Do you recognize this?"

"I don't know what that is. Is that yours?"

"It's an earring. That woman ... Katrina ... she was wearing this at our housewarming party. What's it doing on the floor of one of our bedrooms?"

"Jesus, Lisa. You actually remember what someone was wearing two weeks ago? I have no idea why you found it. Maybe she lost it there."

"Really? And it never occurred to her that she did? Or maybe she came looking for it. Is that something you forgot to tell me?"

His eyes narrowed. "Look, I don't know why you have this weird fixation on that Katrina chick. According to you, she's dead. And, no, I haven't seen her since the party."

Lisa bit her lip, letting the full weight of the "according to you" sink in. Whether or not he was lying about the earring, David had revealed he did not believe her description of the events in the old house.

She pocketed the earring, grabbed her keys off the table by the door, and shoved her feet into her sneakers. David unsteadily rose from the couch. "Babe, what are you doing?"

"You better not be lying to me, David. Because if I find out you've been screwing around, you can kiss our wedding goodbye."

Panic replaced the ire on David's face. "Lisa ... where are you going?"

She walked out, slamming the door behind her. Rain still fell in buckets. Cupping a hand over her eyes, she ran the three blocks to her SUV. Once inside, she pulled out her cell phone and was soon speaking into the handset.

"Meg, I'm kind of having an emergency here. I just had a fight with David—I think he might be cheating on me. And maybe a lot worse. I just need someone to talk to. Uh-huh. Can we meet? At the cafe? Near the university, right? I'll be there in fifteen minutes."

After ending the call, Lisa did a U-turn in the middle of the street and drove to a main intersection. She took a right and then went straight, headed in the direction of the University of Toledo.

***

As Lisa's car raced towards her destination, a gray Volvo traveling in the opposite direction zipped past her and turned onto a side street. The car drove past rows of family homes, eventually stopping in front of the desolate Victorian mansion.

The Volvo idled in the street for a half minute, then rolled forward several car lengths and pulled into an open parking spot.

Chapter Twenty-nine

Dr. Stein stepped out of her Volvo onto the wet asphalt. Her yellow rain jacket covered her sweater and slacks, and she had a handbag slung over one shoulder. She crossed the street, pausing on the sidewalk to take in the sight before her. The Victorian mansion had clearly once been elegant and noble, but was now ramshackle and forlorn. Falling rain smeared black soot down its exterior.

I can see why Lisa found this so disturbing.

She ducked under the yellow tape that ran the perimeter of the lot and rushed towards the front porch. With each step, her sneakers sunk into damp earth with a *slorp* sound.

A window from a neighboring house squealed open. "I wouldn't go in there!" a voice called out. "The police were all up in that place yesterday."

Dr. Stein turned to see a woman peering out from the house to the right. "It's fine," she said. "I work with the police. I wanted to have a look at the place."

The neighbor scowled and yanked her window shut.

After patting rain off her coat, Dr. Stein walked to the mansion's front door. A bronze knob hung loose, obviously broken, perhaps by the police investigators who'd trampled through the house the previous day. She gave a gentle push and the door swung back, eager to welcome a new visitor.

She rummaged through her handbag and pulled out a miniature flashlight. With a click, a bluish LED beam came on. The device was made for looking through glove compartments, not entire rooms, but it would provide enough illumination to get around.

She stepped through the doorway into what appeared to be an entrance room; what was called an antechamber in the old days. Despite the burn marks on the walls and floor, she found herself envisioning well-dressed families from a hundred years past marching into the space, shouting stories of the day's adventures.

An open doorway led her to the next room, empty and unremarkable aside from four small depressions in the wood floor marking the corners of a long rectangle. Once, there had been a table here, and this had been a dining area.

In the far wall, an open archway connected to the mansion's turret. But more interesting was a closer doorway. She passed through it and beamed her flashlight at a jumble of exposed pipe and dilapidated cupboards. It was doubtless a kitchen, where mothers and servants had toiled under the thumb of the patriarchy, cooking dinners and desserts for husbands and children.

Even before she'd arrived at the house, Dr. Stein had known her focus would not be the first floor. The top level was where Lisa's hallucinations had come to life; where she'd heard the mysterious voice and seen the body with the missing eyes. So Dr. Stein retreated back into the living room and walked into the turret. There, a circular staircase rounded its way upward. Despite fire-scarred rails and balusters, the grand design of the stairs affirmed an era of architecture long since faded from the American zeitgeist.

She gripped the scabrous handrail, moving slowly and carefully up two flights, testing each tread with her foot before putting her weight upon it. When she stepped off at the third level, she heard the patter of rain on the ceiling. Cut into a wall on her right was a hallway with four closed doors, two staggered at each side. The corridor ended at a fifth door that was wide open.

Dr. Stein walked to the end of the hallway and peered into the room. Light from the outside slunk in through two gabled dormer windows, revealing a space empty of furniture. Numerous shoe prints—signs of the recent visit by the police—disrupted the layer of dust on the floor.

With nothing more to see, Dr. Stein turned to the nearest closed door and tested the knob. The door rolled back to reveal a gloomy chamber with a few blades of light cutting through the poorly fitted boards covering the windows. She stepped inside, her sneakers scattering dust. A charred pullover desk stood against a wall, close to a metal skeleton of what had once been a filing cabinet. Cobwebs, long since abandoned by their arachnid architects, hung loosely in the corners.

Utterly unremarkable.

She decided to bypass the other rooms in the hallway and see if there was anything noteworthy on the floor beneath her. After descending the staircase, she discovered a layout similar to the top level. To her right was, again, a corridor with four closed doors. She walked to the second one on the left and opened it. Inside was what had once been a bedroom, but now only contained a blackened steel bedframe with rusted springs.

She moved on to the room across the hall. It appeared to be identical to the office upstairs: a burned pullover desk next to a skeletonized filing cabinet. She stepped into the room and walked to the desk, curious about its pedigree. Affixed to the skirt was a brass, oval-shaped marker imprinted with a brand: Hamilton Co. Had it not been so damaged, the desk would have been a valuable antique.

Ducking under cobwebs, she moved to the center of the room and ran her flashlight over the interior paneling. Flaps of charred wallpaper clung to burned plywood. Flames had etched disturbing patterns into the walls, patterns perfectly suited for paintings in the abstract expressionist style.

For a moment, Dr. Stein thought she was seeing smoke. Then she realized her eyes were playing tricks on her; dark splotches of shadow were becoming imprinted on her retina, giving the illusion of gloomy clouds that moved about the chamber.

She moved back into the hallway and stood in the corridor. While the mansion certainly had a macabre quality, she'd seen nothing unusual. And what had she expected? Ghosts? Demons? A monstrous voice of the sort Lisa had claimed to hear the night her father had been killed?

Such ideas were preposterous. Utterly out of the bounds of reality.

So why was she even here?

A thought flashed into her mind. What if she'd been prompted to visit the house by some unconscious part of her psyche that believed Lisa's visions were more than simple fantasies? Perhaps somewhere in the bowels of her rational and scientifically grounded consciousness was that immortal *id*, a child terrorized by a fear of the dark and unknown. Coming to the ruined house had been a necessary step to soothe that child's nerves and reassure her there were no demons or monsters hiding in the shadows.

Dr. Stein chuckled softly. Even a lifelong student of psychology such as herself could still be duped by the brain's furtive machinations. However, the game was now up. It was time to return home and formulate the next steps in Lisa's treatment.

She walked down the corridor, heading to the hallway opening. As she passed the second room on the left, a sound slipped out. Like a footstep.

Perhaps the slats of the wood floor shifting as they often did in old houses?

There could be no harm in investigating.

When Dr. Stein opened the door and flashed her light into the interior, her eyes widened in surprise.

The room was identical to the others with the boarded windows, pullover desks, and filing cabinets. Why so many offices in one house?

She walked to the desk: another Hamilton Co. Her flashlight revealed sections of wall with artistic patterns scrawled into the charred wood. The patterns looked exactly as those in the previous room.

She aimed the flashlight at the floor and saw it was covered with shoe prints. The police? No, she recognized the pattern of the soles.

Her own sneakers.

She'd been in this room before. But how was that possible? Had she gotten confused when traveling through the hallway?

Again, the illusion of moving shadows visited her. She held up the flashlight, but its glow could not cut through the shroud. Unease began to ferment within her; candle flames of dread that flickered at the base of her spine. She reminded herself this was her limbic system initiating the body's fight-or-flight response. The feeling was not rational; it was the result of a fear of the dark that had been encoded into humankind's primal self eons ago. She needed only to empower her cerebral cortex to overrule the anxiety that was inflaming her reptilian basal ganglia.

She inhaled deeply and stared into the dark cloud gathering before her. Two glistening orbs appeared, each reflecting the glow of her flashlight. They were eyes. Eyes that belonged to a figure. And when that figure stepped forward, Dr. Stein had to summon all of her scientific faculties to keep her mind from shattering into a thousand shards of psychic debris.

Chapter Thirty

"You get me out of here and I'll kill you quick, *ese*. Otherwise, I take my time, you know? The way I like to."

The shackled prisoner named Vasquez twisted his face into a sneer, narrowing his eyes into a death stare that sent nervous jolts through Jeremiah's chest. They'd been on the road for thirty minutes and he guessed the van was now somewhere on the Ohio Turnpike.

Vasquez had turned out to be a real charmer. Once the vehicle had gotten onto the open road, the tattooed convict had begun spewing profane condemnations of prison guards and the Ohio state justice system. While Jeremiah didn't disagree with the sentiments, he'd opted to remain silent. Vasquez had interpreted this as a sign of intimidation, and his tirade had become more and more threatening.

Jeremiah tried to avoid eye contact. Vazquez was presumably a new member of the prison population, but it was possible he'd been in Grand March for years. If that were so, he might eventually realize that Jeremiah was not a guard, but a fellow inmate.

Earlier, Jeremiah had noticed a single camera mounted off the ceiling at the front of the cargo hold. This meant Bautista could see what was happening in the back of the van, though his eyes would doubtless stay mainly on the road. Next to the camera was a three-inch speaker. The driver's voice had crackled out of it twice so far, informing his passengers of the light traffic conditions.

Still scowling, Vasquez said, "You not talking, *ese*. That's pissing me off. I'll give you one last chance. Or you gonna scream like a *chica* when I'm working you."

A trip from the prison to downtown would take around an hour, an hour and fifteen minutes, max. They were probably traveling through the rural country outside of Toledo right now, but soon they'd be in the heavily trafficked areas approaching the city.

"You gonna be crying like a little bitch. You gonna be begging me to kill you."

It had to be around 5:15 p.m. The sky would stay light for another hour.

"Maybe I'll make you my woman before I kill you, *ese*. What you think about that?"

Jeremiah raised the shotgun and pointed it at Vazquez's throat. The prisoner's eyes went wide, then narrowed as a smile crossed his lips. "*Cabrón*, you ain't got the—"

The shotgun stock jerked against Jeremiah's shoulder a millisecond after he squeezed the trigger. Oddly, it seemed to take a moment for a deafening boom to fill the van.

Vazquez's Adam's apple burst open with syrupy gore, the metal wall behind him suddenly pasted with what looked like a full bottle's worth of barbeque sauce mixed with shards of bone.

A plume of smoke rose from the shotgun barrel and the instantly dead prisoner teetered in his seat, an expression of incredulity frozen on his face. As a river of blood poured out of Vasquez's mangled neck and down his shirt, his body seemed to shift comfortably back against the wall of the van.

Jeremiah set the shotgun on the floor and stood as tall as he could in the cabin. He looked into the camera. "Pull over! There's been an accident!"

Bautista came over the speaker. "Hunt? What the fuck happened? I heard a—"

"*Pull over!*"

The van moved rightward two lanes, slowing and eventually rolling to a stop on what felt like a bed of gravel. The highway shoulder.

The speaker again crackled to life. "Hunt, what the fuck is going on in there? Did you fire your weapon?"

"Ohmigod, ohmigod," Jeremiah chanted hysterically. "You've got to get me out of here. I'm having a panic attack! I'm having a panic attack!"

"Jesus, fuck, no," Bautista grumbled, and the speaker went dead. Jeremiah heard the driver's door fling open and seconds later, the rear doors chirped. A key turned in the lock, and the back of the van opened. Bautista stood in the afternoon light, his hands wrapped around his service revolver.

"What the hell's going on in there?" the compact CO shouted.

Jeremiah leaped out of the van and gasped for air. He pointed back at the body of Vazquez. "Look at him. I think he's dead!"

Bautista hoisted himself into the vehicle and approached the blood-soaked prisoner. "You 'think' he's dead, Hunt? His head is barely hanging on his neck! What the hell happened here? Command is going to fuck us in our eye holes!"

"Look in his hand," Jeremiah said. "He had a knife."

"So you shot him? He was fuckin' handcuffed!"

Jeremiah looked around at the surrounding area. Bautista had stopped the van on the right shoulder of the highway. A frontage road ran parallel, about thirty yards to the right. Beyond that was a rural neighborhood of farms and homes, widely spaced apart. On the other side of the highway, a field of pumpkins stretched to the end of the world.

The traffic rolling by was light, a car every hundred yards or so. But Highway Patrol would stop to investigate if they saw a prison van parked on the side of the road.

Bautista's voice reverberated in the van. "Oh, man. I don't see any knife, Hunt. What the fuck have you gotten us into?"

Jeremiah hopped back into the vehicle and picked the shotgun off the floor. Bautista had holstered his revolver and was on his knees searching for the mythical weapon.

Jeremiah placed the barrel of the shotgun against the back of the kneeling guard's neck. "Give me your gun."

Bautista froze. "What's going on, man?"

"If you're trying to stall for time to figure out how to disarm me, we both know it's not going to happen. So give me your gun."

Bautista's hands trembled as he unfastened the snap of his holster, withdrew his revolver, and held it out to his side. Jeremiah grabbed the weapon and tucked it into the front of his pants.

A heavy wheeze came from Bautista's mouth. "Puh-Please, man. I've got a family, bro. I just had a daughter, man. Please don't kill me."

A plan was forming in Jeremiah's mind. But there were many variables to consider.

Could he afford to let Bautista live?

He rotated the shotgun in the air so that he held the stock with his left hand while stabilizing the barrel in his right. With a jerking movement, he thrust the butt of the rifle at the back of Bautista's head. The guard fell forward and rolled into a fetal position on the floor.

"Ow! What the fuck, man?"

"Sorry," Jeremiah said. He crashed the barrel into Bautista's temple and watched the guard jerk and go limp. Then he leaned down and pinched hard on Bautista's eyelid. No person could pretend to be unconscious through that kind of pain. Bautista didn't move.

Jeremiah hopped out of the van, locked the doors, grabbed the ring of keys, and walked to the open driver's door. He plopped himself in the front seat, leaned across the interior, and popped open the glove box. A vehicle manual and two shotgun shells sat inside. He shoved Bautista's revolver into the compartment and slapped it shut.

He found the van's key on Bautista's key ring and smiled when the engine roared to life. Thank God his old man had stuck around long enough to teach him to drive a stick shift before being chased off by his mother's crazed rants. Within seconds, he'd merged into the sparse traffic.

He took the next exit and drove onto the frontage road, where the houses were separated from each other by at least a hundred yards. Ahead was a single-story yellow house with an aged Datsun parked in an open garage. A sign planted in the front lawn encouraged people to vote for a certain politician because "She Will Preserve the Rights of Seniors!"

Jeremiah turned onto the yellow house's long driveway and parked in front of the garage. Seconds later, he was ringing the doorbell.

Slow footsteps came from inside the house. A wooden door rolled open and a thin, gray-haired woman dressed in a flannel sweater and jeans peered through the mesh of the screen door. "Can I help you?"

Jeremiah pointed to the prison ID badge affixed to his chest. "I'm with the Ohio state prison system, Ma'am. I have to use your phone. We just lost a prisoner in transit, and I need to notify the authorities."

"Oh my lord. Come in. The phone is on the kitchen counter." A gold wedding band sparkled on her ring finger as she pointed behind her.

Jeremiah opened the screen and stepped inside the house, scanning the layout as he went. A short hallway led to a kitchen area. Beyond that was a living room filled with two sofas, a giant bookshelf full of books, and a large television. Photographs of various adults and toddlers hung off the walls. Sons and daughters, probably, and grandchildren.

He turned to the woman. "Ma'am, my partner was hurt in the escape. He could use some medical attention. Is your husband available to help?"

The woman's face fell. "I'm sorry ... Barney's dead. He's been gone for three years now. It's just me and the cats in the house."

Jeremiah stepped onto the kitchen's porcelain tiles. On a laminate countertop were piles of notebooks; a rotary telephone; and a key ring linking several keys, a few plastic loyalty shopping cards, and a tiny flashlight marked with a Datsun logo.

Jeremiah stared at the phone. He tapped two fingers on the kitchen counter, lost in thought.

"Officer?" the woman behind him said. "Do you need to make your call?"

He turned and smiled. "Actually, I know exactly what I need to do."

Chapter Thirty-one

The interior of the Counter-Culture Café modeled a hip ambience designed to attract students from the nearby University of Toledo campus. Books and magazines lay scattered across coffee tables, sofas and chairs, making the space look more like a scholar's living room than a coffee shop. At 5:30 p.m. on a Sunday, baristas behind the counter were serving drinks and pastries to a diverse array of customers that included families seeking safe harbor from the rain, college students hunkered over laptops, and jogging fanatics determined not to let the weather keep them from burning carbs.

Next to a window with a view of the sidewalk, Lisa and Meg gathered at a circular table painted with a checkerboard design. Both women held steaming cups of coffee.

Over the past year, Lisa had engaged Meg in many discussions about relationships, work and politics, and she appreciated her co-worker's willingness to consider a subject deeply before offering her opinion. Lisa trusted Meg. She trusted her enough to tell her what had happened during the visit to the sanitarium earlier that day and the revelation that Dr. Stein had altered Lisa's memories. And she also recounted the discovery of Katrina's earring in the bedroom and David's angry response.

After hearing it all, Meg took a sip of coffee and leaned back in her chair. "Wow ... that's a lot to absorb in a couple hours."

"Tell me about it. You must think I'm crazy."

"Well, I've always thought that," Meg said with a smirk. "But, I don't think you've gotten any crazier. You've experienced more crap in your twenty-six years than most people do in their whole lives. You're entitled to be a little kooky. And spooky." She hummed the first notes of *Addams Family* theme and snapped her fingers.

Lisa couldn't help smiling. "Thanks, I think. But I realize what this must sound like. Am I really saying that some kind of *thing* killed my father? Lots of folks would say I should be locked up with my mom."

Meg backhanded the idea away. "I don't think you need to beat yourself up over it. If it seems real to you, that's real enough." She paused. "And Dr. Stein says she erased your childhood memories?"

"In a nutshell, yes. She didn't quite admit to it. The conversation got pretty heated."

"But you don't remember anything? About that night, I mean? When your dad was killed?"

Lisa pursed her lips. "Sometimes I feel like there's something floating around in my head. Not actual memories … more like sensations. Nothing I can see or hear, just a sense of something horrible happening. Or about to happen. Or having just happened. It's hard to explain. Sometimes it's hard to know what you've actually experienced—"

"—and what you've been told you've experienced!" Meg finished the sentence. "I know what you mean. I lived in Florida until I was six and we had a neighbor who had a collection of birds. For years, my family would tell this story about how I snuck into her house as a toddler and opened up the cages for her parakeets, letting them poop all over her furniture. And I could even remember doing it myself."

"And?"

"A couple of years back, my folks went back to the old neighborhood. And the woman was still there. My dad reminded her of the story, but she said that it wasn't me. It was my older sister. She even said that by the time I was old enough to walk, she'd already given away her birds. So I couldn't have done it. But I still have the memory."

Lisa let out a sigh. "It's so hard to know what's real."

"Totally. And we've all had those dreams where you wake up and you're convinced they actually happened."

"I always have the one where my teeth are falling out. I think Jung had something to say about that. It means I'm insecure in some way. Or I'm pregnant. I can't remember which."

"I have ones where I meet a great guy and fall in love," Meg said with a wistful smile. "I should know better."

Lisa laughed. There was a moment of silence, and she breathed in the scent of nearby cinnamon cookies. She took a sip of coffee and looked at her friend. "Look, Meg, we've never talked about this before, but what do you believe? I mean, spiritually. Do you believe in God?"

Meg swirled a wooden stirrer in her coffee. "Well, my family are believers. Church every Sunday, the whole nine yards. I guess as I've grown up, I've drifted a bit. It's hard to make everything you read in Sunday school map to the world you see around you, you know? But, I think there's something good out there in the universe. And you can call it God."

"And angels?"

"I can't dismiss some of the stories I've heard. People who say someone or something appeared to help them just when they needed it. Or people who appear just in time to comfort folks on their deathbed. Who am I to say they're not what we call angels?"

"What about guardian angels?"

Meg chuckled. "Girl! Now you're getting all *Caressed by Heaven* on me."

"I've been thinking. If you can have a guardian angel—someone who protects you and watches out for you—couldn't you have the opposite of that? A demon or something? A creature that's out to destroy you?"

Meg gasped and Lisa wondered if she'd gone too far. After all, she was no longer raising idle questions about spirituality, but revealing ideas that could be fairly classified as paranoid. Her gut tightened as she waited for an answer.

Brow furrowed, Meg spoke slowly. "I've heard of different cultures that have beliefs like that. They think if a person is cursed, some kind of creature from hell becomes focused on their destruction. But don't you think this is getting kind of out there, honey? Is this what you think is going on? Some demon is out to get you?"

"I don't know. It sounds crazy. I never would've considered something like this a month ago. But there's either more to this world than I understand, or I really am going insane."

A supportive smile flashed across Meg's face, but she said nothing. A pop ballad about the agonies of teenage love flowed from the cafe's stereo system. Background conversations rose in Lisa's ears. Normal people discussing everyday topics. Babies on the way, planned high school dances, going back to college for career development.

Nothing about being tormented by a beast from hell.

Meg leaned forward. "So what are you going to do about David?"

Lisa shrugged. "When I found the earring, I was so angry. And, uh, frightened, I guess. I mean, I saw ... or I think I saw Katrina's body. If she was having a fling with David and he didn't want me to find out, maybe he—"

"Whoa, whoa, slow your roll, girl. You find an earring on the floor and you go right to accusing your fiancé of murder?"

Heat warmed Lisa's cheeks. "Well, I mean, I don't know. You don't think it's possible?"

"Anything's possible, I guess. But it seems more likely Katrina just dropped the earring by accident. Or maybe it isn't even her earring. Maybe somebody who came by when the house was being shown dropped it."

Lisa forced a smile. "You're right. Of course, you're right. It could have just been an accident." She gave a heavy sigh. "This is why I wanted to talk to you. I spiral in my own brain. I need a clear set of eyes on things."

"I'm always happy to help." Meg said. She took her lower lip under her teeth and a nervous look crossed her face. "While we're getting all confessional, maybe I should tell you something. When you and David got engaged, I got a little jealous. I guess I hadn't realized how close the two of you had gotten and I thought now you were going to leave me to my lonely pity party of one."

"What? Meg, no. I would never—"

Her friend waved the concern away. "Don't worry, Lisa. I'm going to be fine. But every time I see you and David together, I think you have a great relationship. It would be such a waste if you lost it over something stupid. I mean, we all have our little fears and jealousies. Until you know for sure what happened, you shouldn't make any rash decisions. I think you need to talk to him."

"You're right. I'm just embarrassed to go back there after screaming at him."

"Girl, if you do get married, you're gonna do some screaming at your man. You better get used to it."

A laugh blurted from Lisa's throat. Her visit with Meg had done just what she'd hoped it would, buoying her spirits and soothing her nerves. Now she had a clearer view of her situation. Maybe things weren't as bad as she'd thought.

They sipped the last of their drinks, gathered their coats and handbags, and walked outside where the rain had slowed to a sprinkle.

As they stood under the cover of the café's awning, Meg pressed a hand to Lisa's shoulder. "Talk to David," she said. "See if you can get to the bottom of all this. But, you know, if it turns out he was messing around, well ..."—her eyes sparkled—"you gonna have to do some ass whooping. Nobody messes with my girl."

Lisa grinned, raising her fists in a boxer's stance. "Of course I will. And thank you, Meg. For everything."

"It's going to be okay. You just gotta have a little faith."

Meg opened her arms for an embrace that Lisa joined. It felt good to have a friend, to know at least one person was on her side.

Chapter Thirty-two

In a private room in the McArthur Psychiatric Hospital, Margarita Kallman slumped in her wheelchair. The chamber's interior, painted and carpeted entirely in shades of calming blue, held a single-sized bed, a small kitchenette, and a plastic dresser. Hanging in one corner of the ceiling, a video monitor flashed a montage of pleasant imagery across its screen. A radiant sunset, a bucolic mountain vista, a sandy beach ...

Margarita faced the bed, her back to the kitchen sink. Though the video screen was in her field of vision, she stared at the wall underneath it instead.

A mix of images, sounds, and fragrances stirred in her consciousness. She saw the botanical garden and smelled the bitter scents of the vines and flowers. She heard the voice of her daughter, Lisa, as a small child, asking for a glass of milk. That sound was burned away by the sparkling blue ocean that emerged on the video screen. Then a clatter of footsteps in the sanitarium hallway. Lisa again, but now a young woman, speaking in the garden. The terrible sense of confusion caused by Lisa's words. Margarita had no conscious narrative to explain the jumbled perceptions. They existed as an interminable filmstrip projected into her mind.

The footsteps in the hallway grew louder, then a familiar beep sounded. The door opened and a figure in a white uniform entered.

Margarita continued staring at the wall.

"Hello, Mrs. Kallman," said a musical voice belonging to Molly, the older nurse. "It's time for your pills."

The pills. They made the already confusing world more incoherent. But they also brought sleep. And sleep was a pleasant departure, the only time Margarita truly felt at peace. Until the nightmares came.

Brown fingers placed three pills in Margarita's right hand. "I'll get you some water, Mrs. Kallman." Margarita sensed the nurse moving to the sink. Pipes in the wall hissed, then Molly handed Margarita a small paper cup filled with cold liquid.

"Take your medicine now, hon."

Margarita lifted the pills to her lips. They tasted as they always did. Bitter. Like tree bark and chalk. She swallowed them in one gulp.

"That's a good girl," Molly said. Margarita ignored the condescending praise and continued staring ahead, avoiding the nurse's face. Why couldn't she just be left alone?

"Do you think it's time to get into bed, Mrs. Kallman? You can still watch the screen from there."

Margarita made no effort to move.

"I'll help you up." The stout nurse put a hand under each of Margarita's armpits and lifted her to her feet. She guided Margarita to sit on the bed.

"Your daughter came by for a visit today. That must've been nice."

The words sparked the ghost of a memory in Margarita's mind. Lisa. Had she been here earlier?

Molly placed her hand on Margarita's shoulder. "Your daughter is a very special young woman. I've always liked Lisa. I've always thought she was …"

The thoughts swirling in the tempest of Margarita's brain struggled to order themselves. Lisa *had* been here. And Margarita had warned her daughter of something. But what?

Molly finished her sentence. But her voice dropped two octaves, now drenched in phlegm and spit.

"... A STUPID WHORE!"

Margarita gasped, but it was the smell that filled the room—the suffocating, nostril-burning stench of rot—that sent a jolt of electric terror crackling down her spine.

The memories returned. Standing in the doorway as Derek went into their daughter's room. Derek opening Lisa's closet. The inhuman and monstrous green hand reaching out, its skinless muscle undulating like a colony of worms.

That same hand was now upon Margarita, pushing against her face. The room spun as she was pressed backwards into the bed. When she opened her mouth, vocal cords that had experienced twenty years of near silence burned as she screamed.

***

The terror-stricken cry echoed in the hallway outside Margarita's room, filtering into the rooms of her neighbors. Several patients, lost in their own delusions, began to mimic the cry. Soon, plaintive and mocking howls of the insane filled the corridor.

Hearing the commotion, an orderly stepped out into the hallway and pounded his hand against the wall. "*Shut the fuck up!*" he shouted.

Chapter Thirty-three

The old woman showed no fear when Jeremiah ordered her to march into the bathroom. Her tired eyes expressed only resignation, as if she'd suspected something was amiss from the moment he'd appeared at her door. He needed no weapon to give weight to his threats; he was at least seventy pounds heavier than her and he could easily snap her neck with his bare hands.

When they were both standing on linoleum bathroom tile, he went through her pockets, looking for a cell phone she could use to call the police. Finding only loose change and gum wrappers, he ordered her to sit in the bathtub. The bulky mirror above the sink was obviously a medicine cabinet, and he popped it open to reveal three shelves of bottles and ointment tubes. He found some insomnia medication and handed five pills to the woman. She gulped them down, muttering that perhaps now she would be reunited with her Barney in heaven.

"You're out of luck," Jeremiah said. "I don't plan on killing you." She replied with a spiteful look that seemed to say, "Don't do me any favors."

He walked out of the bathroom and closed the door. It swung outwards into the hallway, giving him an idea. He went to the living room bookcase and swept its shelves free of fantasy novels and ceramic knickknacks. Grunting, he dragged the heavy furniture into the hallway and leaned it against the bathroom door. The weak old woman would have no chance of escaping.

The Datsun keys sat on the kitchen counter. He grabbed them, walked to the outside driveway, and peered at the surrounding area. Neighboring houses on each side were at least five hundred feet away.

He went into the garage and backed the Datsun out to the driveway, then he pulled the prison van into the garage stall. Grabbing Bautista's revolver and two stray shotgun shells, he hopped out of the van and flipped the wall switch, watching the garage door rumble shut. Now there was nothing unusual for the neighbors to notice.

He opened the van's rear doors, where Bautista lay unconscious on the floor. Above him, a blood-soaked Vasquez slumped forward on his metal seat, his dead eyes staring at his shoes.

For a half minute, Jeremiah gazed at the face of the man he'd murdered. The gang member had clearly been a bastard, one who'd doubtless left a trail of victims during his short time on earth. But Jeremiah hadn't pulled the trigger as part of some vigilante bid at justice. Rather, killing Vasquez was a necessary step in the path towards freedom.

He wondered whether it should bother him. Perhaps it did, somewhere deep in his soul. It was something to contemplate. But later, once this was finished.

He turned his attention to the silver handcuffs hooked to Bautista's belt. He hopped into the van, unlocked the metal bracelets, and placed the handcuffs in his pocket. Gripping the unconscious man's ankles, he dragged him into the house.

After dumping Bautista on the hallway floor, Jeremiah pulled the bookcase to one side. He opened the bathroom door, and the old woman looked at him sleepily. "Get out of the tub. Sit down on the floor."

She yawned and did as she was told.

An aluminum grip bar jutted out from a section of wall between the toilet and bathtub stall. Jeremiah dragged Bautista into the bathroom and heaved his body to a sitting position on the toilet. He grabbed the handcuffs, snapped one bracelet around Bautista's wrist, passed the other behind the arc of the grip bar, and secured it on the woman. When they woke up, the two captives would need to pry the bar from the wall before they could get free.

Satisfied with the arrangement, he stepped out of the bathroom and pushed the bookcase back to block the door. He needed only a few hours; short of killing his captives, this was the best solution.

He stepped into the living room where a laptop computer sat open on a desk. In the center of a high-resolution picture of a sunset was a password prompt.

Tension tingled in his gut as he approached the computer. He'd always heard that stupid people used the word "password" as their password. He tried it to no avail. So he took a series of guesses: '1234abc', '1234ABC', '1234%'. None of them worked.

What now? Back to the bathroom where he'd have to wake the sleeping woman and threaten her with violence to get the code?

An idea struck him. He typed "Barney" into the prompt box and pressed the Return key. A screen full of desktop icons appeared.

After a quick web search, he brought up a white pages website for the Toledo region and typed in the name Lisa Kallman. The returned results showed the age range of each individual listed. Only one was in her twenties. Jeremiah inserted that address into a mapping website and studied the location. He knew the area well; when he was a kid, his best friend had lived nearby.

He jotted the address on a slip of paper, folded it into his pocket, and walked out the front door to the waiting Datsun.

Chapter Thirty-four

The skies above the Old West End smeared into pink and purple as the sun dropped beneath the horizon. Billowy clouds hung in the air, framed by the glow of the day's last light. Though the thunderstorm had quieted, an occasional bolt of lightning still shot from the heavens as if to say, "I'm not done yet."

David Hague slumped on the green plaid couch, alone in the darkened living room. Snot stains mottled his t-shirt. Tears warmed his cheeks. Minutes ago, when he'd looked at his reflection in the darkened glass of his phone screen, he'd seen that his eyes were red with inflamed blood vessels

His fingers were wrapped around a vodka bottle but, for the first time in his life, the booze brought no pleasure, nor did it chase the anguish away. Nonetheless, he continued taking deep sips, his Adam's apple undulating as the clear liquid burned his throat. After one long swig, he brought the bottle to eye level. Only a third of its contents remained.

Hopefully, Lisa would be home soon. Or maybe that would be the worst thing that could happen.

"You've really screwed up this time," David muttered to himself. Out of all the women he'd dated, Lisa had been the least willing to accept his affections. Instead of being impressed with his charms and appearance, she'd seemed wary of those qualities. Wooing her had required a surfeit of patience. For every moment he'd made her laugh, or brought a smile to her face, there had been one where she retreated back into her shell, becoming quiet and distant. Earning her trust, and showing her that the world did not seek her destruction, had made David a better man.

But now he was about to lose the only woman who'd ever really mattered to him. And all his charisma, all his lawyer's tact, could not win her back.

Katrina. That had been his fatal mistake. But how could he have known the exotic beauty would vanish after their indiscretion, raising people's suspicions and resurfacing Lisa's long dormant paranoia? Now his fiancée was hearing and seeing things that were not there.

Of course, it wasn't only paranoia that had inflamed her mistrust. It was his own stupidity. Why had he chosen his new house for a liaison? Why not get a hotel room, or finagle his way into Katrina's apartment? Like he had with all the others?

And yet, he knew why. He loved Lisa for her innocence, her purity, but he also resented those same traits. In his better moments, he would swell with pride at the fact that such an angelic woman stood by his side. But the feeling would pass and he'd feel her eyes judging him, relishing her moral superiority. The urge to spite such condescension would overwhelm him.

And what better way to deliver that spite than by engaging in a sexual betrayal right underneath her nose?

Creaking floorboards interrupted his thoughts. It came from upstairs. Had Lisa returned? Had he been so inebriated that he hadn't even noticed her walk in through the front door?

He rose from the couch. One hand gripped the vodka bottle and the other he held out in front of him, necessary to keep his balance.

The sky, visible through the front window, had gone black, drenching the house in shadow. But in his inebriated state, he couldn't remember where the light switch was.

Cautiously, slowly, he made his way up the stairs.

"Lisa? Are you up there?"

There was a moment of quiet. Then more creaks nearby.

"Lisa, babe. I'm so sorry. I've been so stupid."

Silence. Then an almost imperceptible sound. Sniggering?

"Baby, I'm coming up." David used the handrail to guide him up the rest of the stairs. Then he saw it: a figure stood halfway down the hallway.

A woman silhouetted by the moonlight coming in through the window of Lisa's office.

"Lisa?" He squinted in the dark.

"No," replied a sweetly feminine voice. "Not Lisa."

The figure reached into a handbag slung across her shoulder and removed a small rectangle. There was a metallic click followed by a flickering flame. The woman lifted the lighter to a cigarette dangling between her red lips.

"Katrina!" David exclaimed. "Lisa thinks you're dead!"

His former paramour exhaled a long plume of smoke, and the lighter's flame vanished. But not before David saw her outfit. It was the black blouse and white cigarette pants he'd last seen her in. Around her neck was a red silk scarf.

"Wherever did she get such an idea?" Katrina replied in the dark. "As you can see, I am quite alive."

David took a few teetering steps down the hallway. "They said you'd disappeared. Sharon said she called you and you never answered."

"Sharon is not my mother. I go where I want. I simply decided to leave for a while." The bright nub of the cigarette glowed and David saw Katrina's eyes drift to the vodka in his hand.

She exhaled. "Aren't you going to offer a lady a drink?"

He plodded towards her and raised the bottle. Her warm fingers pressed against his as she took it from him. She brought the container to her lips and cocked her head back. David gaped in disbelief as she downed the remaining liquor, each eager swallow accompanied by the soft rise and fall of the red fabric covering her throat.

Finished, Katrina brought the bottle down to her side and let it drop to the floor.

"Shit ... that's good."

David took a step closer. The smell hit him, a sickly sweet aroma of cheap perfume. His eyes watered. "Jesus. What are you wearing?"

"I wanted to smell good for you, baby."

The cloying fragrance caused a wave of vertigo to overwhelm his sense of balance. He staggered backwards, and Katrina moved to steady him. Her taut hands grabbed both sides of his torso. Despite her petite size, she seemed more than capable of holding him up.

"Easy baby," she cooed. "You need to lie down." She wiggled her shoulder underneath his armpit and murmured for him to lean on her for support. He didn't resist as she led him into the guest bedroom, where he collapsed onto the bed. She perched on the edge of the mattress, brushing his cheek, muttering indecipherable words.

The spinning slowed and his faculties returned. He looked at the beautiful woman kneeling over him, and the emotional weight of the situation felt like a boulder. A woman whom he'd recently threatened with physical violence was now tending to his needs. A great shame washed over him. He struggled to speak.

"I've made so many mistakes, Katrina. I shouldn't have been with you. I shouldn't have treated you the way I did. I was just high on my own bullshit. I thought I could fool everyone."

"It's okay, baby. You don't have to explain yourself to me. You never do." She drew a hand down his neck and across his chest.

"No, you don't understand. We can't do this. Lisa can't see us together. I love her."

Katrina smiled. "I know you do, baby. But what happens between us is between us, right? Lisa doesn't have to know." She leaned in and kissed David's neck. Her mouth moved under his ear and she whispered, "You know I can give you things Lisa will never give you." As she cooed, her hand ran down his chest and slipped into his sweatpants.

David sobbed and squirmed on the bed. "I can't, Katrina. I'm sorry."

She brought her lips to his face and kissed him softly. Her hand, now enveloped by his pants, massaged him. "Let me make you feel good, baby. You deserve to feel good."

He gritted his teeth and closed his eyes. He couldn't tell whether he was speaking aloud or in his mind when he repeated the phrase, "I'm sorry." But this time he spoke not to Katrina, but to Lisa. Wherever she was.

He placed his hands on the sides of Katrina's covered breasts. He pulled her towards him, mashing his lips against hers. Their wet tongues fought and engaged each other and for a dozen rapturous seconds, he bathed in the ecstasy of the moment. Then Katrina drew back, slipped her hands under his white T-shirt and guided it off his body. She did the same to his sweatpants and boxers, and he lay naked on the bed.

The silken haired woman smiled and wriggled out of her blouse. Her pants slid off her like a second skin, dripping to the floor. She now wore only her neck scarf and a pair of black embroidered panties. But David had only a few seconds to observe the underwear before it too fled her body.

The light reflecting off the outside clouds filtered in and outlined Katrina's soft, milky flesh. Her form was a tantalizing combination of smooth skin and feminine curves. A volcanic blast of desire burned in his groin.

The coy expression on her face told him she was eager to satiate his needs. She returned to the bed and straddled his hips. His heart stuttered as her warmth enveloped him. He gasped.

Katrina smiled. "You okay, baby?"

"Jesus ... that feels so good."

Katrina began a rhythmic gyration with her body. David caressed her thighs and then gripped her hard buttocks. His biceps flexed as he pulled her closer to him, onto him, and then relaxed when she pulled back. The sensations were beyond anything he'd ever felt; waves of pleasure traveling the length of his body.

Lightning flashed, illuminating the room. Thunder arrived seconds later. He looked past Katrina to the tall, oval dress mirror in the far corner of the room. In the reflection, he watched the gray shape of their undulating, interconnected bodies.

Still feeling rapturous bliss, he looked into Katrina's eyes. Strange thoughts wormed into his mind. "It doesn't make sense … Lisa said she saw your body …"

"Don't worry about her, lover. Just do what you want with me." She reached down, unfastened his left hand from her buttock, and placed it around her scarf-covered neck.

There was another lightning blast, and the room was lit again. David's eyes darted towards the mirror. In the millisecond the electrical flash bathed the room, he saw an image that froze his heart.

Running down the middle of Katrina's back was a long, vertical gash. The cut started underneath the folds of the scarf wrapped around her neck, traveled down the length of her spine, and stopped just below her waist. The two loose flaps of skin that jacketed the wound were stitched together by what looked to be pieces of shoelace. And in the wound, where one might expect to see bloody muscle or bone, a dark, oily flesh seethed and churned, like the surface of a lake disturbed by a passing motorboat.

David's heart pounded against his chest. Someone, or some*thing*, was wearing the skin of Katrina Chen!

He turned to the woman atop him. Her eyes, once unknowable, burned with rage.

He forced the question out. "What … are … you?"

She opened her mouth to answer. The voice that spoke was not her normal lilting tone, but a guttural snarl, smacking with phlegm and spittle.

"Sorry, babe. Am I not your type?"

David screamed and tried to push the thing off his body, but 'Katrina' possessed a strength belied by her small size. She pressed down on him, pushing his body into the mattress. At once, the phallic pleasures of lovemaking became painful. A hissing sound, like a chorus of snakes, was immediately followed by the smell of burning flesh. He thrashed in the bed and pounded at the body on top of him. The thing's fingers caught his throat in a vice grip. His lungs burned as oxygen dried within them. There was pain. Down below. So much pain.

He clawed at her flesh. The chalky skin, once taut, tore off in wide, meaty strips, exposing more of the strange pulsating muscle underneath. He dug his fingers into the creature's eyes, but succeeded only in ripping away the mask of Katrina's face.

A crushing panic weighed down his body. His throbbing veins and booming heart threatened to burst out of his skin.

The powerful hands stayed locked around David's throat. He thrashed to the left, and then jerked right, heaving his fists against the creature's chest. To his surprise, the tactic worked. The thing toppled off him and fell to the floor.

Sharp, jagged knives of pain emanated from somewhere below his waist. He looked down and saw that he had no penis, only a bloody, steaming orifice.

"Oh my God!" he screamed. "What have you done to me?"

A figure rose in the shadows. Only seconds before, its size and form had matched that of Katrina; now it was well past six feet, with the build of an athlete. Its skinless muscles were not fibrous, but resembled oozing, quivering clay the color of swampy vegetation.

The horror of the thing's body was surpassed by its face. A mass of greenish meat tightly covered its skull. Red, angry eyes hovered above an upturned nose. Thin lips pulled back over razor sharp animal teeth.

The creature again spoke in its hideous voice. "What's the matter, David? Am I a lousy lay?"

Sobs rushed out of David's throat as he pushed himself up on the bed. This couldn't be real. It had to be a dream. Some kind of nightmare. Or a hallucination caused by the booze.

But the pain ... the pain ... what would make it go away?

The creature raised its right hand and stepped towards David. It held out an open palm as if offering an invisible gift.

A piece of bone the length and shape of a kitchen knife suddenly protruded from its wrist. The beast rammed the white blade into David's chest.

David felt himself slip back down to the bed. Warm, salty liquid rose in his throat, dripping out of his mouth with a gurgle. His hearing went quiet.

"Lisa ..." he murmured. His body relaxed. The shadows closed in on his field of vision and everything went dark.

***

Standing in the moonlight, the creature removed the bony extension from David's chest. It flipped his body over and sliced a long incision in the torso, starting from the lumbar spine and finishing at the base of the neck. A dark sheet of blood spread out from the wound, spilling across the body and seeping into the bedsheets.

The creature muttered strange words as it rolled David's body back over. It then sliced a line around the full radius of the neck. More blood flowed.

With a slurping sound, the bone blade retracted into the greenish forearm. The beast slipped its fingers into the gash around David's throat and began the slow process of parting the flesh from muscles and bone. When the process was complete, it lifted the bloody helmet in the air. The monster's thin lips curled into a smile. It dangled the hanging flesh over the crown of its skull and its quivering head muscles reshaped themselves to fit the slot that had once been David's neck. After some adjustment, the dead skin mask came to fit perfectly.

Wearing its new face, the monster walked to the oval mirror. It studied its reflection for several moments, then spoke in a perfect mimic of David's voice.

"Lisa ... *I'm back.*"

Chapter Thirty-five

Jeremiah pulled the red Datsun to a curb in the Toledo neighborhood known as Five Points. Gray and olive houses abutted cracked and uneven sidewalks. Cricket chirps broke through the hum of evening traffic on nearby Interstate-75.

He killed the engine and peered through the mosaic of raindrops spattered on his driver's side window. A two-story, multi-family quadplex stood back from a grassy lawn across the street. Lights shone through the windows of two units on the ground floor. The second floor apartments were accessible via stairs that ran up each side; their drawn shades made it hard to tell if anyone was home.

According to the Internet, Lisa Kallman lived in apartment four. A marker on the stairs indicated it was the second-story unit on the right side.

Jeremiah stepped out of the car, his body squeezed into a pink raincoat he'd found in the backseat. The olive covered duffle sack in his grip sagged with the weight of the shotgun and revolver.

Rain dampened his hair. He took several steps towards the multiplex, then paused, gut tightening. There was still time for a new plan. He could get back into the car and drive. Away from the police force that had to be searching for him. Towards a freedom he'd craved for two decades.

But what was more important? Freedom or vengeance?

He resumed walking to the stairs that led to apartment four. As he got a better view of the building's right side, he saw a darkened window. Lisa Kallman might be inside, perhaps asleep. If not, he'd go back to the car and wait.

He mounted the steps. From around the corner, a door squeaked open. When he was midway up the stairs, a voice came from behind him.

"Are you here to look at the apartment?"

He turned. A middle-aged woman wearing a bathrobe and hair curlers looked up at him. She sheltered herself from the rain with a tattered umbrella.

"Excuse me?" Jeremiah said.

"I'm Becca Davidson. I manage the house. I live in apartment one. Did you see the ad in the paper?"

He blinked, confused. "I'm sorry ... does Lisa Kallman live here?"

The woman smiled. "Oh, heavens no. Lisa vacated at the end of last month."

Jeremiah let out a quiet groan. He wracked his brain for a lie to explain his presence. "Uh, I'm her uncle. We haven't seen each other in some time and nobody told me she'd moved."

"Yep, she found a nice fellah, and they got a house together. Lovely couple. Lisa was such a good tenant. I hated to see her go. I hope things work out for her."

"You wouldn't happen to know her new address?"

The woman looked hesitant.

"Her dad was my step-brother," Jeremiah offered. "He was ... well, she probably told you about what happened."

"Oh yes," the woman said. "And I read the book by her psychologist." She shook her head. "Such a terrible tragedy. Thank goodness they put that awful man away."

Jeremiah nodded. "Yes ma'am. Justice was served. Lisa's the only family I have left and I'd really like to see her." He sunk his head into his neck, trying to make himself look small. Just a tiny, unthreatening man in a pink raincoat.

The manager looked back at her apartment. "I do have her address around somewhere. I have to send her deposit back. Let me look." She disappeared around the corner and Jeremiah heard a door open and close. He walked down the stairs and stood in the front yard as speckles of rain fell on him. He set the duffle by his feet.

The woman opened her door and peered out. With a musical tone, she exclaimed, "Found it. Do you need a pen?"

"Yes ma'am. I don't have any paper either."

"Let me write it down for you." She left the door to her apartment open and disappeared inside. Seconds later, she reappeared with two index cards, one marked, the other blank. As she leaned against the side of her door, she copied the address onto the blank card and handed it to Jeremiah.

"Thank you, ma'am." He shielded the card from the rain and examined the scribbling.

"Know where that is? I drew a little map for you."

"I think so. The Old West End?"

"That's right. Just take the surface streets south and you'll be there in no time."

"I appreciate it." He hoisted the duffle over his shoulder and ambled towards the Datsun. When he reached the driver's door, the woman called to him.

"Tell Lisa I said hi. We all sure miss her around here."

Jeremiah turned and waved. "I'll be sure to give her your message."

Chapter Thirty-six

Lisa arrived back at her West End neighborhood to find that rarest of gifts, a parking space in front of her house. The phrase, "thank Heaven for small favors," popped into her head, immediately followed by the notion it might be no favor at all. She'd been dreading her return home and the conversation she'd have to have with David. Putting off that interaction for even a few minutes would have felt like a small victory.

A gust of wind wheezed against the car window as she let out a long sigh. Outside, leaves fluttered over the sidewalk like angry birds who'd found themselves tossed out of their nests.

She left her SUV and made her way to the front steps of her house. No lights were visible through the curtained windows. Maybe David wasn't even home. Of course, his absence would merely delay the inevitable. Would she now have to sit in the living room into the morning hours, waiting for him to stumble drunkenly across the threshold?

She unlocked the door and stepped into the shadowed interior. Fumbling along the wall, she flipped the switch for the chandelier light hanging above the stairwell. The space remained dark. She walked over to a lamp on an end table beside the couch and turned its switch. Nothing. A glance at the digital clocks in the entertainment center confirmed they were also dead.

"Great," Lisa muttered. The power was out. She'd seen lights in neighboring homes, so the outage was only in her house. Had the fuses blown?

"David?" she called out. "What happened to the lights?"

No answer.

She locked the front door and ran the security chain through its track. After hanging her raincoat on the coatrack, she went to the kitchen and pulled open a cabinet drawer. Several flashlights and candles piled next to spare batteries. She picked out a hefty plastic flashlight with a six-inch lens and flipped it on. When the bright LED light bathed the room, her simmering anxiety cooled a bit. She was now well-armed to go tromping through the basement to find the fuse box.

The bowels of houses always creeped her out, especially in the dark, but she knew she'd need to work past her silly fears if she was going to get the power back on. There was no bogeyman waiting down there as she swung open the basement door.

Eyeing the grain of the wooden steps lit in the flashlight beam, Lisa started her descent. The planks creaked and groaned as she went, but eventually, she stepped onto the smooth concrete floor.

Moonlight drifted in through windows near the ceiling to reveal a basement as wide and as long as the house above. A washer and dryer set cast angular shadows across the floor. Two of David's old recliners and dozens of storage boxes stood in a gray corner, pressed up against brick walls. Wooden support columns were spaced throughout the room, running from concrete blocks on the floor up to the ceiling.

Outside, the wind was shaking the milkweed shrubs planted along the base of the house. It caused silhouettes to scamper across the walls like two-dimensional rats fleeing to unseen hiding places.

David had shown her the fuse box several days after their move. From what she remembered, it was mounted somewhere on the far wall. Shivering in the cool air, she started walking across the room. At the midpoint, her foot brushed against something solid and there was a loud clatter. She aimed the flashlight towards the sound and watched an empty vodka bottle rotate to a stop.

She gnawed at her lower lip. Was David's drinking habit worse than she'd suspected? Was he now hiding bottles of liquor throughout the house?

She pushed the thought from her mind, and walked to the wall housing the fuse box. The metal door opened with a squeal and she shined her light on the glass cylinders inside. Every one was clouded with dried smoke.

"Lisa!"

She shrieked and spun around, frantically slashing her flashlight over the walls and floor in search of the source. David stood in the middle of the room, dressed in unusually formal attire: leather boots, well-pressed slacks held up with a leather belt, and a wool sweater. The buttoned collar of a dress shirt stuck up through the neck of the sweater, pressing against the bottom of his chin.

His face did not match the tenor of his clothes. His skin was haggard and gray, like he'd aged a decade overnight. Underneath disheveled hair, his eyes squinted in the light.

"Jesus Christ!" Lisa exclaimed. "You scared the crap out of me."

"Sorry." His face was flat, expressionless.

"What are you doing down here?"

"I was upstairs," he said. "The lights went out all at once. I figured an electrical surge had blown the fuses, so I came down here. But I got confused. I'd ... I'd been drinking. I lay down on one of the couches and just drifted off to sleep. I didn't wake up until I heard you walking around just now." He paused and scowled. "Can you please not shine the light in my face?"

Lisa lowered the beam. "So, um, what do we do now?"

She was asking about the fuses, but he seemed to interpret the question in the context of their relationship. "All I can do is beg you to forgive me. You were right about Katrina. It was the stupidest thing I've ever done. And you have every right to hate me. But, please, don't call off the wedding. If you leave me, I'll die. I swear, baby, I'll die."

His words clawed at her heart. She'd hoped her suspicions were some terrible mistake, some confusion that David could explain away and then everything would return to normal. But that dream was now shattered. The future and all its promises—the wedding, a family, a normal life—hung in grave jeopardy.

And David thought all he had to do to make it right was beg?

She glared at him. "What I don't understand is why? Why did you do it? Didn't our life together mean anything to you?"

His eyes receded into the shadows under his brow. "I can't control myself. I've never been able to. I get these urges ... to drink, to screw. And I can't turn them off. I know I'm only going to hurt myself. And the people I love." He paused and gave a weary smile. "Sometimes I feel like I'm not even myself. It's like the face staring back in the mirror isn't even me."

Lisa lowered her eyes; she couldn't even look at him. "I should have known better. When you first started coming around to the children's center, asking me out, I thought you seemed too good to be true. Boys ... men ... had always been scared of my past. But not you. You seemed almost perfect."

David took a step forward, his face twisting into that of a repentant child. "I'm not perfect. I never was. You're the one who's perfect. I know what I've done is wrong. But I'll make it up to you. One day at a time, baby. One minute at a time. For the rest of my life. Just let me make it up to you."

Heat flushed Lisa's neck. Her eyes grew moist. "I'm sorry, David. You're asking too much."

He got down on one knee. Tears streamed down his cheeks. "Please, Lisa. I don't know what I'll do without you. I'll die without you. Just say you'll love me. Say you won't leave me. Please."

She felt discomforted by the pathetic man-child kneeling before her. In their relationship, David had always been the strong one, the one in control. Now he was a blubbering toddler, begging for his mother's forgiveness. His open hands offered Lisa the power in their relationship. But for reasons she couldn't fully understand, she wasn't sure she wanted it.

"David," Lisa said. "Please, just get up."

He rose. He honked his nose and then wiped it with the side of one hand, looking at her forlornly. "Help me, baby. Please, help me."

She met his sad, wet eyes. The mournfulness in his lost puppy dog gaze pulled at her, igniting a quiver that spread from her lower lip to her entire jaw. Then something deep inside her cracked. She lurched forward and threw her arms around him. "Oh God, honey. Maybe we can make it work, baby. Maybe we can get through this."

She felt David release the breath he'd been holding. He uttered a strange little laugh and leaned into her embrace, his arms running over her back. "Thank you, Lisa. Thank you so much. I will make it up to you. I won't let you down again."

A pungent odor wafted into Lisa's nose. She paused, carefully weighing her next words. Finally, she let out a nervous chuckle and said, "You really need to quit drinking, babe. You smell like a sewer."

"I'll stop," David mumbled. His arms dropped to his sides as he stepped away from her embrace. "When I'm *GOOD AND FUCKING READY!*"

His open palm smacked Lisa's jaw. She toppled backwards, her head knocking against the concrete. The flashlight clattered on the floor and she slid down the wall.

She lifted her stunned gaze to David. His shadowed form towered above her, his glinting eyes drilling into her.

"David, what—"

He swung his boot into the side of her ribs, setting off an explosion of pain. She screamed, but used the force of the blow to roll herself sideways on to her hands and knees. She tried to run, but felt David's hand wrap around her ponytail. With a sharp tug, he yanked her to the floor and squatted across her pelvis, pressing his forearm onto her chest. With his free hand, he struck her cheek, setting her face on fire again.

Her palms grew wet. Frantic bursts of animal fear pulsed in her chest.

The sneering contempt in David's eyes told her their entire relationship had been a lie. How had he disguised this vicious rage when they took walks in the park or engaged in sweet talk over candlelit dinners? While making love?

He wrapped his hands around her neck. "Time's up, bitch. Get ready for hell."

The pieces suddenly fell into place. Between desperate gasps for air, she forced words out. "You ... You killed Katrina ..."

"Did I, my dear? Perhaps it was you. A woman traumatized by her father's murder grows up with a dark side she can't control. A separate personality that destroys anything that threatens her, including her fiancé's lover. Then she turns on him and he's forced to kill her." He smiled, tightening his grip on her throat. "I think the police will buy it, don't you?"

Lisa flailed her arms across the concrete floor, searching for something, anything, to use as a weapon. Her right hand connected with the grip of the flashlight. She swung it upward in a wide arc, bludgeoning him across his temple. He screamed and clawed at the air.

Still pressed against the floor, Lisa raised her legs and wrapped her ankles around David's throat. Twisting to one side, she pulled him off her and ran towards the stairs. Before she got to the first step, David's hand snared her ankle. She toppled forward, dropping the flashlight and grabbing at the wooden planks before her body hit the steps.

She drew her other foot back and kicked him in the forehead. He cried out and his grip relaxed.

Scooping up the flashlight, she scampered up the stairs, looking back as David's silhouette rose at the bottom of the steps. She bolted into the hallway, heading towards the front door.

A single question burned in her brain. Did she have enough time to draw back the chain and undo the latch?

There was a crash as David threw open the cellar door, followed by thuds of his stomping feet. He'd be upon her in seconds.

Lurching to the left, Lisa started up the stairs. David raced after her, his obscenities filling the air. Before she arrived on the second floor, she twisted around and heaved the flashlight at him. It bounced off his head and fell to the landing.

She ran through the hallway and into their bedroom, locking the door behind her. Several long strides took her to David's nightstand, where she yanked open the drawer and hefted the Glock in both hands.

Pounding shook the door. At first, she thought David was using his fists, until she realized he was throwing his whole body against the center panel. His mocking voice sounded between strikes. "Open the door, Lisa. I want to get out. Let me out."

She aimed the Glock at the pulsating wood. Could he get through by brute force alone?

The wood splintered and a square section of the panel fell to the floor. David reached through the opening and wrapped his hand around the doorknob.

The next seconds fragmented into slow-moving images.

David's voice dropped an octave. *"Open the door!"*

A flash of recognition sparked in Lisa's subconscious.

The door swung open and David lunged towards her. She squeezed the trigger and a flash lit the room. A dark stain appeared under David's collarbone.

He kept coming.

Lisa fired again. Bright flash. A burst of fabric from the sweater near David's kidney. Yet he still rushed towards her.

Too low! She was aiming too low!

He was only a few feet away and coming fast. She raised the pistol level with his face. The thunderous retort of a third gunshot filled the room. Dark liquid spattered across his forehead.

David dropped to the carpet.

A high-pitched sound rang in Lisa's ears. Smoke curled out of the Glock's barrel as she held it out in front of her. Her heart thudded in her chest, her hands trembled as she lowered the gun to one side.

With her gaze fixed ahead, she approached the doorway, fighting every instinct to look down at her former lover.

Shadows drenched the hallway as she walked towards her office. Once inside, she set the handgun on her desk and sat in her chair. A drumbeat of falling rain on the rooftop tapped off the passing moments until a moaning gust of wind rose up and drowned it out.

Using the light of her cell phone, Lisa opened a drawer and rummaged through papers and pens, eventually finding Devin McCuddy's business card. She began pressing his phone number on her keypad. Three digits in, she stopped.

Her eyes fixed on an object on her desk. The wingless statue of St. Michael lay on its back next to a yellow legal pad and several scattered pens.

"I thought you might like that back," rasped a voice from the hallway.

Chapter Thirty-seven

Lisa struggled to take in the sight before her. David—the man she'd just shot and left for dead—stood in the doorway to her office. His sweater and shirt were gone, and oozing purple bullet holes marked his torso. Dark liquid trickled from the two-inch hole in his forehead, flowing down his cheek past the wicked grin on his face.

How was he still alive? The question confounded her, as did the cause of the bloodless, open gash that ran across his exposed neck like a choker necklace.

She grabbed the Glock off the desk, yet his eyes mocked her.

There was no escaping while his muscular form blocked the doorway. She rose from her chair and moved to one side of the desk, where she paused to weigh her options.

Her fiancé—*former* fiancé, it could now be safely assumed—stepped into the room. He raised one arm and flexed his bicep in a bodybuilder pose. To her horror, the muscles underneath the flesh squirmed and rippled like a pit of snakes. The skin began to tear, revealing a strange, green-gray substance underneath.

She choked out her words. "My god, David ... what ...?"

He pirouetted around to expose his back. Two flaps of skin ran the length of his spine, hanging open like a jacket. Inside the wound was more of the weird muscle covered by a glistening membrane of black tar.

Keeping his back to her, David rotated his head—an impossible, inhuman action—until his cobalt eyes stared at her. In a low, grating voice, he said, "Poor David. I guess I really got under his skin."

The insanity of the moment scraped Lisa's mind. What she was seeing defied all rules of logic and science. Was this an elaborate hallucination? A fevered dream? Had she gone mad? Any of those options was preferable to accepting what was before her.

David twirled his body back around and held his arms open, as if expecting her to join him in an embrace. Then his head snapped back so that he stared skyward. His rounded Adam's apple began to undulate and a hissing gurgle came from his throat. A steaming, milky fluid erupted out of his mouth, ears, nose and eyes. It poured down his neck and chest.

Lisa gagged when she realized the white liquid was not only dampening David's skin and clothes, but disintegrating them. The surface of his chest and arms curled like paper caught in a flame and split from his body. The flesh around his fingers flitted away like digits snipped off a glove. The torrent of steaming fluid quickly washed away the cloth of his pants and the soft pink underneath.

David's face was the last part to be eradicated. As the vomit flowed from his orifices, strips of his cheeks and nose tore loose and fell to the floor. Lips that had been pressed against Lisa's so many times steamed and melted. With a few more seconds, all that remained of his visage were those fiery, glowering eyes.

Finally, the humanoid figure ceased its expulsion of fluid. The last drops of the pearly acid oozed through the crevices and corners of exposed claylike flesh, dripping down and burning into the floorboards.

"Do you remember me, Lisa?" came the voice. "I've been waiting for our reunion. Indeed, I would have visited you sooner, but your friend stopped me." It nodded towards the broken Saint Michael statue on the desk.

Lisa staggered and dropped to one knee. The floodgates of her mind broke open. She was a child again, lying on her bed in the dark. Her father burst into the room and turned on the lights, her mother just behind him. Daddy opened the closet door and the hand … the hand made of the same greenish flesh as the thing before her reached out and grabbed him by the throat. It pulled him into the closet. Then the horrible sound, the ripping. Her father's head tossed at her. Lisa and her mother frozen in fear, incapable of processing what they were seeing, yet acutely aware of what would come—the monster would leap out and slay them where they stood.

But that did not happen. Instead, they heard the voice.

"It would be a gift to kill you now, Lisa. But I will see you again. Soon."

Now Lisa kneeled in her office, her chest quaking with sobs. The grief of a seven-year-old girl washed through her. An emotional wound never truly healed ripped wide open.

"You … killed … Daddy!" she stammered between gasps for air.

"Yes. I wanted to cause you pain. The same pain you caused me. I wanted to begin your suffering on that night. But this long anticipation will only make your destruction sweeter."

Part of Lisa wanted to curl into a ball and dissolve into her own terror. But inside her was a voice that allowed no surrender. *Fight*, it screamed. *Don't give in!*

Placing the muzzle of the pistol on the ground, she pushed herself to standing. The thing in the doorway glared at her. "Are you ready to die, Lisa?"

With quivering hands, she pointed the gun at the beast.

The phlegm-drenched voice chortled. "Foolish girl. That can't kill me."

But it can hurt you. She fired two shots into its face. It toppled backwards, bounced off the doorframe, and fell into the corner of the room.

Her adrenaline surged. She leaped forward and ran through the door, into the hallway. A quick look behind showed the thing was not following. She reached the stairs and began taking them three at a time. The flashlight lay ahead of her, its wide beam cutting through the dark.

Her legs froze when she saw the creature standing at the bottom of the stairs, glowering up at her.

Extraneous light from the flashlight beam illuminated the monster's features. It snorted, jerked its head to one side, and then spat. A bullet clattered somewhere across the room. The creature repeated the action and expelled a second projectile.

"You're starting to give me a real headache, Lisa. Why don't you just die like a good little girl?"

The monster took several steps up the stairs. When it came into the glare of the flashlight's beam, its flesh began to smoke. The pained look that crossed its face sparked two realizations in Lisa's mind.

When the creature had murdered her father twenty years ago, it had never left the confines of the darkened closet.

David—or the thing wearing David's skin—had scowled at the light when she'd shined it on him in the basement.

Lisa raised the gun and fired into the illuminated flesh of the creature's pectoral muscle. This time, the monster screamed, falling back onto the darkened living room floor. Sounds like the moans of a wounded animal came out of the shadows.

The beast was hurt, but Lisa would not risk going past it, not when there were other ways to get out of the house. She retreated up the stairs, down the dark hallway and into the guest bedroom. The room was immaculate, the perfectly made bed bathed in rays of moonlight coming through the window. She jammed the gun into her front pocket and pushed on the window lift. With a screech, the framed glass slid open. Powerful winds seethed through the evening air.

She threw a glance behind her. Nothing. She heaved her torso through the open window and out onto the roof. Cold and wet shingles dampened her palms. Then something grabbed her leg. She looked back and saw the creature in the bedroom, one hand wrapped around her ankle.

She screamed into the roaring wind. "*Help! Help me!*" With her free foot, she kicked the thing in its face. It laughed. It was safe in the dark, where her flailing blows could not hurt it. She was helpless as the beast dragged her back in through the window, down to the bedroom floor, where the air shot out of her lungs. The monster straddled her waist. A stream of acidic foam dripped from its sneering mouth, burning the fabric of her sweater.

"You hurt me, Lisa. But not in the way I will hurt you. Are you ready for pain?"

Lisa's eyes darted around the room, searching for a weapon or an escape. But there was nothing. Only the shadows coming to life. They rose out of the darkest corners and swirled before her like inky serpents set to feast upon her body. Then the cold, black gloom settled over her eyes, blocking the moon's light.

Chapter Thirty-eight

Standing on the damp sidewalk outside Lisa Kallman's current residence, Jeremiah ran through his body's complaints in his head. The handles of the heavy duffle bag dug into his shoulder. The revolver tucked into the small of his back felt cold against his flesh. He pulled the old woman's pink raincoat closer, hoping the thin plastic would fend off some of the nighttime chill.

The curtains in the yellow house were drawn, with no light inside. A few minutes ago, the Datsun's dashboard clock had read 10 p.m. So Kallman and her fiancé were either out for the evening or they were early-to-bed types.

He jogged up the porch steps and peered into a small, diamond-shaped window cut into the front door. Gray outlines of standard living furniture—couches, tables, an entertainment center—were visible in the gloom. A single beam of light shone from somewhere to the right, out of his field of view.

His chest swelled as he sipped cool air into his lungs. He had to control his nerves, to stay calm, stay sharp.

When a new rush of oxygenated courage took hold, he turned the doorknob, not at all surprised to find it locked. He leaned his weight against the door and determined the dead bolt had been set. Fortunately, he'd done his share of break-ins in the past; he knew a home's rear was always less secure than the front.

Jeremiah padded down the steps to the sidewalk. Only a few cars had passed since he'd arrived and the street was empty. He walked to the house's west side and looked at the windows of the neighboring residence. Two men in bathrobes stood in a well-lit kitchen drinking martinis. The younger man held a small pug to his chest and smiled as he rubbed the animal's belly.

Sounds of swelling violins and brass seeped through the walls of the house. A famous symphonic piece was playing loudly through the stereo. Good. The music would drown out any sounds that might otherwise draw attention.

He retreated to the sidewalk and walked to the other side of the Kallman house. There, a two-story home rose up behind several trees, no lights coming from its windows.

With a final look to see if anyone was watching, he ducked into the space between the two houses. Creeping through the shadows, he scanned the windows of the Kallman residence, again finding no light or signs of activity.

After rounding the rear, he came upon a seven-foot tall fence. He hooked his fingers into the slats and heaved himself up and over the top, coming down on soft earth on the other side.

Crouching low, he made his way across the yard and up the porch steps. A wide rectangular window was cut into the wall. Just past it, he saw the silver glint of a refrigerator.

He stepped to the door and turned the knob. As before, it was locked, but this time, there was no deadbolt. He pulled the Datsun's key ring from his pocket and inserted one of the plastic shopping cards into the slit between the door and doorframe. With a little work, he pushed the bolt back into its slot. Then he eased the door open, trying to make as little noise as possible.

His heart galloped in his chest as he stared into the open space. So much for staying calm.

He slipped into the house and shut the door behind him. The laminate tiles chilled his knees when he kneeled to unzip the duffel bag. He hefted the shotgun in his hand and slung the empty bag back over his shoulder. No reason to leave any evidence.

It was hard to see in the shadows, but he quelled the urge to flip a light switch. Here, he was a predator, and the darkness was his friend.

He moved through the kitchen, noting that the counters were clean, and the sink empty of dishes. Even with only the moonlight coming in through the windows, the floor sparkled. The space gave off the ambience of a magazine-perfect home for two American lovers with their whole lives in front of them.

Time to ruin that little dream.

The first door in the hallway was wide open. When he stepped through it, he found himself in an office with a wooden desk set on a soft carpet. Even in the dim light, he could read the spines of the books in the bookcase set against the far wall. Reference material on the American legal system.

Had Lisa Kallman become a lawyer? Or had her lover?

More importantly: did he care? He left the room.

The next door hung on its hinges, slightly ajar. Jeremiah peered through the crack and saw stairs leading to a cellar. Unlikely anyone would be down there.

The end of the hallway opened to the living room on his right. As he looked around, it struck him as odd that none of the electronic gadgetry in the entertainment center had any lights. Had the power gone out? Was that why the house was dark?

He contemplated these questions for a few moments until something else caught his attention. The single beam of light he'd seen from the front door appeared to be shining out of the obscured stairwell.

He paused. A flashlight? If so, it was too still to be held in a person's hands. But why would someone leave a flashlight lying on the stairs?

One possibility occurred to him. The electricity in the house had died and someone upstairs had attempted to come down to the main floor. They'd fallen in the dark, and had been knocked unconscious or broken their neck, and now lay on the steps next to the beaming flashlight.

The irony stung Jeremiah. Had he come all this way, only to find his planned victim already dead?

But maybe that wasn't the case. Perhaps Lisa or her fiancé had heard him entering the house and they were now waiting on the stairs, armed with a gun, poised to shoot whoever came around the corner.

For the second time that day, Jeremiah questioned what he was doing. With a little help from a mysterious friend, he'd pulled off an impossible escape from prison. Why wasn't he making his way into Canada or somewhere down south? Was it so important that he come face-to-face with the woman who had imprisoned him with her lies? A woman who might now be standing in the shadows, waiting to put a bullet in his gut?

He snapped himself out of his anxious musings. He was not a little boy afraid of the dark. He was not a child dependent on the crazed prayers of his mother for protection.

He'd already killed a man to come this far. There was no going back.

A wheezing moan came from somewhere outside the house. It took a few seconds for Jeremiah to recognize it as the blowing wind. The sound faded to silence, immediately followed by light taps. The rain was back, using the roof as its own personal percussion kit.

He pressed forward and approached the stairwell. Ducking low, he rounded the corner and aimed the shotgun up where a person's midsection might be. As he'd suspected, a flashlight was there, lying on one step. But there was no unconscious body, nor an armed occupant. The empty stairwell simply led to a landing, then turned towards a second floor.

There were many explanations for the abandoned flashlight. Perhaps Lisa and her lover had been drinking and, in a giggling rush towards the bedroom, let it fall to the floor.

He made his way up the stairwell, pausing to pick up the flashlight. This would give him a clear view of anything he might shoot at.

At the top of the stairs, a dark hallway emerged. He pointed the flashlight beam towards the floor and used the residual light to guide his movement. Midway down, he passed an empty bathroom. Beyond that was a hallway that branched left. He shined his light and saw that it ended at an office.

Returning his attention to the corridor's main stretch, Jeremiah saw a partially closed door. Stilling his breath, he crept forward and used the toe of his boot to push it open. The first thing he saw was a single-sized bed with sheets and a blanket neatly folded at the top: probably a guest bedroom. If Lisa and her lover were not home, it would be an ideal place to hide and wait.

He stepped into the room. Moonlight and cool night air trickled in through an open window.

A bolt of lightning crackled outside and Jeremiah saw a figure standing in the far corner of the room. As darkness returned, he lurched aside, his grip tightening on the shotgun and flashlight. But the yellow beam revealed only himself. Or, more accurately, his reflection in a tall oval mirror in the corner.

As thunder growled outside, both discomfort and joy swelled in his chest. He was struck first by how old his mirror image looked. Fleshy bags bulged under his eyes. The crevices around his cheeks etched out a grimace he hadn't been aware he'd been wearing.

But he also relished seeing himself standing in an environment so different from the concrete of prison. The room he was in reminded him of his childhood bedroom. And, if he ignored the shotgun in his hands, he looked like a normal person going about their evening. Not someone who'd spent twenty years in a hell of rock and steel.

Then he noticed a flicker in his mirror image, somewhere near the center of his belly.

He looked down and saw nothing. When he returned his gaze to the mirror, he saw the flicker was now a tiny figure running towards him. The person was getting bigger with every moment. It was as if a film projector was superimposing the image of the runner over his own reflection.

As it came closer, he recognized the figure. It was her, Lisa Kallman. She was running towards him from the other side of the mirror. As Jeremiah's heartbeat thudded, she grew closer, closer, until she was only a few feet away in the inverted world on the other side of the glass.

Before he could comprehend what he was seeing, the mirror exploded. Shards of silver scattered across the room. Lisa Kallman erupted out of the oval frame, collided with Jeremiah, and sent them both flying backwards.

Chapter Thirty-nine

When the creature held Lisa to the floor, the mist-like shadows had voraciously consumed all light. Then the beast had vanished, leaving her flailing in the dark, effectively blinded, though the image of her monstrous opponent took a moment to fade from her retinas.

The shadowy void quelled more than her ability to see. She quickly discovered she couldn't feel the ground under her feet. In fact, she couldn't tell whether she stood upright, lay supine or prostrate, or hung upside down. Both gravity and her kinesthetic sense had vanished.

Confused as she was in her new environment, she stayed silent. If she couldn't see the creature, perhaps it couldn't see her. She floated in the dark space and took deep breaths to calm her nervous system.

Until she realized there was no air.

Tingling anxiety flared in her chest. Her hands clawed into the black, a desperate bid to find air by touch somehow.

But, as the moments passed, her lungs did not ache, and her body lost no strength. Air seemed to be inconsequential in this bizarre environment.

She began to detect blurry images in the gloom. A series of horizontal stripes hung in space twenty feet away. The lines existed in a dreamy haze, but she recognized them as a row of beveled balusters rising out of the circular staircase of the derelict Victorian mansion. She was observing them as if she was floating sideways, a distance away.

She looked around, and other sights emerged. A room with a bed and metal toilet appeared in the distant murk. A prison cell? Near it was the bare outline of the bedroom she shared with David, as it would be viewed from one of its darkest corners. And then a similar view of their kitchen.

Gradually, ghostly images of more than a dozen locations appeared, all cordoned off by cloudy pillars of shadow. Some places she recognized, like her mother's empty chamber in the sanitarium, but others she did not.

What was she seeing? Had the creature killed her and now her soul was experiencing the afterlife? Was this heaven? Or hell? Or some purgatory stuck between the two?

Familiar slurping laughter sounded throughout the space. Or in her head. It was hard to tell which. The beast was close.

"Don't worry, Lisa," came the voice. "I haven't forgotten about you."

Her darting eyes caught glimpses of the monster's silhouette as it passed in front of the dim vistas before her. Its shadowed form would appear, then vanish, only to reappear a distance away.

"I can play this game until eternity. How about you?"

She scooped her arms through space in an attempt to propel herself forward like a swimmer performing the breaststroke. While she sensed movement, the pockets of imagery that surrounded her remained frustratingly distant.

The spittle-drenched voice sounded again, now louder and closer. "It's time to end this. Before others arrive."

She rolled her body, searching for any sign of the creature. Coming to a rest, she clenched her teeth and prepared for the worst. It was no surprise when hot breath touched her neck and the stink of rotting plants filled her nose.

"Game over, Lisa."

She looked towards the gurgling voice and saw the barest hint of red eyes. A monstrous hand appeared, a sharp bone protruding from its wrist.

Her intestines rolled in her belly. She hoped death would be painless. But why would the beast grant her that favor?

A beam of light appeared behind her. It was not bright, but in the pitch-black realm, it carried an almost physical presence.

The creature sensed it, too. It screamed and vanished into the shadow.

Turning towards the yellow glow, Lisa saw it shone through an oval portal in the distance, a curious eye peering into a shadowy swamp. The streaks of light started strong, but faded as they projected deeper into the void.

With the radiance came a partial return of gravity. Her legs dropped, as if pulled by invisible hands, and one foot connected with what felt like a platform of cotton. She dragged her other foot forward and located even firmer ground. With another step, the luminous pathway upon which she walked took on the consistency of mud. She began staggering towards the floating doorway.

As she moved, the images behind the oval became more discernible. There was a figure, a man. The beam poured out of his hand. Lisa prayed he would not leave and take the light with him.

The surface underneath her sneakers grew firmer, and she was able to accelerate. It felt like jogging on sand at the edge of an ocean.

Then a snarl sounded in the shadows. The creature was closing in. *Just keep running*, she told herself. *Only a few more seconds.*

Her heart jolted when she recognized the figure in the doorway. Jeremiah O'Brien. He stood in the guest room of her house, holding a flashlight and a shotgun.

A choice loomed before her: go through the portal and face a hardened criminal who had every reason to seek her death, or stay in the shadows and battle a demon.

Man or monster?

It was really no choice at all.

Chapter Forty

After crashing through the mirror, Lisa bounced off Jeremiah O'Brien and landed near the bedroom's entrance. O'Brien tumbled backwards, losing his grip on the flashlight, which somersaulted through the air and landed on the bed.

She rolled upright on the floor, mirror shards cracking under her weight and slicing into her flesh. O'Brien lay against the far wall, blinking rapidly. The oval mirror frame stood a half dozen feet away, but the space that had once held reflective glass was now an eerie blackness.

The beast had been close behind her when she'd crossed over. There was little time to act and she'd need all the help she could get. "O'Brien! Can you hear me?"

The convict moaned and rubbed his eyes with one hand, while his other stayed wrapped around the shotgun grip.

A rasping voice filled the room. "Lisa, I'm beginning to think you don't like my company." She gaped in horror as the creature stepped out of the mirror's black screen. As one foot set down on the bedroom floor, it placed its hands on the inside of the oval frame and heaved. The wood splintered into pieces and fell to the floor.

She looked to O'Brien. "Use your gun. Shoot it!"

O'Brien pressed his back against the wall, his bulging eyes glued to the monstrosity that had just appeared out of nothing.

The creature laughed and moved closer to the room's center. Lisa again shouted, "Shoot it!" but O'Brien did not move.

She half-rolled-half-leaped to where O'Brien sat and grabbed the shotgun out of his hands. She aimed it at the creature and pulled the trigger.

The beast stood blanketed by the shadows from which it drew strength. It stumbled back a step as the shotgun pellets blasted its chest, then returned to its full stature, a growl rising in its throat.

She needed to weaken the monster. The flashlight lay on the bed, several feet away from her, but close to O'Brien. She turned to him. "I don't have time to explain this. Shine the flashlight on its chest. Just do it!"

O'Brien moved quickly this time, grabbing the light and swinging it around. The creature, realizing Lisa's plan, lurched towards them, but as the beam of light crossed its torso, she fired twice. Greenish skin burst open like clay hit with firecrackers. Black blood spattered against the wall.

Screams filled the air as the monster clutched its wounds. Lisa raised the shotgun and shouted at O'Brien. *"His face! Aim the light at his face!"*

O'Brien brought the light to the creature's scowling visage. Another shotgun blast lit up the room, but not before the beast ducked into a corner where shadows folded over it like a blanket. O'Brien aimed the flashlight into the dark, revealing only empty space. Then the hideous voice echoed off the walls.

"You know where to find me, Lisa. Let's not waste another twenty years."

Chapter Forty-one

Jeremiah gripped the headboard of the bed and hoisted himself up. His brain whirled like a washing machine as it laundered through his growing list of questions. How had Lisa Kallman gotten into the room by crashing through a mirror? Where had she come from? And most importantly …

"What the fucking fuck was that *thing*?"

"That's what just killed my fiancé," the woman across the room from him said. "And my father twenty years ago." She paused, clucked her tongue, and added, "If I had to guess, it's what set you up for his murder."

The answers only bore more questions, but Jeremiah's mind was racing too fast to put them to words.

Plus, that shotgun in Lisa's hands was distracting him. He gave it a wary glance. "You're pretty handy with that thing."

She hefted the weapon. "I had a foster dad who taught me to shoot. I think he'd been hoping for a boy."

Jeremiah grunted and moved his eyes away from the shotgun. "You still haven't answered my question about that refugee from a horror movie … What the hell is it? Some kind of maniac in a funny suit?"

A heavy sigh left Lisa's lips. "I wouldn't bother explaining if you hadn't just seen what you'd seen. That thing is some kind of monster. Like a demon. It can teleport through shadows. And it can trap people in the dark. It ensnared me in some strange darkness, like another dimension, where it's been hiding and watching our world. I was only able to escape when the light from your flashlight came through the mirror."

She delivered the explanation with a nonchalance that confounded Jeremiah. "Another dimension?" he repeated slowly. "Escape through a mirror? What kind of *Stranger Things* bullshit are you trying to sell me here?"

"Think about it, O'Brien. You just saw me crash through the looking glass like I was Alice in goddamned Wonderland. Explain that with your regular laws of physics."

He couldn't, he knew that. His mouth flapped open and closed as he struggled for a response. In the end, he could only grit his teeth.

"That creature has powers," Lisa insisted. "When I was a child, it used them to appear in my closet. When my father opened the door, it tore his head off."

Anger hit Jeremiah hot and fast. "So you *knew* I didn't kill your father? Why the hell didn't you say so at my trial?"

Lisa's fingers tensed on the shotgun grip, her knuckles turning white. "I'm sorry about that. I was a little girl. They sent me to a psychologist and I told her what I'd seen, but she didn't believe me. So she changed my memories. I suppose she just thought she was trying to help. In her own egotistical way."

The apology did nothing to calm Jeremiah's rage. For a moment, he gestated in the realization his life had been laid to waste by a cruel twist of fate. The anger simmered in his gut, burning into his lungs, only cooling when he felt the cold steel of the service revolver pressed into the crook of his back. He wasn't nearly as helpless as the pretty redhead before him might think.

Lisa lifted the shotgun. "What you were planning on doing with this?"

"What do you think?" he spat. "You sent me to prison. I was gonna get revenge."

"Prison ..." she repeated. "Shouldn't you still be there?"

He threw her a snarky look. "Well, you know ... good behavior."

"Get serious, O'Brien."

He took a breath. "A few days ago, I saved a guard from another prisoner's attack. He wanted to thank me, so he smuggled me out of prison."

"A guard just let you out? Do I look like a moron?"

"You think I care if you believe me? It's the damn truth."

Lisa's brow furrowed, and she began speaking slowly, as if talking to a three-year-old. "Look, this thing ... whatever it is ... it can disguise itself as people by wearing their skin. It was pretending to be my fiancé earlier tonight."

"It wears their *skin*?" Jeremiah shrugged off a shiver of disgust. "That's pretty weird. But what's your point?"

"Are you sure it really was a guard who let you out?"

Jeremiah recalled CO Baker's gray pallor and listless behavior. The young man's eyes had been pulled back into his face, as if to hide any dark truths that might be revealed by their close examination.

"But why?" Jeremiah asked. "Why would this demon of yours want to break me out of prison?"

"It's been tormenting me for weeks, making its presence known in bizarre ways. Maybe it knew you'd come for me. Maybe that's how it gets its kicks."

A clamping pressure tightened around Jeremiah's head, two steel thumbs pushing into his temples. A wave of vertigo made him nauseous. "I don't understand any of this. I never saw that thing before in my life. Hell, I'm still not even sure I did see it."

"Trust me, you did. And unless you want to keep seeing it for the rest of your life, you'll help me kill it. Tonight."

He choked back a laugh. "I'll do *what*?"

The narrow-eyed look Lisa gave jolted him like a slap across the face. "There's an abandoned house a few blocks from here," she said. "It has no electricity, and it's always dark inside, filled with shadows. This thing likes it there. We need to go there, find it, and kill it."

"You want to take me *monster hunting*?"

"O'Brien, remind me what you came here to do? It seems like you're a pretty brave man when you're about to gun down a defenseless woman. But if you want revenge against the thing that got you locked up twenty years ago, you're going to have to grow a pair. Preferably made out of brass."

The heat of rage returned to his chest. "What about the police? The army? The fucking dogcatcher? They should be the ones handling this, you know? Not us."

"Do you really think anyone who hasn't seen this thing is going to believe it exists? If we don't deal with this tonight, we're going to spend the rest of our lives waiting for it to appear out of nowhere and drag us into the dark."

"*Us?* I got no beef with this thing. Why shouldn't I just walk the fuck out of here?"

"This monster killed my fiancé, O'Brien. It had no problem letting you rot in prison for two decades. It can move through the shadows. Do you really think it'll just let you roam free?"

Jeremiah rubbed his hip as if massaging a bruise. His fingers pressed into muscle inches away from the gun.

Lisa seemed to sense no answer was coming to her question. "If we go after this thing now, tonight, we do it on our terms. We know it has weaknesses. It can be harmed in the light. It can bleed whatever it is that it bleeds."

His hand slid behind his back and wrapped around the handle of the revolver. It was now or never. Once he had Lisa Kallman at gunpoint, he could tie her up, grab her car, and drive to the southern border. Or take her as a hostage and …

The schemes withered in his head as quickly as he conceived them. His grip on the weapon faltered.

Why couldn't he take control of the situation? Why couldn't he put his plan into action?

And yet, he knew why. He'd come to this house to see if he had the courage to kill the woman standing in front of him. He'd envisioned her on her knees, begging for her life.

But this Lisa Kallman was not the timid young girl he'd watched moving into a house in his neighborhood twenty years ago. Nor was she the anxious woman he'd observed at his parole hearing almost a dozen days back.

This Lisa Kallman was a fighter.

Everything he'd seen since she'd burst out of the mirror still confused him. They were events that required the existence of supernatural forces and beings he'd always presumed to be impossible. But he recognized Lisa was offering him gifts he desperately wanted. Closure. Justice. Revenge.

A chance at living the rest of his days in peace.

He dropped his arms to his side, leaving the gun tucked into the hollow of his back. "All right. But what's your plan? We just walk over there and start shooting?"

"Not at all." She gave him a wry smile and walked to the door. "Follow me. We need to prepare."

Chapter Forty-two

He floated in the blackness, cursing the agonies brought on by the metal shards caught in his flesh. The pain nearly blocked out all thought, all consciousness, leaving him a wild beast tormented by shrieking nerve endings.

But the dark was a salve. The cold, creeping hands of the shadow caressed his skin, slipping into his wounds and chasing the pain away. One by one, invisible fingers plucked the gray pellets from his innards and tossed them aside. Slowly, the shadow healed him.

He grunted, musing on the irony. The shadow had not always been his friend. When he'd been of the light, he'd feared the shadow's confines. He'd known that, were he unable to cross the murky swamp of the shadow floor, he would be sucked into its bowels where no amount of light could save him.

An electric jolt shot through his nervous system, forcing a whimper from his throat. His hands balled into fists, and a cracking sound cut into the air. When the pain mitigated, he opened his palm and looked at the crushed remains of the trinket he'd held, the wingless statue that had protected her for so long.

Humans were foolish. With their mythos and holy texts, they came so close to understanding the true nature of their universe. But those very tools kept them from seeing the truth. Because they did not understand their own legends. And they could not reconcile their twin lords of science and religion.

In the minds of humans, creatures of dark or light existed only in ethereal otherworlds far removed from material reality. To these ghostly realms, humans had banished white-winged angels and beings such as him, what they would call demons. But though he was powerful, he shared much with the evolved denizens of earth. Like them, fluids pumped through the tunnels of his body, bringing him life.

Another stab of pain drove him to call out a name that had once been so familiar. His own. "Yug'yu."

The agony burning through his body withered when he focused his anger on the girl. She had brought him so much misery and he would make her pay.

He'd already begun his initial torments. By exerting his control over the weakest minds around her—the children and animals—he'd driven her to question her own sanity. It brought him great delight to watch her reverting to the fragmented state he'd left her in after taking her father.

Another agonized blast wracked his body. His healing would take time, but that did not matter. Time moved differently in the shadows. This was the humans' greatest gap in their understanding of the universe. They viewed space and time as fixed concepts defined by unbreakable rules. But human perceptions were limited by the way their brains had evolved to interpret their environment. Yug'yu knew differently. He knew how to bypass the dimensions of space and time. He could dig tunnels through the dark and travel from one realm of time to another. This was the great power of the shadows.

Those same shadows now fulfilled their duties, closing his wounds and rebuilding his strength. When the girl and her confederate came, he would be ready. And he would exact the vengeance for which he had waited so long.

Part Three

Chapter Forty-three

Standing on the lawn of the desolate house, Lisa shivered as a breeze flittered into the crevices of her jacket, leaving goose bumps in its wake. The mansion towered above her, its turreted window-eye seeming watchful for any approaching interlopers. She recalled when she'd first seen the structure and declared it to be passive, even tragic. How wrong she'd been. It was terror incarnate.

Beside her, Jeremiah shifted his boots on the yellowing grass. "If I were some kind of hideous monster, this is where I'd live," he muttered.

Though the storm had broken in the past hour, nebulous clouds lit by a full moon floated in the night sky. Lights shone from a few windows in nearby houses, but most people in the quiet Toledo neighborhood had gone to sleep.

Lisa could not let the house—or Jeremiah—sense her fear. And fear—or rather *terror*—primal and raw, was what she was feeling. It rose within her, swirling up and down her spine, tensing her muscles and churning her intestines with nausea. She wanted to run to some faraway place where she could curl up in a ball and cry for her mother and father.

A new thought struck like a dissonant chord from a pipe organ. Her dreams of a marriage, a family, *a normal life* ... those were all gone. They'd vanished when she'd fired a bullet at what she thought was her fiancé. Or perhaps even before that, when she'd found the ruby earring, the proof of

David's betrayal. Until that moment, she'd been living with the mistaken belief the fates would allow her a chance at peace and happiness. She no longer suffered under that delusion. And with the realization that she had nothing left to lose, came a strange calm that caused her fears to dissipate. At least for a little while.

She tightened her grip on the handles of the gray duffel bag and looked at Jeremiah. "Let's go."

They crossed the lawn, ascended the porch steps and walked to the front door. It hung on its hinges, slightly ajar, offering a combination of welcome and menace. Lisa nudged the door open to reveal a foyer. Shadows shrouded most of the interior, leaving only a few sections of the floor brightened by moonbeams sliding in through cracks in the walls.

Jeremiah scratched the nape of his neck. "Are you sure this is a good idea? There's not some other way we can handle this?"

"We already had this discussion," Lisa replied. "We either deal with this thing now, or we spend the rest of our quite possibly short lives jumping every time a shadow moves. And believe me, they will."

She stepped into the house and Jeremiah followed. Now that they were safe from the prying eyes of neighbors, she set down the bag and began removing items: David's Glock, two kitchen knives, Jeremiah's shotgun, and a service revolver he'd sheepishly confessed to having hidden in his belt. They'd duct-taped flashlights to the barrels of the guns and penlights to the handles of the knives, ensuring light would bathe anything they shot or stabbed.

Lisa examined the arsenal spread out before them. She slipped one of the flashlight-knives into her belt and picked up the Glock. Jeremiah hung the shotgun off his shoulder using a length of rope he'd found at her house as a sling. He grabbed the revolver and the remaining knives.

With a mutual nod, they switched on the flashlights attached to their handguns and waved the beams across the walls and floors.

"So what are we looking for, exactly?" Jeremiah asked.

"You know damn well what. We need to find that thing. And kill it."

"And we just go through the entire house? You said the only time you saw it was on the third floor."

Lisa chewed her lip. He had a point; the creature seemed to prefer the top level of the house. But that didn't mean it couldn't appear anywhere. Essentially, they were waiting for it to come to them. And for that to happen, they needed to offer themselves as bait.

But it seemed best to keep that idea to herself.

"Let's start on this floor," she said. "We'll go through the house. And remember … *stick together.*"

Jeremiah scoffed. "A couple of hours ago, I was planning on killing you. You might want to keep that in mind before you start ordering me around."

"I think you know that killing me now would only be doing me a favor."

Jeremiah followed her into the dining room, their crisscrossing beams of light causing shadows to spasm across the floor. But, despite the disconcerting imagery, the space was empty, no different from when she'd last been in the house. And a quick search of the kitchen also revealed nothing of interest.

"Now what?" Jeremiah said.

"Upstairs."

They crossed the dining room and went through the arch that led to the circular staircase. Lisa paused before the first step. She'd been up these stairs once before, but she couldn't ignore how dangerous they looked, with their rotting wooden slats and cracked balusters.

Jeremiah choked out a laugh. "I thought entering Hell meant you had to go down."

She didn't smile at the joke. "C'mon."

Cautiously, she mounted the steps, feeling a tickle of relief when she heard Jeremiah following behind her.

On the second floor, only a little exterior light slipped through the boarded windows, which made them even more dependent on their flashlights. The yellow beams darted about, revealing blackened floors, flame-scarred walls, and decaying spider webs hanging from the ceiling.

"You know, we have two kinds of cells in our eyes, right?" Jeremiah said. "One sees brightness, the other sees color."

Lisa sighed, in no mood for a science lesson. "I know. Rods and cones."

"Exactly. And there are three types of cone cells that each fire at different colors. Red, green, and blue."

She paused at the start of the hallway that led to the bedrooms, shining her light into its depths. Without turning around, she said, "You don't sound stupid, O'Brien. How'd you end up as a criminal? Why didn't you do something with your life?"

She sensed the sting of her words as she uttered them. Several moments passed before he mumbled a response.

"You don't know what it's like to be cursed."

Chuckling, she stepped into the hallway. "I'm beginning to think I do."

As she moved, Lisa replayed the interaction in her head. Perhaps she'd been too harsh. After all, Jeremiah had not slaughtered her father, nor had he planted false memories in her mind. For all the years she'd spent hating the man, she'd been the one in the wrong. And, for reasons she didn't entirely fathom, he was working with her now, trying to track down whatever this monstrosity was.

Perhaps now was the time to make peace. Before God-knows-what happened to them.

"O'Brien," she started. "I don't claim to understand you. I don't know why your life ended up the way it did. But I appreciate you being here. And I think ... I think what we're doing is something we need to do together."

She paused in her tracks, giving him time to consider her words.

Moments passed, and there was only silence. No footsteps, no breathing.

"Jeremiah?"

She whirled around and saw that he was gone.

Chapter Forty-four

Cords of fear tightened around Lisa's throat. She called out for Jeremiah again, aiming her flashlight at the spot she'd last heard his footsteps. There was no disturbed dust, no spatters of blood. Only a dark, empty hallway.

She was alone. *Alone.* The realization shook her core. Her heart thundered in her chest and needle pricks raced down her back and arms. The terror she'd felt on the front lawn returned.

Calm down. You're having a panic attack!

She'd have to work quickly to manage the fear that was threatening to overwhelm her senses. Keeping her grip on the Glock, she leaned forward and put her hands on her knees. She took a deep breath, held it, and then exhaled. After she repeated the process two more times, her sprinting pulse slowed, and her lungs opened to accept air. While the anxiety of the moment did not completely vanish, it diminished.

Where had Jeremiah gone? Had the beast gotten to him? Or had he left of his own accord? She backed out of the hallway and jogged to a boarded-up window, careful to avoid burned-edged gaps in the floor as she went. When she peered through the slats to the front yard, she didn't see what she most feared: the sight of the escaped prisoner scampering across dead grass, fleeing to safety.

Was he in another section of the house? Should she call out to him? Maybe, but doing so might alert the creature to her location.

As she stood paralyzed by indecision, the sound of creaking wood floated in the air, followed by a tired sob. The noises had come from the hallway she'd just been in. Perhaps from one of the bedrooms?

She crept back into hallway and stopped at the first closed door. The knob turned easily in her grasp, and she stepped into the room. Her flashlight beam ran across the interior: the room was empty aside from a rusted bedframe pressed against the far wall. A thick layer of dust and ash covered the floor, disturbed in one area by a scattering of shoe prints. Perhaps Katrina had visited this room before her death? Or the police when they'd searched the house?

None of those answers sat well with Lisa. Neither did the blots of shadow that seemed to shift and churn in her beam of light.

Thud-thud. Thud-thud. Her heart pumped in her chest, flooding her ears with tingling warmth.

That same heart sputtered when her light revealed a pair of fleshy legs standing in one corner.

She screamed, jerking the pistol forward. "Don't move!"

Who was it? Jeremiah? The beast?

Naked and trembling, Dr. Gretchen Stein stepped out of the shadows and into the flashlight's beam. Her hands were clasped around her elbows. Bruises and dirt marked her doughy body. Dried blood splotched around gashes on her arms and chest.

But most disturbing was the expression on the woman's face. Lisa knew Dr. Stein to be reasoned and cerebral—a woman of profound self-control. Now, the psychologist's lips twisted into a crazed smile and her glassy eyes darted across the room.

"Gretchen?" Lisa said. "What are you doing here?"

Dr. Stein giggled. "Oh goody ... you've arrived ... that means he'll have to let me go."

Lisa kept her gun aimed at the woman. "I don't understand. How did you get here?"

Cracked lips drew back to reveal a rictus grin of brown teeth and gray gums. "You told me the house upset you, Lisa. I had to see what was wrong with it. So I would know what was wrong with you. I was so foolish ..." Her words ended with a sad laugh.

Lisa felt a sense of déjà vu, the same she'd felt when she saw David. She was being confronted with someone she'd known for years who now seemed vastly different. Of course, it turned out not to be David. And perhaps it wasn't really Dr. Stein.

The giggling woman moved closer. Lisa tightened her grip on the gun. "Stay where you are!"

"I'm not going to hurt you, my dear. But he will. He's going to do things to you so much worse than what he did to me."

Lisa circled the woman, inspecting her body. While the therapist's flabby flesh had many bruises and cuts, there was no long gash down her back. Perhaps this was the real Dr. Stein.

"Gretchen, what happened to you? How long have you been here?"

The doctor held her crazed smile for a few moments, then her face curled into an expression of torment. She began to weep. "It lasted forever. It was so cold and there was only darkness, only black. He tortured me." Her whimpering speech mutated into a hiss as she fell to her knees. "He was inside me."

Aghast, Lisa kneeled beside the woman. "I need to get you to a hospital. Can you walk?"

Dr. Stein's head tilted and madness once again flowered in her bloodshot eyes. "Oh, you're not going anywhere, my dear. If I couldn't escape this house, what makes you think you can? He sees you all the time, and says you must be punished. You'll pay for what you did."

The words stabbed Lisa like a blade in the gut. Dr. Stein had spent endless hours consoling her after the trauma of her father's death. Whatever the therapist's faults, her dedication to her young patient had never been in doubt. And now this same woman was reveling at the thought of Lisa's destruction.

As her stomach rolled in her belly, Lisa recoiled from the madwoman on the floor and fled the room.

She turned towards the hallway and saw a shape holding a flashlight. Jeremiah stood a dozen feet away, black revolver in one hand, shotgun slung over his shoulder.

Or was it Jeremiah? Lisa pointed the Glock at his chest. "Where have you been?"

He looked stunned. "I was about to ask you the same thing. You were in front of me and then you just stepped into the dark and disappeared."

"What are you talking about, O'Brien? You were the one that vanished. I turned around, and you were gone."

Jeremiah ran his flashlight beam over the walls and ceiling. "It's this house. It's playing tricks on us."

"Or maybe you aren't who you say you are." Lisa narrowed her eyes. "How do I know you're not that thing?"

His eyes bulged. "We've only been separated for a couple of seconds. Besides, how do I know you're not the monster? You said it took over the body of your boyfriend."

Lisa's fingers dug into the grip on her pistol, the flashlight bathing Jeremiah with its yellow ray. "I have to know I can trust you," she said. "Take off your shirt. I need to see your body."

"This is insane. Now is not the time for a strip search. It could be watching us right now!"

"Do it!"

Jeremiah lowered his gun. "Lisa, you have to trust me. I'm not some monster."

Her arms grew heavy, as if weighted by sandbags. It was too much: first seeing Dr. Stein, now not knowing whether she stood across from the real Jeremiah. She was tired of second guessing her senses and instincts. Tired of searching for cracks on the surface of reality. If trusting someone meant her death, then so be it.

She let her hands fall to her side. The light from her pistol coned into the floor.

Jeremiah mouthed the words, *"thank you."*

Then he raised his gun and fired.

Chapter Forty-five

The beam from Jeremiah's flashlight was blinding. Lisa's visual field flared into a screen of white stippled with sharp black and red dots. Time slowed to a crawl.

The next gunshot sounded far in the distance, its reverberations echoing in her head. Her legs turned to jelly and she crumpled to the floor.

After an indeterminate period—*seconds? Minutes?*—her brain clicked back on in a hard reboot. She couldn't feel any pain, but it offered little relief; she'd heard of soldiers wounded in war who'd not realized the extent of their injuries for hours.

Another gunshot. Then another, and a third; they crashed together in a disjointed rhythm. By the sixth report, her eyes had adjusted to her surroundings. She was lying on the floor. Jeremiah was shooting at where she'd just been standing. No. Shooting *next* to that spot.

She twisted and looked down the hallway. Jeremiah's flashlight beam cut through the dark like a laser, stopping on the flesh of the beast where fresh bullet wounds spat black fluid. Lisa heard a wailing noise that she realized was a monster screaming.

She scrambled to her feet beside Jeremiah. He'd stopped firing but was still aiming his flashlight down the corridor. The creature had vanished.

Jeremiah tilted his head, keeping his eyes focused straight ahead. "It came out of the shadows behind you."

"Well, I guess I know you're not it," she said dryly. "Let's get out of this hallway. I don't like these tight quarters."

They retreated to the second-floor foyer. A preternatural gloom drenched the area, absorbing any exterior light. Only the direct beams of their flashlights could cut through the dark fog.

"Stand back to back," Lisa whispered. "We need total visibility of this space. This thing is in its element and it will come for us."

"I'm pretty sure whispering won't help," Jeremiah said in a hushed reply.

She grinned. "You're a turd, O'Brien."

They stood with their backs together, scanning the room with flashlights mounted on their guns. They held the position for a minute, then two. The seconds of a third began ticking by.

"Maybe he gave up and went home," Jeremiah murmured.

A figure swooped towards Lisa, a jagged blade protruding from its wrist. Even as the claw dug into her bicep, she swung the Glock towards the attacking form. Two flares lit up the room, but the creature was gone.

Jeremiah gaped at her. "What happened?"

She clenched her teeth, ignoring the liquid warmth dripping down her arm. "Don't look at me. Keep your eyes in front of you."

"Okay. But I—*Argh!*" Lisa turned to see the beast pull its bone blade from Jeremiah's thigh. The convict swept his gun around, firing into empty shadow.

Lisa scanned the dark and pressed her shoulder close to Jeremiah's. "Are you okay?"

He grimaced, blood pouring down his leg. "In this weird haze, he can just tear us to pieces. We can't see him coming."

"This is our best chance. Here we have room to move. Stay focused."

Another movement. Off to the side. The creature darted between them, and they both spun, firing their weapons in concert, smiling when they heard guttural screams.

"Watch yourself," Lisa said, noticing the distance separating them. Jeremiah grunted, one hand tight around the grip of his gun, the other staunching the blood flowing from his leg.

Wisping shadows rose around him, and suddenly the thing was there, ramming its blade below his ribs. He moaned, dropped his revolver, and fell to the floor.

Lisa opened fire and the creature slunk back into the shadows.

Her gut churned in rage at their shared helplessness. They were easy targets for a predator that could appear and vanish with ease.

An odor of rot assaulted her nostrils. Hot breath warmed her neck. The bone blade sliced at her forearm, causing her to drop her gun. A fist cracked against the base of her skull and she toppled forward.

Face down on the floor, she pushed back against the fog clouding her brain. She rolled over, forcing her blurring eyes to scan the room. Motes of dust flickered in a single blade of moonlight that cut through the dark. In her stunned state, she stared as the particles danced in the air like fireflies.

Then the beast stepped into the light. Its two red orbs bore down on her, feasting on her vulnerability. Teary crevices in its flesh marked bullet wounds already starting to heal.

Parts of the creature's neck and chest began to throb and pulse, as if the skin was holding back eels struggling to break free. Greenish flesh heaved into tiny hills or receded onto valleys.

After several seconds of the grotesque undulation, the creature sneezed, releasing a pillow-sized mass of yellow goo. Lisa cried out as demon snot splattered across her torso, enveloped her arms and chest, and glued her to the floor.

The creature wiped its nose and mouth. "That should put an end to your impertinence, Lisa. Now you'll be much easier to deal with."

She struggled as the sticky material took on the density of chewed bubble gum. She looked at Jeremiah's motionless form splayed across the blackened floorboards.

The Glock lay only a foot away, but with her arms ensnared, it might as well have been miles. She glared at the beast. "God damn you, bastard. I'll see you dragged into hell."

There was a slurping sound as the bone claw retracted into the monster's wrist. A cruel smile grazed its lips. "I almost forgot, my dear. I have something for you." It pushed a hand into the flesh of its stomach and began to explore the viscera underneath. After a moment of grunting, it pulled a glistening oval shape into the moonlight.

Lisa gagged, choking on waves of revulsion.

Margarita Kallman's head, drenched in a dripping, transparent jelly, dangled from ribbons of wet hair. The woman's bulging eyes intimated the terror of her final moments.

The beast gurgled. "Now you've got a matching set, Lisa. One for each parent."

There was a flash and a loud pop from the room's periphery. As the creature lurched sideways, Margarita's head fell from its grasp and clunked on the floor. Lisa turned to see Jeremiah standing upright, wisps of smoke curling from the muzzle of the shotgun strapped around his shoulder. The convict swayed unsteadily, but his expression was resolute.

"Prepare to die, fucker," Jeremiah said. He flicked the switch of the flashlight taped to the shotgun and a wide beam spread to the corner of the room, where the monster was climbing to its feet. There was another thunderous blast, and the beast howled as inky liquid erupted from its chest.

Lisa watched Jeremiah squeeze the trigger a third time, but there was only a hollow click. The empty shotgun dangled at his side as he reached into his belt and pulled out two kitchen knives. He switched on the attached penlights and staggered towards the monster with a lurching gait slowed by his leg and gut wounds.

As Jeremiah came closer, the creature dove into a patch of shadow and vanished.

"He hasn't gone anywhere," Lisa warned. "But you've pissed him off, and when he's angry, he doesn't think straight."

The shadows remained still. Jeremiah kneeled beside Lisa and hacked one of his blades into the gooey substance.

"This plan of yours isn't working," he said. "This thing is just tearing us to pieces. We've got to get out of here. Maybe you can convince the cops to come back and bring the kind of firepower that can take this thing down."

Lisa chewed her lip. He was right. What had she been thinking, coming to the abandoned house to face a super-powered demon?

There was an abrupt movement behind Jeremiah. "Turn around!" she shouted.

He spun and stabbed one of his glowing knives into the chest of the approaching monster, smiling as the blade went deep. Then, as Lisa watched in horror, the pleasure on Jeremiah's face turned to fear as his arm was pulled into the monster's body. Within seconds, the appendage was absorbed up to the elbow. A sizzling sound filled the room, coupled with Jeremiah's scream.

The air filled with curling smoke and the acrid smell of burning flesh. There was a sickening crack before Jeremiah fell to the floor. He lay there moaning and grasping at the steaming stump where his arm had been.

Lisa pushed her arms against the sticky substance wrapped around her. Jeremiah's blade had loosened it enough, and with a great effort, she managed to tear free. She reached for the Glock, but a green fist clamped down on her hand.

The creature crouched beside her. "No, no, no. Little girls shouldn't play with guns." It drew back its palm and slapped her face, following up with a punch to her forehead. Blots of light sparkled at the edge of her vision. When a third blow landed on her jaw, a rush of copper liquid filled her throat.

Lisa spat out a bolus of blood, glowering at the monster. It smiled and raised its fist. The next blow came down hard and everything went black.

Chapter Forty-six

Lisa woke to a fiery ache spread across her body. One eye was swollen halfway shut. Her jaw throbbed, and her tongue scraped over patches of coagulated blood on the roof of her mouth.

She lay face up, her arms fixed to her sides by the same mucous straitjacket from which she'd previously escaped, though it now felt like a leathery wrap. Rolling from side to side confirmed she was not stuck to the floor, but that was of little solace when her movements were so constricted.

A steady glow came from her left. One of the kitchen knives lay on the floor, its attached penlight beaming on one of the charred walls, dimly illuminating the surrounding area. She was no longer in the second floor foyer, but in the attic bedroom with the angled ceiling where she'd discovered Katrina Chen's body.

Heavy pellets of rain pummeled the roof. A flash of lightning burst through an open, paneless window, followed by a thunderous crunch that sounded like an automobile being crushed by boulders.

Lisa was not alone. Jeremiah moaned on the floor a dozen feet away, cradling what remained of his left arm. The now empty shotgun hung around his shoulder, the attached flashlight deadened. A few feet away, the demon-creature sat with its back against the wall. Like its human captives, the monster seemed injured and spent. It pushed fingers into its flesh, tweezing out bullets and shotgun pellets, and tossing them to the floor.

The beast smiled wickedly. "Our princess awakes." It stood and walked towards her, stopping near her restrained body.

Though her jaw muscles were tight and sore, Lisa managed to spit in its direction.

The beast peered at her. For a moment, its eyes showed not anger, but the curiosity of a child examining the translucent wings of an insect discovered under a rock. Then the sneer returned, as if, upon reflection, it decided she deserved only contempt.

Inhuman lips parted and the phlegm-drenched voice filled the room. "Hell isn't hot, Lisa. It's cold. But you'll find out soon enough."

"Why?" she struggled to ask, staring into the creature's eyes. "What do you want with me?"

It grimaced and turned away.

Again, Lisa forced her bruised tongue to form words. "Who ... are you?"

The beast laughed. "Don't you recognize your very own guardian angel?"

She choked on the coppery liquid pooling in the back of her throat. "You're ... from heaven?" she asked between coughs. "From God?"

"Ah, you *Jung-ne*. Your understanding of your world is, in some ways, remarkable. And in other ways, so pathetic."

Lisa blinked several times, as if that would bring clarity to the beast's words.

Rising to its full height, the creature emitted a heavy sigh and ran one hand over the muscles of its torso. The flesh began to move and form images akin to the bas-reliefs found on the walls of ancient temples. The shapes were at first unfamiliar, but Lisa soon recognized a lone standing figure: the tall and winged angel who'd walked along the storming sea in the dream she'd had weeks ago.

Seeing her recognition, the demon smiled. "My world is far from here, not even in this universe. But my species is connected to yours. We evolved as you *Jung-ne* did, when it was understood that you would be of importance. When the makers realized you would be part of the redemption."

As the creature spoke, the images on its chest transformed, first to a swarm of planets, then to strange rotund creatures with extended tentacles.

Were these the makers? Lisa thought.

"But *Jung-ne* were prone to danger," the beast continued, "often of your own design. And the makers came to understand you would need protection. Thus, certain members of your species were granted the watchful eye of one of mine. A patron to protect you as you made your way through your world."

Lisa huffed. "So you're supposed to be protecting me? You're doing a shit job."

The monster made an impatient snort. "My species comes from a land of light. But if we are called to your world, we need to first travel through a barrier dimension. A realm we call the shadow floor."

A burst of lightning flashed through the window, illuminating the imagery on the creature's chest. Lisa saw the lone angel treading warily through a sea of moving shadows.

The creature smiled at the figure rising out of its fibrous belly muscle. "For some of us, this journey is complete when we arrive in your world and hide in the rays of the sun, granting protection to our wards. But not all are successful. Some are overwhelmed by the darkness of the shadow floor. And we are damned to spend eternity in this purgatory, writhing as black humors bleed into our veins, dim our light, and desiccate our souls. We suffer an endless death and our wards on your world are forced to confront their fates alone."

Lisa's mind reeled. Extra-dimensional angels journeying through a netherworld of shadow to aid their human charges? It seemed inconceivable. And yet, had she not just discussed with Meg the possibility of something beyond the physical world? Some kind of greater reality? "I ... I don't understand. You were my protector? And the darkness trapped you? How did you get here? To our world?"

"You were in danger," the creature said. "And though I was ensnared in the mire, the call to protect you still drew me. I was able to follow the beacon light of my ward out of the shadow floor and into your world. Because I had a strength possessed by few of my kind."

Lisa struggled against her bonds. "I was in danger? When I was a little girl, you mean? What danger?"

The creature chortled and walked to Jeremiah's quivering body. It leaned down and placed a hand on his cheek. "Why don't you tell her, my friend?"

Jeremiah moaned, but it was impossible to tell whether it was in response to the monster or to visions only he could see.

Not satisfied, the demon grabbed Jeremiah by the back of his head and yanked him to a sitting position. It pointed an olive finger at the man's anguished face. "He was the entity that threatened you. You were a young child, and he had seen you. He had watched you for days. And the desire for young flesh churned in his loins."

Lisa felt a wave of nausea pass through her belly. She stared at Jeremiah. "Is this true? You were going to …?"

Jeremiah blinked and returned her gaze. "I told you," he said as spittle dribbled out of his mouth and down his chin. "You don't know what it's like to be cursed."

The creature released its grip, letting him collapse back to the floor.

Lisa looked at the monster. "But you *didn't* protect me from him. You killed my father! You tormented me! Why?"

The beast again flashed a smile dripping with wickedness and derision. "As you humans have long understood, everything has its opposite. When I arrived in your world, I was no longer a creature of the light. The journey across the shadow floor had turned my heart black and my flesh dark. Light was no longer my strength and the shadow no longer my weakness. I was freed from the urge to protect you. Instead, the entire weight of my soul sought your damnation." Its burning, furious eyes radiated malice. "Your guardian angel became a demon!"

Heart twisting in her chest, Lisa shuddered and turned away from the cruel mien across the monster's face. Her mind was a cauldron of confusion, but one thought broke through the surface. "That was twenty years ago!" she said. "Why did you wait all this time?"

The monstrous eyes clouded. "After I killed your father, you gained a different kind of protection." It lifted an arm and reached into the soft flesh of its belly. After a moment of exploration, it pulled out several small objects and tossed them in the air. Like dice, pieces of the broken St. Michael clattered on the floor.

"In some ways, you *Jung-ne* are quite clever. Your totems work, though you do not always understand why."

Lisa glared at the creature. She now understood all that had befallen her. And she knew what it meant for her fate.

"Go ahead then," she sputtered. "Kill me."

The wooden floor squealed under the creature as it moved closer. "You misunderstand my intentions, Lisa. I don't want you to die. I'm taking you with me to the shadow floor. I want you to experience what I did: the darkness filling your veins and cracking your bones. Your inner light snuffed out by soul-corrupting black."

She struggled against the substance binding her arms. "You won't get away with this. Our gods ... the makers ... they'll stop you."

A wet laugh emanated from the beast's throat. "The realm of the shadow floor has permeated this structure, this house. No one, not even the makers, can see or hear what happens within these walls."

Her chest grew tight. She felt the desperation in her body, her muscles aching to move, to run away. She no longer feared the release of death, but eternal damnation in the underworld was another matter.

The creature extended the bone claw from the underside of its open palm. It crouched beside her and waved the blade in her face.

"But before we leave, I want to you to experience the last agony you can feel in this world of flesh. I want you to feel your warm blood dripping across your body, the screams of your nerves being severed."

The hand drew back, and the white bone shimmered in the moon's glow. Lisa sucked in a deep breath, preparing herself for the tortuous moments that were sure to follow.

Chapter Forty-seven

There was a blast of lightning, followed immediately by thunder. Then a second yellow flare filled the room, and another crashing sound, different from the first. Not thunder. The roar of the shotgun.

The creature's hand ripped apart and Lisa felt chunks of clay flesh rain on her skin. The bone blade clattered against the floor, as the monster screamed.

Jeremiah stood in the corner of the room. He held the rifle with his one good hand, shining the flashlight directly at the monster's face.

"You shouldn't have assumed the shotgun was empty, motherfucker. I picked up a couple of extra shells today."

The creature grabbed its stump. "So our pedophile has a heart of gold. I've no quarrel with you, Jeremiah. Leave us."

Teetering on unsteady feet, Jeremiah scowled. "Fuck you, monster. Now get away from her."

The beast took several steps back, tracked by Jeremiah's flashlight as it moved. "We aren't enemies. You know what I can do. I can become anyone you want, my friend. I can become any child you desire." As it spoke, the demon's bas-relief chest showed images of young boys and girls.

"You don't know me so good," replied Jeremiah. He squeezed the trigger.

Another blast filled the room. The monster screamed as dark fluid spattered out of its torso.

Lisa rolled herself over, struggling against her confines. She felt blindly against the floorboards until her fingers brushed against the bone claw. Holding it parallel to her forearm, she tilted her wrist sideways and began cutting at the constricting jacket of snot that trapped her. As she whittled away, she kept her attention on the battle playing out before her.

Jeremiah dropped the spent shotgun. He grabbed a knife from his belt and flicked on the flashlight.

The creature, oozing oily blood from its wounds, glared at its knife-wielding attacker. "That was a mistake." The flesh of its chest seethed and undulated. Then it opened its mouth and vomited gallons of white fluid at Jeremiah. Lisa recognized the steaming liquid not as the binding mucus that had ensnared her, but as the acid the monster had used to dissolve its way out of David's skin.

The sizzling liquid washed over Jeremiah's head and torso, burning his flesh, and prompting an earsplitting scream. His eyes melted in their sockets, translucent jelly running down cheeks which sloughed apart. His chest crumpled into an oozing sinkhole. The hand that gripped the knife became a knot of gore and bone.

Lisa watched in horror as Jeremiah's upper body transformed into a slab of crimson meat and collapsed to the floor. There, pieces of bone and muscle steamed in an expanding pool of blood and acid.

The beast's howling laughter filled the room, its eyes blazing. "You're on your own, dear girl. Just as you've always been."

Lisa felt the bonds of hardened snot start to break away under the probing edge of the bone claw. Pressing against her confines, the shell broke apart, allowing her to roll upright.

Another blast of lightning filled the room. The creature recoiled, shielding its eyes, and at once, Lisa knew what to do.

Bellowing thunder filled the air. The monster lurched forward. Lisa swung the bone blade in a wide arc, driving the thing back. As it dodged the blade, Lisa saw its eyes bulge in alarm.

She darted forward and swung the blade again, this time catching the meat of the creature's shoulder. It jerked back in pain and she seized her opportunity. She ran to a dormer window and kicked out the grilles. The cool night air caressed her as she hopped onto the windowsill and grabbed the overhang. She could hear movement back in the room as she pulled herself onto the slant of the roof.

The beast would follow. It had to.

Rain spattered against her face as she perched on the incline, leaning forward to steady herself. Hooking her fingers into the roof's crevices, she made her way to the top. She rose unsteadily, searching for the demon along the moonlit rooftop.

A spider's web of lightning lit the sky and she saw the beast standing by the cylindrical turret that rose out of the roof's far corner. The wounds on its chest were closed and a frail, infant-like hand now protruded from the stem of its right arm. The monster was healing itself.

A grimace contorted its face. "I'm tiring of these games, Lisa. I need to take you back with me to hell."

"Then stop hiding in the dark, demon."

It took several steps towards her. Moonlight dripped from the sky and the creature's skin steamed in the glow. The light, however limited, was to Lisa's advantage. If the beast wanted to capture her, it would need to play on her turf.

It lashed sideways with a chopping hand, nearly connecting with her ribs. She jerked back, and her foot slipped several inches on the wet shakes, almost sending her tumbling down the incline. She tried to steady her galloping heart and brought herself back to standing.

The moon's rays still singed the monster's flesh. Its undulating muscles oozed and folded in upon themselves, as if seeking refuge from the injurious beams of light.

The beast stepped forward and swung an unsteady fist at her. She ducked low and felt only a bare impact on her shoulder. In return, she shoved the blade upwards into its gut. Its glowering eyes showed no acknowledgement of the wound.

For a moment, they simply stared at each other.

"I had a dream about you," Lisa said. "About when you were good. An angel."

"You've been in my dreams as well," it replied. "And will continue to be until I free myself from you." The creature gulped a mouthful of air, its diaphragm expanding. Lisa pulled her blade out and ducked as a mass of viscous muck shot out of the creature's mouth and sailed over her. Staying low, she pushed her shoulder into the creature's wounded belly. It toppled backwards, landing on the roof and sliding towards the edge until its claws halted its descent. It climbed to the top ridge, where it steadied itself against the turret tower.

"You don't have it in you," the thing said as Lisa approached. "You have not faced the horrors I have in the shadow floor. You cannot kill me."

Her eyes narrowed. "You say you want to be released, demon? Let me indulge you."

She thrust the blade forward. It slid easily into the creature's throat and then out the back of its neck where it embedded itself in the wooden turret.

Pinned in place, the thing choked on the torrents of black blood pouring from its mouth. Its steaming hands clawed at the air.

Lisa released her grip on the weapon and stepped back, eager to watch her tormentor die.

But the red eyes still glowed with life. Phlegm-drenched words rose out of a shattered throat. "This is not how it ends, Lisa. I dragged myself from the depths of hell to find you. I can do so ag—"

Lightning crackled in the sky. The air shuddered as a single bolt of electricity, thrown by the gods above, struck the bone dagger. The beast throbbed and sizzled as millions of volts of electricity surged through the crevices and cracks of its body.

But the demon was not the only target of the storm's ire. More electric bolts flashed, striking the wooden turret and the top ridge of the roof. Lisa ran across the shakes towards the gabled dormer windows, intent on climbing back into the safety of the attic room. She was almost there when a bolt of lightning blasted the roof into fragments and she toppled into a chasm of darkness.

Chapter Forty-eight

Lisa sputtered to consciousness, amazed that her back could hurt so much all at once. The impact upon landing had knocked the air out of her lungs and they throbbed with an ache that brought tears to her eyes. She could move, barely, but was content to lie where she was, staring at the dots of light floating above her.

She scanned the edges of her peripheral vision, realizing she was on the third floor in the attic room with the slanted ceilings.

She groaned and rolled to one side. Jeremiah's remains lay several feet away, flesh still steaming. She paused, contemplating what had motivated the newly freed prisoner to sacrifice himself for her. Twenty years earlier, he'd stalked her as a pedophile and just this evening, he'd arrived at her doorstep intending to kill her. But she understood. He was finally free from his demons. Just as she was hers.

Oxygen seeped into her lungs, and she mustered the strength to stand. She looked up at the hole in the roof. Red embers flickered on the perimeter of the house's gaping wound. Beyond that, glittering stars floated in the cloudless night sky.

Moving slowly, she walked into the hallway, when a thought shook her. *Dr. Stein.* Was she still in the house? Some part of Lisa would have been content to let her therapist rot in the bowels of the grim tomb, but, for better or worse, the older woman was now the closest thing Lisa had to family. And family was important.

Dr. Stein had been in the bedroom on the second floor. Lisa trudged down the stairs and approached the doorway. The metal bedframe stood against the wall, and footprints were still visible on the floor, but the psychologist was not to be seen.

"Gretchen?" Lisa's voice hovered just below a whisper. Then it dawned on her she no longer had to fear being heard. "Dr. Stein?" she called out.

No answer. Had the deranged therapist fled the burned house? Or was she trapped in its ever-shifting corridors and rooms? But was that even possible now? With the creature and its mysterious powers gone, had the house returned to normal?

She stepped back into the hallway and sniffed the air. Smoke tickled her nostrils. Had the simmering embers of the roof caught fire? If so, it was vital she find Dr. Stein and get them both out of the house as soon as possible.

Lisa darted to the next bedroom. It was darker than the rest. "Gretchen?" she called out, again receiving no reply.

The bedroom seemed, in some impossible-to-define way, unwell. Lisa felt a goose bump-hardening chill, though there was no cool breeze to justify it. She exited the room. If she couldn't find Dr. Stein, she'd go to the neighbors and call the police.

She stopped when a barrage of smoke danced before her, filling the top of the hallway. Except she wasn't in the hallway. It was another bedroom. A stab of panic cut into her chest.

The house was playing its games again.

She looked at the floor. The shoe prints were there. She was back in the first room.

She found the door, yanked it open, and walked into the same room she'd just exited. Distant crackles of fire now accompanied the billowing smoke.

Again, she found the door and stepped through into the same room. She turned to find the door she'd entered by, but smoke obscured her view. She reached her arms out, searching for the knob. It was gone, in a way that only made sense according to the house's twisted logic.

Tears wet her eyes. It wasn't fair. After everything she'd been through, to end like this? She'd defeated her demon and earned the peace she'd sought her entire life. And the house was going to snatch this victory out of her grasp at the last minute? *No*, she decided. She wouldn't let it. She'd walk through a thousand doors if she had to. Whatever it took to get free.

Lisa stumbled forward, her palms making contact with a wall. She felt her way to the frame of a doorway. She threw the door open and was met by a six-foot tall screen of flames. The heat pushed her back, and she could almost feel her skin tighten under the intensity. She slammed the door shut, but not before plumes of black smoke saturated the room and poured into her mouth, choking her. Hot needles stabbed her lungs. A coughing spasm wracked her body. She fought the urge to vomit, and dropped to one knee, her throat burning.

Then the tension abated, and she felt as if she were floating. Was the smoke already limiting the oxygen going to her brain? It didn't matter. A blissful warmth rose up her spine. She slid to the floor, lured by the promise of sleep.

This was no defeat, she realized; this was nothing to be ashamed of. Perhaps it was the only ending that made sense.

Lisa's eyes closed, shielding her pupils from the heat of the approaching flames. And as the dancing orange spirits surrounded her, the world went dark.

Chapter Forty-nine

The first thing Lisa was aware of was a kiss. A gentle caress across her lips conveying only love. Love without lust or expectation. It was unlike any kiss she'd ever received.

The black smoke was drawn from her lungs and replaced with oxygen. She had never thought about the taste of air—she'd never thought it had a taste—but at that moment, it was the sweetest substance she had ever consumed.

Powerful arms lifted her off the floor. She heard the crackling flames, but their sounds were muted, as if far in the distance, perhaps in another world. Her heavy eyelids fluttered open only for a second before being drawn shut by the weight of sleep. In that moment, she saw foggy blots of warm light.

"Where …?" she murmured, keeping her eyes closed.

The answer came not in words but thoughts not bound to any language. Whatever their medium, their meaning was clear.

"You are safe. Rest. Let yourself sleep."

Seconds later—or perhaps minutes, maybe hours—Lisa felt herself being placed on cold, damp earth. While it was not uncomfortable, it prodded her from her reverie. This time, her eyes opened easily, and she found herself looking at a great, bright light, a circular portal. She wondered if this was the end. She'd heard of people who'd momentarily died during surgery and reported seeing a tunnel of light. But as her eyes cleared, she realized she was staring past the cloudless sky above her into a full, glowing moon.

The Victorian mansion was many feet away, its roof and turret engulfed in flames. She was lying in the front yard, past the yellow perimeter tape, close to the sidewalk.

Her gaze was drawn to movement on the front porch. She saw the back of a creature—tall, winged and gleaming white—as it entered the burning building.

"Wait ..." she tried to shout, but her voice was hoarse and weak. And then it didn't matter. The being vanished. If it had ever truly been there at all.

She settled back on the damp dirt, feeling it mold to her shape. Her breathing settled, and a smile crossed her lips. In the distance, wailing sirens grew closer.

Chapter Fifty

In the weeks after the fire, Lisa felt as if she were experiencing life anew. Gone was the nagging anxiety that had followed her through her childhood and teenage years into adulthood. No longer did she feel cursed because of the tragedy that had come to define her past.

She mourned the loss of her mother, but understood Margarita had been avenged. And she felt confident the woman had found the peace that had been stolen from her decades ago.

Lisa's feelings about David were more conflicted, but she sensed that with time, she could honor at least parts of his memory.

The Toledo Police Department, however, did not share her sanguine attitude towards the recent events. They were very interested in a woman whose fiancé, mother, and therapist had vanished under mysterious circumstances. During questioning, Lisa insisted she knew nothing of the missing people's whereabouts. She could only describe how the man who'd murdered her father had shown up at her doorstep and dragged her at gunpoint into the depths of a nearby abandoned mansion. There, in the attic, he'd beaten her so severely that she'd slipped into unconsciousness. She'd awakened hours later on the front lawn to discover that the mansion was burning.

A police investigation into the matter revealed that parts of her story could be corroborated. A woman who lived next door to the house had seen a man and woman matching Lisa and Jeremiah's description standing in the front yard late in the evening. And crime lab scientists identified DNA from the charred human remains found inside as that of the escaped prisoner.

Two weeks after the incident, the police requested Lisa come to the neighborhood precinct for a third round of questions. After several hours of interrogation, the police still had no reason to charge Lisa with a crime, so they let her go. She walked down the steps of the station, onto a busy street.

"Good day, lass."

Lisa turned. McCuddy stood on the sidewalk in a rumpled gray jacket, sipping coffee from a paper cup. She rushed to embrace him, a wide grin on her face. "I'm so glad to see you," she said.

McCuddy held her for a second, then stepped back. He frowned as his eyes trailed over the bruises still visible on her face. "Does that hurt?"

She touched her cheek. "It's getting better. You must have heard what's going on."

"Of course," he said. "Policemen like to gossip, you know? We're worse than bored housewives."

She looked at the ground. She'd known this conversation would come and not be easy. But it was necessary. "I've told them what I know, Devin. I don't know what happened to David or my mom. Or Dr. Stein. They're just ... gone."

The detective exhaled a sigh and tossed his empty coffee cup in a garbage bin. "Come, lass. Let's take a walk."

They strolled for several blocks. McCuddy asked about Lisa's house and her job and whether he could be of any help. She was acutely aware he was steering the conversation away from both her ordeal and the suspicions swirling around her.

After several minutes, they stepped onto Promenade Park, a city recreation area located on the edge of the Maumee River. A few families were enduring the chilly November breeze while they picnicked near the large sculptures rising out of the park grounds. Office workers on their lunch break strolled over stone pathways that meandered across fields of grass.

McCuddy and Lisa walked towards a row of short iron posts connected with heavy chains that lined the river's edge.

"Did you ever find it?" McCuddy asked.

"Find what?"

"The statue, dear. St. Michael."

"Oh, no. I'm sorry, but I don't know what happened to it."

His brow furrowed. "After you lost the statue, lass. Is that when your troubles began?"

Lisa's chest tightened, but she was determined not to let the tension show. "What do you mean?"

"I have to confess something. I told a wee lie. I never got that statue in Italy."

She pursed her lips, unsure where the detective was going. "What do you mean? Where'd you get it?"

"My family, my dear. In Ireland. We always had them around the house. My dear mum swore they could protect a person. We used to give them to each other on Christmas. There were never any surprises in the stockings in my house."

Lisa felt a cool breeze glaze over her neck. "So why'd you give it to me?"

McCuddy looked across the river before answering. "I've seen many things in my line of work. Including things I can't claim to fully understand. When I saw you that night those years ago, I dunno ... something just told me you would need it."

She stayed quiet, but looked at the man she'd always considered her friend and protector. All thoughts that needed to be expressed passed silently between them.

The detective smiled. "My dear, do you ever think about leaving Ohio?"

"Sometimes. I have ever since my father died. But I don't know. I like it here. I like our ... my house."

McCuddy placed a ruddy thumb under the fold of his chin. "I'm sorry to say this, but you should think long and hard on the subject. My fellow officers are not going to give up easily. They're convinced something in your story isn't right. But if you were no longer in the city, or the state ... well, you wouldn't be their problem anymore, would you?"

"I guess not."

"It's a decision you'll need to make. And sooner rather than later."

She looked around the surrounding area. A Sandhill Crane dropped from the sky and landed on the grass a dozen yards away. In the distance, the Anthony Wayne Bridge loomed across the expanse of the river, connecting the busy downtown district to the less commercial neighborhoods to the east.

Her eyes grew wet. "But I like Toledo. It's home to me. I'd miss you. And Meg."

McCuddy put a hand on her shoulder. "Come now, lass. Home is wherever your heart is. You know that. And friends can always visit."

She wiped her tears and leaned into McCuddy's chest. For a minute, they stood in silence as the gentle waves of the river lapped against the shore. Then Lisa straightened up and looked at the sky, past the clouds and atmosphere, to the heavens beyond. "You know," she said. "I never used to believe in all this stuff. I never thought it was real."

"What do you mean?" McCuddy asked. "You never thought what was real?"

She scrunched up her face. "Gods. And monsters."

McCuddy reached for the crucifix hanging from his neck. He rubbed the pendant between his thumb and index finger.

"And angels?" he asked.

The question caught Lisa off guard. But so did the smile it brought to her face.

"Them too."

Epilogue

Several months later, Lisa sold her yellow American Foursquare in the Old West End and left Toledo. She moved across the country to California where she enrolled in the graduate program at San Francisco State University and spent two years earning a doctorate in psychology. Upon graduation, she relocated ninety miles east to Sacramento and took a job at a clinic for children with depression and emotional issues. There she treated many youths lost to the torments of their minds.

She fell in with a small group of friends who found her likeable, if somewhat distant. Some tried to set her up on dates, but their efforts were always politely resisted. Lisa seemed to be focused entirely on her work and the support she could provide to her clients.

One day, she arrived at her clinic in anticipation of a meeting with a new patient. She walked into a conference room and saw a small boy of eight or nine with his mother and father. The family huddled together on a couch and looked around with weary, sleepless eyes.

With a friendly, relaxed demeanor, Lisa introduced herself and settled into an office chair. She asked the family to describe the reasons for their visit. As the parents recounted their recent experience, she saw the obvious love and concern they had for their son, Amit, who stayed silent.

When the mother and father finished talking, Lisa smiled and asked for a moment alone with the child. The two adults nervously rose from the couch and walked into the outside hallway.

Alone with Amit, Lisa stood from her chair and approached the child as he folded into the confines of the couch. She bent over, placed her hands on her knees, and smiled at him. His eyes darted across her face, briefly met her gaze, then dropped to his lap.

"So what do you think about this, Amit?" Lisa asked. "You heard what your mom and dad said. Does that sound like what's been going on?"

The boy's lips grew tight. She could hear his teeth grinding in his mouth.

"Please tell me, Amit. I want to hear what you think is happening."

He continued to evade her eyes, but for the first time since she'd entered the room, he spoke, muttering, "You won't believe me."

She squatted before him, making herself small and unthreatening, balancing herself on the balls of her feet and placing one hand on the arm of the couch. "Don't be so sure. I can tell you're a very brave boy. Why don't you tell me what's going on?"

Amit said nothing. But when he tilted his head and looked at her, Lisa felt his dark brown pupils exploring the contours of her face, perhaps searching for some indication she could be trusted. She took it as a sign to keep talking.

"Your parents said you hear voices at night?"

He nodded. She let the silence settle, listening to an instinct that said he would not let it last.

Amit brought his hands into his lap, and his fingers began to fidget. "It never lets me go to sleep. I hear it after the lights go out. In the closet of my room."

"What does it sound like?"

"A monster. Like ..." He paused, then pushed air through his larynx, forcing out a wet gurgle.

Lisa's face remained still, showing no sign of recognition. "Do you understand the voice? Does it say things to you?"

He began taking quick gulps of air. "It says ... it says it will kill them!"

Lisa nodded towards the door through which Amit's parents had just left. "Your mom and dad?"

"Yes," he replied. He was crying now, glistening tears of dread snaking down his cheeks.

She placed an arm on Amit's shoulder and let him weep. Neither of them spoke for a full minute. Then the boy raised his head and gave her a mournful look. "I told you you wouldn't believe me."

The cords of muscle in Lisa's neck grew taut. She met Amit's frightened eyes with her own determined gaze and placed her palm on his cheek. "Amit, I want you to listen to me. I do believe you. I know the voice you hear is real. And I know what it is."

His jaw dropped and his eyes bulged in their sockets. Then something akin to hope passed over his face.

"But most importantly," Lisa said. "I know how to make the monster go away. For good."

Your Reviews Help

Thanks for reading "What Waits in the Shadows." I hope you enjoyed this book and if so, please drop by Amazon and Goodreads and leave a review.

Amazon: https://www.amazon.com/dp/B0CSGDQZTL

Goodreads: https://www.goodreads.com/book/show/205155858-what-waits-in-the-shadows

Also, word of mouth is one of the best ways for news of an entertaining book to spread, so please tell your friends, either in person or online.

See you at the next one,

Wil Forbis

2024

Acknowledgements

Heartfelt thanks go to the many beta readers and ARC readers who provided valuable feedback for this book, including but not limited to:

Daniel Menacher, Damien Lee, Deborah Forbis, Ali Marae, John Saleeby, Steve Anderson, Alison Newchurch, Christopher Kelly, Dan Izen, Alison Marae, Peter Jones, Patricia Sterling, Heather Ann Larson, Kevin Johnson, and Kimberlee Jenson.

ABOUT THE AUTHOR

Wil Forbis is an author of both fiction and nonfiction residing in San Diego, California, USA. His short stories have been included in several anthologies.

In addition to his writing endeavors, he is an accomplished professional musician.

"What Waits in the Shadows" is his first novel. It will be followed by a slasher horror novel, "Anonymous," coming soon.

Visit https://www.thehorrorofwilforbis.com/ to sign up for his newsletter and receive a free short story.

Made in United States
Troutdale, OR
02/16/2024